FIXING TO DIE

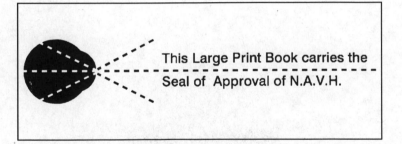

A SOUTHERN LADIES MYSTERY

FIXING TO DIE

MIRANDA JAMES

WHEELER PUBLISHING
A part of Gale, a Cengage Company

GALE
A Cengage Company

Farmington Hills, Mich • San Francisco • New York • Waterville, Maine
Meriden, Conn • Mason, Ohio • Chicago

LIBRARY OF CONGRESS CIP DATA ON FILE.
CATALOGUING IN PUBLICATION FOR THIS BOOK
IS AVAILABLE FROM THE LIBRARY OF CONGRESS

ISBN-13: 978-1-4328-4492-9 (softcover)

Published in 2018 by arrangement with The Berkley Publishing Group, an imprint of Penguin Publishing Group, a division of Penguin Random House LLC

Printed in Mexico
1 2 3 4 5 6 7 22 21 20 19 18

*This book is lovingly dedicated to
Megan Bladen-Blinkoff,
with thanks for many years of
friendship and support.*

ACKNOWLEDGMENTS

The hard work and dedication of my agent, Nancy Yost, and her associates — Sarah E. Younger, Natanya Wheeler, and Amy Rosenbaum — make my life easier in so many ways. Thank you all for everything you do.

My wonderful editor, Michelle Vega, is truly a gift; it makes all the difference in the world to have an editor who "gets" you and your characters so thoroughly. Jen Monroe, ace assistant, and Roxanne Jones, PR diva, are unfailingly helpful, and I appreciate them more than they realize.

My crazy writing schedule over the past year hasn't given my critique partners — Amy Sharp, Bob Miller, Julie Herman, Kay Finch, Kay Kendall, and Laura Elvebak — much of an opportunity to give direct feedback. They have helped me immeasurably over the years, and I like to think they are assisting my subconscious every time I sit down to write. The same goes for my two dear friends Pat Orr and Terry Farmer, who have always given me such staunch support.

Finally, my biggest thanks go to my many wonderful readers. You can't know how much it means to me when you tell me that you have enjoyed a book, or that my characters have made you laugh, or that the books have provided welcome distraction from the pressures of daily living. I can ask no higher praise.

CHAPTER 1

"Do you mean to sit there and tell me you think Cliffwood really is haunted?" Miss An'gel Ducote regarded her sister with a frown.

Miss Dickce Ducote shrugged. "There've been stories about that house for decades, Sister. Anyway, you know Natchez is supposed to be one of the most haunted towns in the country."

"Yes, I know," An'gel replied with a sniff. "I just don't ever recall hearing that Cliffwood was *riddled* with ghosts as you put it." Her brow wrinkled as she paused to think. "At least I don't remember hearing Jessamine or her husband, Marshall, ever talk about it."

Dickce snorted. "That old goat. He was too busy running around after women to notice ghosts. How Jessy put up with him for all those years, I'll never know."

"Fifty years ago, women thought they had

to put up with it for the sake of their sons," An'gel said. "Not to mention that Jessy would have starved if Marshall had left her for another woman. She was one of the sweetest girls I ever knew, but she could get lost in her own closet. She'd never have kept a job."

"That's a terrible thing to say about an old sorority sister." Dickce snorted with laughter. "Even if it's true." She laughed again.

"At least Marshall had the good sense to die before he threw away all his money; otherwise she'd have had to sell Cliffwood."

"We've wandered away from the subject." Dickce pointed to the letter An'gel held. "Mary Turner and Henry Howard Catlin are asking for our help. Even if we don't quite believe in ghosts, Mary Turner evidently does."

"I know." An'gel laid the letter aside on her desk. "I suppose we could go spend a few days in Natchez and see what's going on. I suspect there's nothing supernatural about it. Someone's playing tricks on them, I'd say."

"You're probably right," Dickce replied. "I'm game to go ghost-hunting, and I'll bet Benjy will get a hoot out of the whole thing."

"No doubt," An'gel said. Their young

ward, Benjy Stephens, had a lively intelligence and a healthy curiosity, and he would enjoy seeing the antebellum treasures of Natchez, potential apparitions included. "We can't take that for granted, however, and I wouldn't want him to feel obliged to go if he's uncomfortable with the idea."

"I don't think the idea of ghosts will faze him all that much. Besides, Peanut and Endora can help, too," Dickce said. "Animals are supposed to be sensitive to ghosts. If there are any supernatural presences at Cliffwood, they'll let us know."

"Let's hope they don't run across any tortured spirits that need to be laid to rest." An'gel grimaced. "I'll call Mary Turner and tell her we'll come on Monday. That ought to give you enough time to pack."

Dickce rolled her eyes at her sister. "I'm not the one who has to have a different pair of shoes for every outfit I take."

"If you wore anything other than dark colors in the autumn months, you might see the need." An'gel reached for her cell phone. "Why don't you go tell Benjy about the trip and see what he thinks of the idea of ghost-hunting?"

Dickce nodded and walked out of the study.

An'gel skimmed through Mary Turner's

11

letter again. Given the contents, she wasn't surprised that the young woman had chosen to write a letter, rather than simply calling. An'gel appreciated having the time to think about Mary Turner's story rather than having to respond immediately during a live conversation. She did wonder, however, why Mary Turner hadn't e-mailed her after all. She decided she would ask during the call.

She picked up her cell phone and tapped out the number. After three rings, a high, light voice said, "Hello, Mary Turner Catlin speaking."

An'gel identified herself. "Sister and I were discussing your letter, and of course we'd be happy to help you in any way we can."

Before An'gel could continue, Mary Turner broke in. "Oh, Miss An'gel, bless you and Miss Dickce. Henry Howard and I are about to go stark raving mad, and we didn't know whom else to turn to. Grandmother always said the Ducote sisters never lost their heads in a crisis, no matter what." She paused for a moment. "And if this isn't a crisis, I don't know what is. We're completely booked for Thanksgiving in two weeks, and if word gets out about this, we stand to lose a substantial amount."

An'gel heard a strangled sob. "Your grandmother was a dear friend, and Sister and I will do our best to live up to her confidence in us. I'm sorry that you and Henry Howard are so upset by all this. There's got to be a perfectly rational explanation behind what's happening there."

Mary Turner sobbed again, then choked it off. "I pray every day and night that there is, but we . . ." Her voice trailed off.

An'gel frowned. Had Mary Turner hung up? Or had her darn cell phone dropped the call? She waited a moment for Mary Turner to come back on the line, but when she didn't, An'gel ended the call. After about ten seconds she called again. Mary Turner answered immediately.

"I'm so sorry," the young woman said. "But that's the kind of thing that's always happening. Phone calls get cut off, our e-mails don't go anywhere, all kinds of odd things. That's why I wrote you an actual letter instead of e-mailing you."

"Heavens, this really is a mess," An'gel said, shocked by Mary Turner's words. "I wondered why you chose a letter. I can't remember when I last received an actual handwritten letter from anyone."

Mary Turner sounded grim when she responded. "So far the ghosts haven't been able to stop the post office from working."

13

"It's no wonder you and Henry Howard are at your wit's end," An'gel said. "Sister and I will be there around lunchtime on Monday, if that's convenient."

"That's wonderful," Mary Turner said. "We'll never be able to thank you enough."

"We're glad to help," An'gel replied. "Now, there is one thing. We'd like to bring our ward, Benjy, with us, along with our dog and cat, Peanut and Endora. Will that be all right?"

"You bring whomever you want," Mary Turner said. "The more help, the better. I've heard that animals are especially sensitive to the supernatural."

"You and Sister," An'gel muttered. Then she spoke so Mary Turner could hear properly. "Thank you, my dear. Help is on the way."

"See you on Monday."

As An'gel laid the phone aside, she reflected that, by the end of the call, Mary Turner had a new note in her voice. She sounded hopeful, An'gel decided.

She was glad she'd managed to make Mary Turner feel better, but she wondered whether she and Dickce had committed themselves to solving a problem that would turn out to be more than they could handle. She figured a real live human being was

14

playing tricks on the Catlins for some unknown purpose, but Cliffwood was an old house. Many sad and unpleasant things had happened there, particularly before, during, and right after the Civil War.

An'gel didn't believe in ghosts — not really — but there had been odd things that happened at Riverhill over the years. Doors closing on their own, the occasional cold spot in a room, small objects moved from their accustomed spots — nothing all that frightening, An'gel reflected, but odd. *Definitely odd.*

She and Dickce, along with Benjy, would have to keep their wits about them at Cliffwood, she decided. She wouldn't let odd things frighten her away.

The moment Dickce mentioned the word *ghosts* to Benjy, he grinned.

"Awesome." He looked down at the Labradoodle at his feet. "What do you think of that, Peanut? Are you ready to track down some ghosts?"

The dog gazed adoringly into the young man's face and barked twice. Benjy patted his head. "That means *yes.*"

Dickce smiled and continued to stroke the Abyssinian she held in her arms. "What about you, Endora?"

The reddish-brown feline yawned and stretched, then began to purr.

"Sounds like they're both in," Benjy said. "How long do you think we'll be there?"

"I hope it won't take more than a week to get to the bottom of what's going on," Dickce replied.

A snort sounded from the direction of the stove. Dickce looked over to see the housekeeper, Clementine Sprayberry, arms folded over her chest, frowning at her.

"You and Miss An'gel don't need to go hunting ghosts anywhere," Clementine said. "Especially Natchez. I reckon you've heard how haunted it is. You're just asking for trouble if you go and stir things up."

"That's even more awesome." Benjy laughed. "A whole town that's haunted."

"You laugh all you want to," Clementine said. "I bet you'll be the first one out the door ten seconds after some horrible thing wakes you up in the middle of the night and tries to get you."

"What kind of horrible thing?" Dickce felt a chill at the conviction in the housekeeper's voice. She knew Clementine believed in spirits, and she herself had never made up her mind about them.

"No telling." Clementine shook her head. "Terrible things happened all over that town

16

for three hundred years, and you don't know what might still be lurking."

Benjy's expression of amusement faded, Dickce noticed, in the face of Clementine's unrelenting certainty. He turned to Dickce. "How bad can it really be? I don't know anything about Natchez."

"There are a few books on Natchez in An'gel's study," Dickce said. "The town has a fascinating history, and you might want to do some reading before we go. Terrible things happened during the Civil War when the Union Army took over the town, and Natchez was a violent place in its early days. The books will give you all the details that I can't remember."

Benjy brightened. "Would Miss An'gel mind if I went in there right now to look for the books? If she's really busy, I don't want to disturb her."

"I'm sure she wouldn't mind, even if she is busy." Dickce knew her sister was as pleased about Benjy's interest in reading as she was. They had high hopes for him when he started Athena College the coming spring semester.

"Awesome." Benjy rose from his chair, his *sangfroid* seemingly restored. "Come on, Peanut, you know Miss An'gel always likes to see you." The dog loped after the young man as Benjy headed out of the kitchen.

"Whereas you, Missy," Dickce said to the cat still nestled in her arms, "are another story. An'gel can't get over the fact that you prefer me." She chuckled.

"Gracious, the way y'all talk to those animals." Clementine laughed.

Dickce shot the housekeeper a pointed glance. "I've heard you talk to them both plenty of times yourself."

"Well, I reckon so." Clementine turned her attention back to the stove and picked the lid up from a pot of chicken and dumplings. "If y'all are going to treat 'em like people, I guess there's no reason I shouldn't do it, too." She stirred the pot for a moment. "Lunch is just about ready. Ten more minutes."

Dickce sniffed appreciatively. "The perfect thing for a cool fall day."

Clementine looked up from the stove. "Miss Dickce, y'all ever told Benjy about the things that go on here sometimes?"

Dickce stiffened, and Endora squeaked a protest. Dickce forced herself to relax. "What do mean, the things that go on here?"

"You know what I mean," Clementine said. "Doors closing all by themselves, things moving around after I've dusted, and you know I know to put things right back in the exact same place they've been the last hundred years." She sniffed. "Unless you and Miss An'gel are going around behind my back, trying to play tricks on me, you know ain't no earthly thing doing that."

"An'gel and I would certainly never play that kind of trick on you, and you know it." Dickce shook her head at the housekeeper. "I don't have any better explanation for it than you do, and to answer your original question, no, I haven't said anything to Benjy. I don't imagine An'gel has either. Since he has his own quarters above the garage, he probably might not ever notice anything here in the house."

"Maybe so." Clementine focused her attention on the stove again. "Still, y'all might better tell that boy, 'specially before y'all go hunting spirits in Natchez."

"You might be right. I'll discuss it with An'gel." Dickce set the cat on the floor. "Come on, Endora. After I wash my hands, we're going to set the table." To her amusement, the cat, after a yawn and a stretch, padded after her to the powder room under the stairs and waited until Dickce finished her ablutions.

While Dickce set the table, Endora sat in the doorway and watched. After a couple of minutes, apparently bored, she disappeared down the hall. Dickce figured she had gone in search of Peanut and Benjy.

Dickce performed her task without giving much thought to what she was doing. Her thoughts focused on the upcoming trip to Natchez, and their reason for going. She hated to admit it — and she doubted she would admit it to An'gel — but Clementine's dire warning had spooked her a little. As had the housekeeper's reminder about the occasional unsettling experience here at Riverhill. She and An'gel really should tell Benjy, she decided. He ought to know, because someday he would most likely be the owner of the house, since she and An'gel had no blood descendants to inherit from them.

The last piece of cutlery in place, Dickce gazed at the table. Had she forgotten anything?

"Looks fine to me," she murmured.

As she continued to think about the housekeeper's words, Dickce felt a prickle on the back of her neck.

What if Clementine is right? What if we stir up something in that house we can't handle?

CHAPTER 2

Benjy braked the car gently to a halt, shifted into Park, and switched off the ignition. His shoulders ached lightly from the long drive, as did his head, but he figured a little pain was a small price to pay for having arrived at Cliffwood in one piece. Miss Dickce had pouted for a few minutes when Miss An'gel asked him to drive them all the way to Natchez. Miss An'gel refused to budge over her sister's protests. Miss Dickce acted like a good sport and hadn't sulked for long.

If Miss Dickce *had* driven them, Benjy reckoned, she would have received several tickets coming down the Natchez Trace. The speed limit was only fifty miles an hour, and Miss Dickce had trouble driving less than eighty no matter where she was going. He enjoyed the more leisurely pace because it afforded him the opportunity to appreciate the hues of the fall foliage — rich golds and yellows, vibrant reds, browns, and greens.

Where he grew *Fixing to Die* up in Southern California, there was nothing like this panoply of autumn colors.

The scenery during the drive distracted him from the concerns he had about their reason for going to Natchez. At first he had been excited about ghost-hunting with Miss An'gel and Miss Dickce, but during the early hours of the morning he awoke from a disturbing dream and had trouble going back to sleep. In the dream he found himself in his old home in California, pursued by ghosts with terrifying faces. They wanted something from him, but he was never able to discover what. As ghostly hands reached for him and brushed against his face, he awoke to find Peanut licking him and Endora sitting on his chest. Reassured by the presence of his four-legged friends, he had eventually thrown off the immediate effects of the dream and gone back to sleep.

In the early morning light, however, as he prepared for the drive to Natchez, he found it difficult to push away the memories of those horrible faces. The malevolence in them had terrified him in the dream, and he wondered what he and the sisters might find lurking in the atmosphere of Cliffwood. He found himself fretting over that same question now that they had arrived. Their stories of the weird things that happened at Riverhill hadn't made him feel any better, though they assured him nothing really terrible ever happened. He was glad he didn't sleep in the house, though. The ghosts at Riverhill — if that's what they were — had so far not touched anything in his apartment.

"Thank you, Benjy," Miss An'gel said from the seat beside him as she unbuckled her seat belt. "You really are an excellent driver. I thoroughly enjoyed the trip down. Didn't you, Sister?" She turned to glance at Dickce in the backseat. "Especially since I could actually *see* individual trees, rather than a blur as we zoomed by."

Benjy watched Miss Dickce's expression in the rearview mirror. For a moment he thought she was going to stick her tongue out at her elder sister, and he had to suppress a laugh. He had seen her do it before.

Instead, Miss Dickce shrugged. "Yes, it would have been a shame to miss the scenery. The Trace is always beautiful."

Peanut woofed in Benjy's ear. Benjy knew the Labradoodle was eager to get out of the car and explore — and to *do his business,* as the sisters always referred to it. He slid out of the driver's seat and prepared to open the rear door. First, however, he held up his hand, palm toward the window, to let Peanut know he had to stay. The dog whined but remained on the seat when Benjy opened the door. He quickly attached a leash and grabbed a plastic bag.

"I'd better let him explore a little before we go inside," Benjy told the sisters. "Otherwise he might have an accident."

"Excellent idea," Miss Dickce said. "I'll bring Endora while An'gel rings the doorbell to let them know we're here."

While he and Miss Dickce let the animals wander around the neatly clipped expanse of front lawn, Benjy gazed at the house. He had found several pictures of it in a book on antebellum houses Miss An'gel had.

Cliffwood stood on the bluff overlooking the Mississippi River, and when Benjy shifted his stance and gazed to the west for a moment, he could see where the land dropped away, with a hint of water. From the second-story gallery of the house, he knew he would have an excellent view of the river. He turned back to look at the house and recalled what he had read about it.

The original structure was built in the 1780s, but a lightning strike during a fierce storm in 1852 resulted in its complete destruction. The family rebuilt on a grander scale, this time in the Greek revival style popular at the time. Cliffwood had two stories, each surrounded by a gallery on all four sides. Columns lined three sides of the house, and inside there were fifteen rooms. Benjy remembered reading that there were several outbuildings as well, among them a building that would have housed slaves, a kitchen, and a laundry. That had been converted, along with a former dairy and an old carriage house, into suites for the bed-and-breakfast started by Mary Turner's parents in the late 1970s.

Miss An'gel's book hadn't offered any information about ghosts or other supernatural manifestations at Cliffwood, although it did mention such things about other houses, such as Stanton Hall and its spectral Confederate soldiers.

Benjy thought Riverhill, the ancestral home of the Ducote family, was one of the most beautiful and imposing homes he had ever seen. But with its white columns, white walls, and dark shutters, not to mention its grand size, Cliffwood outshone Riverhill. The midday autumn sun seemed to envelop the house in a golden haze, and for a moment Benjy's eyes dazzled from the effect.

"Spectacular, isn't it?" Miss Dickce said. "Look, you'd better pick that up before you tread in it." She pointed at the ground near Benjy's feet.

"What? Oh, yes, ma'am." Benjy stooped, the plastic bag around his hand, to scoop up the bit of business Peanut had left on the immaculate lawn. He stood and gazed at the house again as he pulled the sides of the bag up and tied a knot in it to trap the droppings inside. "I don't think I've ever seen a house as beautiful as that."

Miss Dickce sighed. "I do love Riverhill with all my heart, but every time I come to Cliffwood, I experience such pangs of envy that I feel like a traitor to my family. Well, looks like An'gel finally roused someone with the doorbell. Come along, Endora." She bent slightly, and the cat jumped into her arms.

Benjy and Peanut followed them across the lawn toward the house. They climbed the broad steps that flowed gracefully down in a wide V from the porch and joined An'gel at the open door. She patted the shoulder of a young woman whom Benjy judged to be around thirty-five.

"Mary Turner, this is our ward, Benjy Stephens, and Peanut and Endora." Peanut stepped forward to greet his hostess while Benjy gazed raptly at the lovely young woman who smiled so graciously at him.

She was beautiful, like the Hollywood starlets he had sometimes seen in Los Angeles.

"It sure is nice to meet you, Benjy, and you, too, Peanut and Endora." Mary Turner Catlin stroked the dog's head, and Peanut barked his approval. Endora surveyed her hostess from the safety of Dickce's arms and yawned. Mary Turner laughed in response. "Just like a cat, impressed by no one." She stepped aside. "Y'all come on in. Henry Howard and I will get your bags in later. Right now y'all must be about to perish from hunger, and we have a delicious lunch ready for you."

"I'd like to wash up first," Miss An'gel said, and Miss Dickce echoed her.

"Let me show you to the powder room." Mary Turner led them to the staircase that swept upward in a gentle curve on the right side of the hall. "We've added it since you were here last."

After accepting custody of Endora from Miss Dickce, Benjy gazed around, awed by his surroundings, while their hostess showed the sisters the new powder room. Every piece of furniture he saw looked old. According to what he had read, much of the furniture in the main house dated from the time of the Civil War, with some additions

27

in the 1880s and early 1910s. He spotted a settee that reminded him of one in the front parlor at Riverhill, and the large carpet that covered much of the wooden floor looked like the Aubusson in that same front parlor back home. Benjy wondered how much help Mrs. Catlin and her husband had to keep the room appearing spotless. At Riverhill, the sisters and Clementine spent a lot of time dusting and polishing furniture.

Suddenly recalling his dream, he wondered where unfriendly spirits could be lurking, if there were any here. What if his bedroom was inhibited by one of those nasty horrors? Maybe he could sleep in the car instead. Then he felt ashamed of himself. Neither Miss An'gel nor Miss Dickce had shown any signs of fear in front of him, or expressed any concerns in his hearing. So he told himself to man up and stop acting like a kid.

Mary Turner placed a hand on his arm, pulling Benjy out of his reverie with a slight start.

"Let's take Peanut and Endora to the kitchen and introduce them to Marcelline Beaupré. She's our cook and housekeeper, and she adores animals. I'm sure she'll have a few tidbits for these sweet creatures. If that's okay, of course." She smiled at him.

"Sure, it's fine," Benjy mumbled. He felt shy with this beautiful young woman and berated himself inwardly for being so awkward. He drew a deep breath as he followed Mary Turner. He promised himself he'd do better. He didn't want her thinking he was an antisocial idiot. Or even worse, a scaredy-cat.

An'gel waited, none too patiently, for Dickce to finish in the powder room. Mary Turner and Benjy had not yet returned from the kitchen, and thus far there was no sign of Henry Howard Catlin. An'gel knew that running the bed-and-breakfast kept both wife and husband busy, but she still found it odd that Henry Howard hadn't been present to greet them.

Given the signs of strain she had noticed in Mary Turner's face, though, An'gel would not be surprised if there had been further incidents of the type Mary Turner had mentioned and Henry Howard was busy dealing with another weird happening. An'gel was eager to hear more about what had been going on. She wanted the details of each incident. There had to be a pattern to them, a pattern that could lead to the discovery of their origin. Their *human* origin, she thought with determination.

An'gel wandered from the area outside the powder room to the foot of the stairs. *Surely Dickce will be done soon.* She felt a bit on edge, and she wasn't certain why — unless she expected a ghost to pop up at any moment.

An'gel chuckled at the thought and at once felt more at ease. She ran her right hand along the burnished mahogany of the banister rail. Her eyes followed it as it curved gently upward to the second floor. At the point where it mounted beyond the opening in the ceiling, she noticed an elongated, horizontal shadow in the rough shape of a body in the dim light that emanated from the floor above.

Who was standing there? she wondered. Why wasn't he moving?

An'gel hesitated a moment, then called out. "Henry Howard, is that you? Come on down and say hello."

For a moment nothing happened. Then the shadow disappeared.

It hadn't moved away, An'gel thought, uneasy now. There had been no movement, she was sure of it.

The shadow just vanished as if it had never been there in the first place.

CHAPTER 3

The incident happened so quickly, An'gel began to wonder whether she had really seen a shadow or instead simply imagined it.

No, it was there. I saw it.

"You must have imagined it," she whispered.

You came here looking for ghosts and strange happenings, and your subconscious obliged you.

No, she argued with herself, *it was there. And then it was gone.*

A voice startled her. She turned to face her sister.

"An'gel, what on earth is the matter with you?" Dickce frowned. "You're pale, and your eyes look wild."

"I'm perfectly fine," An'gel replied as she tried to get her heart rate to slow down to its normal rate. Should she tell Dickce what she saw? Or thought she saw?

"You don't have to glare at me," Dickce said, her tone testy. "If you say you're fine, then I guess you're fine. Though you still look a little strange to me."

"I saw something." An'gel hadn't meant to speak, but the words slipped out anyway.

"What did you see?" Dickce asked, her voice low.

"A shadow at the top of the stairs." An'gel shot a quick look at the spot. Nothing there now. She returned her gaze to her sister's face. "A shadow that made me think someone was standing there. A man, I thought." She paused for a quick breath. "And then the shadow just disappeared."

"You mean it moved away?" Now Dickce sounded skeptical.

An'gel shook her head. "No, it never moved. It was there one moment and then suddenly it wasn't."

"Probably some sort of optical illusion," Dickce said. "Honestly, Sister, I think you're just tired and hungry from the drive. Go and wash up, and we'll find Mary Turner and Benjy and have our lunch."

An'gel shot an angry glare at Dickce before she brushed past her to get to the powder room. She glanced in the mirror and was reassured to see that she did not look at all pale. "Maybe Sister was right," she muttered. "I am only hungry and tired."

Her ablutions finished and her equilibrium mostly restored, An'gel left the powder room some moments later to rejoin Dickce. She found her sister, eyes closed, clutching the banister rail of the staircase and shivering.

Alarmed, An'gel laid a hand on Dickce's shoulder. "What is wrong with you? Now you're the one who's pale, and you look like you're going to faint."

Dickce's eyes popped open to stare into An'gel's. "Thank the Lord it's gone now, but while you were in the powder room, I had the sensation of coldness all around me. It lasted only a moment or two, but I still feel chilled."

An'gel regarded her sister with dismay. They had experienced a similar sensation a few times over the years in their grandmother's bedroom at Riverhill and had never been able to explain it to their complete satisfaction. What would they do if Cliffwood really was haunted?

A baritone voice coming from above them startled both sisters. "Hello there, ladies. Sorry I couldn't be here to greet you with Mary Turner."

An'gel glanced up the stairs to see Henry Howard Catlin descending toward them.

"We're delighted to see you, young man." An'gel exchanged a glance with her sister. Should they tell Henry Howard what they had experienced? An'gel decided it could wait until later and shook her head slightly at Dickce.

Their host, his long, lean form clad in worn corduroy trousers and a flannel shirt, pushed his rimless glasses up his nose before he bent to offer first An'gel, then Dickce, a quick peck on the cheek. An'gel noted that his curly chestnut locks now sported a couple of streaks of white, and there were signs of strain in his face. He looked a good ten years older than his thirty-six years, An'gel decided.

"We did wonder where you were," Dickce said, her smile strained. "But I imagine there are a thousand and one things you have to do to make sure the house is ready for Thanksgiving."

Henry Howard sighed. "Make that a thousand and twenty. The way we're going through lightbulbs lately, we ought to have stock in the company. I went up to check your rooms not long before you arrived, and all the bulbs were out. I replaced them for the second time in three weeks. I hope they'll last while you're here." He shook his head. "I can't figure out why it keeps happening."

"That is bizarre," An'gel said. "Have you had an electrician in to look at it? Perhaps there's a fault in the wiring."

Henry Howard gave a weary nod. "My friend Buzz checked it out, and he couldn't find anything wrong."

"Probably a power surge or something of that nature," Dickce said.

"Could be," Henry Howard said equably. "At least that's a better explanation than saying the ghost of Mary Turner's great-great-grandfather did it."

An'gel couldn't decide from the young man's tone whether he was serious or making light of a worrisome situation. If incidents like this were occurring on a regular basis, it was no wonder Mary Turner's nerves were frazzled.

She said as much and waited for their host's reaction.

Henry Howard shrugged. "These things are irritations, but no one has actually been hurt by any of it. Other than our bank balance, that is." After a quick, wry grin, he offered an arm to each sister. "Let's forget about all of that for a while, what do you say, ladies? I don't know about you, but I've got a hankering for some of Marcelline's fresh cornbread with lots of butter."

"With a big glass of sweet tea." An'gel smiled as Henry Howard escorted her and Dickce to the dining room.

There they found Mary Turner and Benjy putting the final touches to the table. There were eight chairs, but the table was set for five — two places at one end, three at the other. An'gel didn't see Peanut or Endora and reckoned they must be in the kitchen with Marcelline.

"Everything looks lovely," Dickce said, and An'gel agreed. Mary Turner had set out white linen napkins along with her grandmother's silver and second-best china. An'gel recognized the pattern right away.

"And smells heavenly," An'gel said, eyeing the bowls of creamed corn, field peas, potato salad, green beans, a plate of cornbread, and a platter of ham — a good Southern meal.

Mary Turner smiled. "Thank you." She turned to Benjy. "I appreciate your help. You've obviously learned well."

An'gel noted that Benjy blushed on being addressed by their young hostess. His eyes appeared to follow her wherever she moved around the table. Mary Turner was a beautiful young woman, of course, and Benjy was still callow in some ways though quite mature in others. She trusted Mary Turner to handle the situation properly.

Henry Howard touched his wife's shoulder briefly, and they exchanged a glance before he pulled out a chair for An'gel to the left of his end of the table. Benjy hastily did the same for Dickce, across from An'gel, then stood looking awkward behind Dickce's chair. Henry Howard helped Mary Turner to her chair at the other end of the table, and she indicated the place to her right to Benjy. Henry Howard walked back to his seat at the head and took his place.

"Henry Howard will say grace." Mary Turner bowed her head. Her guests followed her lead, and Henry Howard intoned a bricf blessing.

For the next few minutes the only conversation consisted of requests for certain dishes to be passed and the requisite thanks for having done so. An'gel tried her creamed corn first and relished the taste. She loved corn, especially when cooked properly. She remarked on this to Mary Turner, who beamed with pleasure on hearing the compliment.

"Marcelline is a treasure," the young woman said. "Her food is always wonderful. I have to watch myself, or I'd be as big as the side of a barn. Wait until you taste the carrot cake she made for us for dessert today. It's the best I've ever had."

"I love carrot cake," Dickce said, "particularly with an ice-cold glass of milk." She eyed her full plate. "If I eat all this, I might not have room for cake." She laughed. "But I'm not going to let any of this go to waste."

An'gel felt happy to see both their young hosts more relaxed. She pushed away thoughts of the odd experiences she and Dickce had earlier by the stairs. Time enough to consider those later, but for now, she wanted to enjoy her meal. She knew that, all too soon, they would have to face the real business of their visit to Natchez.

Benjy, An'gel noticed with some amusement, managed to eat while casting one covert glance after another at their hostess when Mary Turner's attention moved elsewhere. When Mary Turner spoke to Benjy, he managed a few words in response but in such low tones An'gel never could quite catch what he said. She wondered whether their ward actually tasted anything. He didn't appear to notice what he forked into his mouth. She caught Dickce watching Benjy also.

An'gel exchanged a wry glance with Dickce before turning to respond to a remark from Henry Howard about a mutual acquaintance in Athena, Helen Louise Brady.

"I know her well," An'gel said. "Dickce and I visit her bistro at least once a week. Her pastries are superb. How do you know her?"

"She's actually a distant cousin." Henry Howard paused for a moment. "I'm trying to remember the exact relationship. I think her great-grandfather Brady was the youngest brother of my father's great-grandfather. Or something like that." He grinned. "I'd have to dig out the family tree to tell you exactly."

An'gel laughed. "That's close enough. You're cousins of some degree anyway."

"I met her years ago, when I was still in high school," Henry Howard said. "I think she wasn't long back from cooking school in Paris. I remember there was a bit of talk about it because the elder Bradys all thought she had ruined her life by chucking a career as a lawyer in order to cook for other people."

"Thankfully Helen Louise didn't listen to the naysayers," An'gel said, her tone a trifle tart. "She's made a huge success of that bistro."

Henry Howard opened his mouth to reply, but a voice from the doorway into the hall interrupted him.

"Good afternoon, everyone."

Henry Howard turned to see who the speaker was, and An'gel glanced past him to see for herself. The tall, statuesque newcomer smiled as all eyes focused on her.

An'gel eyed the expensive scarlet red silk suit, the white gloves, double strand of pearls, spike red heels, and enormous red hat dripping with white gardenias and jasmine. The red-and-white of her ensemble set off the rich chocolate of the woman's skin, and a gentle wave of an elusive floral scent wafted from her. An'gel sniffed appreciatively.

Henry Howard rose from his chair, dropping his napkin by his plate. "Good afternoon, ma'am. How can I help you?"

The stranger laughed, a low, musical sound. "I need a room, of course, but I must tell you, sir, that it is *I* who have come to help *you.*" She paused for a moment. "The spirits called me here, and I had to come to release them from their earthly torment."

CHAPTER 4

Dickce heard a loud snort of amusement at the woman's announcement and realized with a shock that she was the one who had emitted the sound. Embarrassed, she clutched her napkin to her chest and said, "I'm so sorry, please forgive me. I was just startled."

The woman in red smiled. "I'm not offended. I know there are those who scoff at my work, but when you have a calling like mine, you have to persevere no matter who or what is against you."

The calm assurance in the woman's voice did little to ease Dickce's embarrassment over her gaffe. She would have tried to apologize further, but Henry Howard spoke first.

"I'm sorry, ma'am, but we're not open to the public this week or next." He offered a polite smile, but to Dickce, his tone and body language were not exactly friendly. In

41

fact, she thought he looked ready to usher the stranger out immediately.

"I don't think of myself as *public,*" the woman responded, evidently not in the least offended by Henry Howard's reaction. She dug into the large white handbag hanging on one arm and extracted what appeared to be a business card. She held it out to Henry Howard, and he took it.

"Mrs. Primrose Pace," Henry read aloud. *"Psychic Medium and Expeller of Unwanted Spirits."* He glanced toward his wife, and Mary Turner got up from her chair and came to stand by him. She laid a hand on his arm.

Dickce watched the unfolding scene with interest. Would they allow this woman to stay? If she really did have the abilities she claimed on her business card, Dickce reckoned, she might be helpful. Or then again, she might be a gigantic nuisance.

"Mrs. Pace," Mary Turner said, her tone exhibiting warmth, "it just so happens that my husband and I need the advice of someone who has experience with the supernatural." She flashed a look at her husband. "Even though we are usually closed to the public at this time, I think we can make an exception."

Primrose Pace smiled, and Dickce thought

42

the woman looked a bit smug as she responded to Mary Turner's invitation. "Thank you, Mrs. Catlin. I appreciate you being open-minded. I have no doubt that I will be able to help you."

Henry Howard did not look happy, Dickce thought. She exchanged glances with An'gel, who gave a slight shrug. *Wait and see. If she's a fake, we'll catch her out.* Dickce could hear her sister now. She nodded to indicate she agreed and turned back to watch as Mary Turner led Mrs. Pace from the dining room.

Henry Howard remained where he was for a moment. Then he shook his head and returned to the table. "This will probably be a disaster, but there's no use arguing with my wife when she makes up her mind."

"I think we all understand your reluctance," An'gel said. "Mrs. Pace could be a help, if she's really what she claims to be."

"And if she's not, we'll find that out and get her out of the house," Dickce said.

"I wonder, however, whether she actually knows anything about what's been going on here," An'gel said. "She seemed quite sure of herself."

Henry Howard shrugged. "Everyone who knows anything about Natchez thinks all the antebellum houses here are riddled with

43

ghosts. Lord knows Natchez has been on those ghost-hunting programs on TV enough in recent years. They've never come sniffing around here, though, thank goodness."

"An'gel and I could make some discreet inquiries," Dickce said. "We know a few people here in town besides you and Mary Turner. We could find out whether she's approached anyone else like this."

"Excellent idea," An'gel said.

"Guess so." Henry Howard picked up his fork and moved a few peas around his plate.

"Who else have y'all told about what's going on here?" An'gel asked.

"My friend Buzz for one," Henry Howard replied. "I've known him since we were in first grade together. He's my best friend. I don't think he'd tell anyone because he knows Mary Turner and I don't want this to get around."

"Anyone else?" Dickce said. "What about Marcelline? She must be aware of the situation. Might she have let something slip?"

"Marcelline? No way." Henry Howard shook his head. "She's too loyal to Mary Turner. She'd never go around talking about our business to anyone."

"I'm sure Marcelline wouldn't say a word, if Mary Turner asked her not to," An'gel said. "You mentioned your friend. What about Mary Turner? Does she have a best friend she confides in?"

"Amy Patridge, but she's in England visiting her husband's family. They've been gone over a month and aren't due back for at least three weeks or so." Henry Howard laid his fork aside and leaned back in his chair. "I can't think of anyone else at the moment. You ladies — and Benjy here — are the only people who know anything, as far as I'm aware."

"And we haven't heard the details," Dickce reminded him.

"No, I guess not," Henry Howard said. "I'd rather wait for my wife, though, before we get into all that."

Mary Turner stood in the doorway. "Honey, would you get Mrs. Pace's luggage and take it up to the green bedroom? She'd like to get settled in."

Henry Howard pushed up from his chair, and Dickce could tell he was not happy about something. He turned to face his wife. "The green bedroom? Why are you putting her in there instead of out in the annex?"

Mary Turner looked uncomfortable, Dickce decided. The young woman's words confirmed that.

"She needs to be in the house in order to tune in to the vibrations, or whatever they are," Mary Turner said. "If she really can help us, then I figured she might as well be on the spot instead of in another building."

"Whatever." Henry Howard walked past her and disappeared into the hallway.

After staring at her retreating husband's back for a moment, Mary Turner approached the table and offered her guests an apologetic smile. "I'm sorry our lunch got interrupted like this. Have y'all finished? Are you ready for dessert?"

Dickce glanced at An'gel and Benjy, and they nodded. "I'm ready for dessert," Dickce said. "I've been hankering after carrot cake ever since you first mentioned it." An'gel and Benjy voiced their approval.

"I'll ask Marcelline to bring it in, then." Mary Turner headed back to the door. "I'll start clearing away in a moment."

Once Dickce thought Mary Turner was safely out of earshot, she said in a low tone, "I don't like seeing Mary Turner and Henry Howard at odds over this. I wonder why he's so reluctant to have that woman in the house."

Benjy broke his extended silence. "Mary Turner told me when we took Peanut and Endora to the kitchen before lunch that this is about the only part of the year that they actually get any time to themselves. Usually, that is. They don't take guests the first three weeks of November so they can have a rest."

"And it's bad enough that we're here," An'gel said, "even though we're here to help. Then a stranger shows up and puts herself into the middle of it."

"I would be unhappy myself," Dickce said. "Running a bed-and-breakfast, especially in an old house, must be awfully hard work."

"They do have some help," Benjy said. "There's the housekeeper, Marcelline. She's really nice and loves animals. They also have a couple of ladies who come in three times a week to help clean when they're open for guests."

"That's good," An'gel said. "But back to the subject of Mrs. Pace. I really want to know what brought her here. I'm not sure I believe that she received some kind of psychic message that her services were needed."

"We'll work on that," Dickce said.

Mary Turner reentered the dining room in the company of Marcelline. Dickce and An'gel remembered her from previous visits and greeted her with compliments on the delicious lunch. The housekeeper smiled in acknowledgment of their praise.

Marcelline must be near seventy by now, Dickce reckoned, because she had started working for the family as a teenager when Mary Turner's father was a boy nearly fifty years ago.

Dickce dug into her slice of carrot cake with anticipation. She savored the first mouthful. It tasted heavenly. She told Marcelline so the moment she could speak.

"I'm glad y'all are enjoying it," the house-keeper responded. "There's plenty more if any y'all wants another piece."

"I could probably eat half the cake my-self." Benjy grinned. "This is probably the best cake I ever ate."

Marcelline beamed at him. "Well, you just come get more of it whenever you want, honey. Now, if y'all will excuse me, I got to go start thinking about dinner."

As she resumed her place at the table, Mary Turner said, "Marcelline is happy to have someone besides me and Henry How-ard to cook for. We make do with sand-wiches, salads, and scrambled eggs a lot of the time."

Dickce eyed her hostess's trim figure and suppressed a sigh of envy. She wouldn't mind losing a few pounds but the thought of giving up food like this depressed her. So she was a little plump, what of it? At her age, she decided, she wasn't going to change the habits of eight decades of life.

Henry Howard returned and pulled out his chair. Once seated, he eyed the serving of carrot cake at his place, then pushed it away. Dickce thought he looked grumpy. His next words confirmed that as he cast a resentful glance at his wife.

"Madame Blavatsky loves her room, you'll be delighted to know. Apparently she's already feeling vibrations, or whatever the heck they are."

"Who's Madame Blavatsky?" Benjy asked with a frown. "I thought she said her name was Pace."

Henry Howard scowled, and Mary Turner appeared embarrassed.

Dickce hastened to explain. "Madame Blavatsky was a famous spirit medium in the nineteenth century. She developed a large following, though of course, many people thought she was a fraud."

"Okay, I get it," Benjy said. "You don't believe in this medium gig, do you?" He addressed his question to Henry Howard.

"No. Maybe. I don't know." Henry Howard shook his head. "Something has to explain what the heck's been going on in this house the past couple of months. Either

that, or Mary Turner and I have been hal-
lucinating like crazy."

"I'm about at my wit's end," Mary Turner
said. "This house has made odd noises ever
since I can remember, but the other strange
things . . ." Her voice trailed off for a moment. "Maybe these things happened in
Grandmother's day, and even my dad's
when he was young, but nobody ever said
anything."

"No, I don't remember any talk about
supernatural happenings," An'gel said, "and
we knew your grandmother for many years.
If anything of the kind occurred here, she
never mentioned it to us."

"What kinds of things have occurred?"
Dickce asked. "Henry Howard mentioned
problems with lightbulbs going out unexpectedly, and you told An'gel about issues
with your computers and cell phones."

"Those issues, yes," Mary Turner said.
"I've experienced one really peculiar thing."
She paused to nod in her husband's direction. "Henry Howard hasn't experienced it,
and I don't think he really believes me."

"I never said that." Henry Howard looked
even grumpier. "It's just so weird, that's all.
You'd think as often as I go up and down
those stairs, I would have felt it, too."

"Felt what?" Dickce remembered the sudden aura of cold she had felt earlier. She had to suppress a shiver.

"A sensation of cold near the bottom of the front stairs," Mary Turner said. "It's only happened a few times, but it's always unnerving when it does." She crossed her arms over her chest for a moment, as if hugging herself against the cold.

"I felt it, too," Dickce said. "While An'gel was in the powder room."

"Really?" Mary Turner looked at Henry Howard. "I told you so."

Before Henry Howard could respond, Primrose Pace spoke from the doorway.

"I felt it, too," she said as she advanced into the room. "I must warn you that the spirit causing this is an unhappy one, and if you don't put it to rest, you could be in great danger, Mrs. Catlin."

CHAPTER 5

Does the woman always have to make a dramatic entrance? An'gel wondered, then decided, *Of course she does.* Part of her stock-in-trade.

"Do you have any idea who this angry spirit is, Mrs. Pace?" An'gel asked after a glance at Mary Turner. The young woman appeared to be in shock after the medium's announcement.

Mrs. Pace inclined her head a mere fraction. "Not as yet. She — and I'm pretty sure it's *she* — isn't willing to communicate that at the moment." She paused — for more dramatic effect, An'gel was convinced — then continued in dark tones, "Sometimes the spirits have to be coaxed. We have to treat this one gently if we want her to confide in us."

"Is that the royal *we* you're using?" Henry Howard asked, his tone barely polite. "Do you mean confide in *you*?"

Mrs. Pace shrugged. "Spirits are capricious. This one could decide to reveal itself to anyone it wanted to. Although I must say I am usually the person they choose."

"Naturally," Henry Howard said.

He wasn't taking any trouble to hide his hostility, An'gel thought, somewhat puzzled by his attitude. She had thought him more open-minded than this, though perhaps his behavior resulted from the strain he and Mary Turner had been experiencing in recent weeks. After a moment's further reflection, An'gel put it down to that and resolved that she and Dickce would do their best to put an end to these *manifestations* or whatever they were. If Mrs. Pace turned out to be a hindrance, then An'gel would personally get her out the door.

Mary Turner cleared her throat and took a sip of water. Setting the glass aside, she said, "All I know is, if there is an unfriendly spirit in this house, I want it out as soon as possible."

"I'm sure I can help you," Mrs. Pace said.

Henry Howard snorted but made no other comment. Mrs. Pace didn't appear in the least bothered by his attitude.

"Won't you join us?" Mary Turner indicated the empty chair to her right. "If you would like lunch, I will ask the housekeeper to prepare a plate for you."

Mrs. Pace took her place. "No, thank you, I'm fine." She glanced around the table. "Please, continue with the discussion of the strange events going on here. I need as much information as possible in order to cleanse the house of any lingering spirits."

Mary Turner began to list the types of occurrences and their frequency, and Mrs. Pace focused her gaze on her hostess's face. When Mary Turner mentioned the problems with their cell phones, the medium frowned briefly, An'gel noted with interest.

Was that not something the medium had encountered before? An'gel wondered.

Mrs. Pace said, "Besides the cold spot on the stairs, the lightbulbs, and the interference with the electronics, have there been any other unexplained things happening?"

An'gel decided to mention the odd shadow she had seen earlier. "Right after we arrived," she began, "while I was waiting in the hallway for my turn in the powder room, I happened to glance up the stairs. I saw a shadow that looked vaguely human in form. I thought it might be Henry Howard's, actually. I called out to him, but there was no response, other than that the shadow simply vanished."

"It moved away?" Mary Turner asked.

"No, it was there one moment and gone the next," An'gel said. "There was no movement, more like a light suddenly switched off, if you see what I mean."

"That is really interesting," Mrs. Pace said, her gaze intent on An'gel's face. "Did you feel a sense of menace, or sense the presence of another being anywhere near you?"

An'gel thought for a moment. "Can't recall that I did. Only that shadow. I certainly didn't feel the cold the way Dickce did. Do you think that whatever cast the shadow is also the source of the cold?"

"It's certainly possible," Mrs. Pace replied. "Some spirits can manifest themselves in more than one way."

"Where were you when this happened?" Mary Turner addressed the question to her husband.

"In one of the bedrooms changing the lightbulbs," he said.

"Did you see anything, or anyone, upstairs that could have cast a shadow?" Mary Turner said, still focused on Henry Howard.

He shook his head. "No, not a thing. As far as I know, I was the only person upstairs at the time."

"Mrs. Catlin, have you observed this shadow for yourself? Or you, Mr. Catlin?"

The medium glanced at them in turn.

Henry Howard shook his head. "I haven't."

"I haven't either," Mary Turner said. "Is it significant that Miss An'gel is the only one who has seen it?"

An'gel was wondering the same thing herself, now that she knew no one else had seen it.

"It could very well be important," Mrs. Pace said after a brief silence. "I will have to consult my own spirit guides and ask their advice on this. Now, to finish the original subject of my question. Are these all the strange things that have happened?"

"No," Mary Turner said. "I find things moved from their accustomed places almost every day."

"What kind of things?" An'gel asked.

"Knickknacks, vases, pictures, things on shelves around the house," Mary Turner replied.

"Don't forget about the dictionary," Henry Howard said.

"Dictionary?" Dickce asked. "What does it do, fly around the room?"

An'gel threw her sister a quelling look. Dickce was a little too flippant sometimes.

Mary Turner smiled briefly. "No, it doesn't fly. It never leaves its place. We have it open in the library on one of those old-fashioned book stands. As long as I can remember, it's been open to the same page, because now if I want to look up a word, I do it online."

Henry Howard said, "But now it's on a different page every day, sometimes two or three times a day. This only started happening last week, after we closed down for our annual holiday." He snorted. "Some holiday."

"That's wild," Benjy said. "There's no draft from anywhere that could cause the pages to turn, is there?"

"No, there's isn't," Henry Howard replied. "We thought of that. It's not near a window or a vent, so either someone is sneaking into the house and turning the pages, or else this place really is haunted."

"Do spirits often do things like this?" An'gel addressed her question to Mrs. Pace.

"Oh, my, yes," Mrs. Pace said. "Generally when they are trying to get a message of some kind across." She turned toward Henry Howard. "Have you made a note of the particular pages when they change? If I could look at the ones selected, I might be able to decipher the message."

An'gel was not surprised when Henry Howard laughed in response. His reaction was consistent with his attitude so far.

"I've got way too much to do as it is," he said, "without having to keep track of ghost messages. Sorry, can't help you, but you're welcome to start keeping track if you want."

The way Mary Turner glowered at her husband, An'gel figured Henry Howard was in for a dressing-down when Mary Turner got him alone.

Mrs. Pace rose from the table. "Thank you all. You've given me a great deal of helpful information. Now I think I will retire to my room and attempt to contact my guides." She glanced down at her hostess. "I will speak with you later if I have information to share." She nodded briefly at the rest of the company and then moved in stately fashion from the room.

"She sure puts on a good show," Dickce said. "And maybe she knows what she's talking about."

"She might," An'gel said. "I reserve judgment for now. My dear," she said to Mary Turner, "I think I would like to rest awhile myself, if you don't mind. Which room am I in?"

"The French room," Mary Turner said. "Miss Dickce is next down the hall in the yellow room, with the bathroom you will share between. Is that all right?"

"Certainly," An'gel replied, and Dickce echoed her.

"The French room is my favorite," An'gel said. "I feel honored to have it. I know it was your grandmother's favorite."

Mary Turner smiled. "Yes, she loved that room. Henry Howard, I thought Benjy and the animals would be more comfortable in the annex. Would you mind showing him his room? Number three."

Henry Howard rose from the table. "Sure thing. Come on, Benjy. I think you'll like it out there. Quiet, for one thing, and no weird crap going on."

"That sounds good," Benjy said. "I always get a little bit of a headache when I drive a long way, and a few minutes of quiet will help me get rid of it."

Despite his headache, Benjy somehow managed to look both relieved and disappointed at the news of his lodging in the annex, An'gel was amused to see. She didn't blame him. She wasn't particularly looking forward to any ghostly visits, though she was curious to see what would happen. She might well want a room in the annex herself if things got too spooky in the house, she reckoned.

She and Dickce rose from the table and followed Mary Turner into the hall. Henry

Howard and Benjy disappeared into the kitchen, where they would collect Peanut and Endora before heading on to the annex behind the house.

An'gel ran her hand along the banister rail as she climbed the stairs beside Mary Turner. Dickce trailed behind. An'gel glanced up and was relieved not to see an odd shadow ahead of them. She stepped into the upstairs hall and followed her young hostess to the front bedroom on the right. She waited until Mary Turner opened the door, then stepped inside.

The room had earned its name because of its furnishings and decor. As An'gel recalled it, one of Mary Turner's ancestors had fitted out the room for his youngest sister, who had a passion for all things French. All the furniture had been imported from France at considerable cost not long before the Civil War started, and a down-on-her-luck Frenchwoman from New Orleans had supervised the decoration. An'gel felt she stepped into the past when she walked into this room.

The bed, made of French walnut, had a headboard and footboard with engraved and studded brass panels. The finials were of bronze. The large oak wardrobe had a similar design to that of the engraved bed panels. The commode or chest of drawers that stood beneath the west-facing window was, to An'gel, the prize piece of the collection. Made of ebony with brass and tortoiseshell inlaid marquetry, it was stunning. An'gel also knew that it was valuable, and should Mary Turner ever consider selling it, she could realize a healthy price for it.

There were a few family pictures on the walls, and objects on various surfaces that gave the room a definitely feminine touch. Some of the objects, like a pair of blue Opaline crystal Baccarat vases and an eighteenth-century Meissen shepherdess, had been in the family for generations, An'gel knew.

Her bags stood on the floor near the foot of the bed. An'gel turned to Mary Turner and gave her a quick hug. "I do love this room. Thank you again."

"It's the most beautiful room in the house," Dickce said, not without envy.

"I'm so pleased you're happy with it." Mary Turner paused, and An'gel thought she looked uncomfortable. "I have to be honest with you, though."

"About what, my dear?" An'gel asked.

"This room," Mary Turner said.

When she didn't continue, An'gel said, "Come on now. Out with it. What is it you're afraid to tell me?"

Mary Turner took a deep breath and let it out. "This is the room where things keep moving around. I come in here at least once a day, and every time, something has moved."

CHAPTER 6

An'gel felt an odd flutter in her stomach at Mary Turner's words. "Is this the only room where things are moved around?"

"Well, no," Mary Turner replied. "It's happened a couple of times in other bedrooms and in the library and the front parlor."

"More often in here, though?" Dickce moved to stand beside An'gel as they both regarded their young hostess.

Mary Turner nodded. "Pretty much every day. I'm sorry, I really wasn't thinking clearly about this. I should have told you before bringing you up here. If you'd rather be in another room or out in the annex, I understand."

An'gel considered it for a moment. What would she do if she woke up during the night and found objects being moved around the room? Her heart was strong, despite her age, but was it strong enough for that?

"How about if I stay in here with you?" Dickce said.

An'gel glanced at her sister. Beneath the determination she read in Dickce's expression, she also saw unease. She knew Dickce would fulfill her offer if requested, but she didn't want her sister to feel she had to. "No, that's not necessary. I will stay here on my own."

"We brought mace," Dickce added. "In case the spirits turn out to be human, they'll get a face full of it. Then a bonk on the head with the big flashlights we also brought."

Mary Turner smiled. "I think you'll both be okay. I've been checking this room last thing at night and first thing in the morning, and only once did I find something — one of the Baccarat vases, actually — moved during the night. The activity seems to happen during the day."

"That's interesting," An'gel said. "That inclines me to think that human hands are doing it. Someone sneaking in during the day to do these things but without access at night."

"Who has access during the day?" Dickce said. "Besides you, Henry Howard, and Marcelline."

"When we're not closed, the front door is unlocked all the time until ten p.m. so guests can come and go, and for new arrivals to come check in." Mary Turner frowned. "We used to always keep it locked when we closed down for our holiday, but I guess we haven't been vigilant about it. We leave it unlocked so often it's hard to remember to lock it. We do lock the doors at night, though."

"I think it would be a good idea, until we get this situation sorted out," An'gel said, "to make sure the front and back doors and all the windows are kept locked at all times. The more difficult you make it for whoever is behind all this, the sooner we can figure it out."

"Unless that person has a key," Dickce said. "Have you ever had the locks on the doors changed?"

Mary Turner looked blank for a moment. "I think my parents did that when they started the bed-and-breakfast, because the locks were so old-fashioned. That was a few years before I was born. I know Henry Howard and I haven't had them changed since we took over."

"There's no telling then how many keys could have been lost or given out over the years. I think it's likely that the perpetrator of these *manifestations* has a key and comes and goes how he likes." An'gel actually felt better now that they knew this because it made human agency all the more likely.

"We'll get the locks changed tomorrow," Mary Turner said. "We should have thought of this before now. I feel pretty stupid, frankly."

Dickce patted the young woman's arm. "Don't be too hard on yourself, my dear. We all get comfortable in our routines and don't always think how those routines could be working to our disadvantage. You know what to do now."

"Thanks to you two," Mary Turner said. "I feel better already." She gave Dickce a quick peck on the cheek. "Let me show you to your room now, and Miss An'gel can get settled and rest a little." She turned and headed out of the room, and Dickce, after a last glance at An'gel, followed her.

An'gel stood in place for a moment, then bestirred herself to close the door. *Such simple things, keys,* she thought. It would be interesting to see what happened after new locks were installed. An'gel was willing to bet the manifestations would cease abruptly. With that, she decided she wouldn't mind at all spending the night in this room.

She looked at her suitcases, then at the bed. She really ought to unpack and hang things up, but suddenly she felt too tired. They'd had an early start this morning, and long drives always tired her. Not to mention the rather heavy lunch she had enjoyed. She elected for a brief nap over unpacking and slipped out of her dress. She laid it over the back of a chair before she pulled a night-gown from one of her bags and put it on.

The bedcoverings and linens, she noted with approval, were modern. The bedspread might look like an antique but that was as far as it went. She made herself comfortable in the bed and, not long after her head hit the pillow, dozed off.

When she awoke later and checked her watch, she saw that nearly ninety minutes had passed. She pushed aside the covers and sat up on the side of the bed. After a couple of yawns and a little stretching, she pulled off her nightgown, folded it, and placed it under the pillow. Then she got up from the bed and padded over to the com-mode, over which a mirror hung. Her hair needed attention, of course, but a few strokes of the brush would put it to rights. She turned away to find her handbag, intent on fixing her hair. Where had she put it?

Oh, there it is, on the floor beside the suit-case. She started to reach for her handbag, then froze in place.

The dress she had carefully draped across the back of the chair before she got into bed now lay across the suitcase instead.

A knock at her door startled her out of her inertia. "Just a moment," she called out. Hastily she grabbed the dress and slipped it on. "Come in."

The door opened to admit Dickce. She stopped briefly after two steps into the room, then hurried over to An'gel. "What's wrong, Sister? You're as pale as those sheets on the bed."

An'gel realized her pulse was racing, and she needed to slow down her heartbeat. She moved to the chair and eased herself into it. After a couple of deep breaths, she said, "I'll tell you in a moment. Let me get ahold of myself."

"All right, but you're worrying me." Dickce stood by the chair and patted An'gel's shoulder.

An'gel smiled at her sister. "Sorry to worry you, but I had a shock right before you knocked on the door."

"What happened?" Dickce asked.

"I put my dress across this chair before I lay down for a nap," An'gel said. Her pulse quickened again as she recalled the moment of discovery she was about to relate to her sister. "I was looking for my handbag, and

68

that's when I saw my dress, draped over the suitcase."

"Oh dear Lord." Dickce clapped a hand over her mouth and stared at An'gel in dismay. She stumbled to the bed and sat on the edge, still regarding her sister. "That's creepy."

"It certainly is." An'gel's tone was grim. "Someone came into my room while I was asleep and deliberately moved my dress in order to frighten me."

"You didn't hear anything?"

"No, I didn't." An'gel nearly snapped the words out. "I would have woken up if I'd heard anything. Whoever it was managed to do it without alerting me."

Dickce's gaze swept the room. She got up from the bed and walked back to the door. She swung it back and forth on its hinges. There was no noticeable sound. "That explains part of it. These doors are kept well oiled. Mine doesn't make a sound cither."

"Not like the doors upstairs at Riverhill," An'gel remarked. "We really should oil them, but the only time I think about it is at night when I'm ready to go to bed." She laughed suddenly. "We're getting away from the main point. Someone is trying to send a message, obviously, by coming in and moving my dress."

"What do you mean, a message?" Dickce went back to the bed and resumed her former perch.

"The gauntlet has been flung down," An'gel replied.

Dickce nodded. "I see what you mean. The person behind all this isn't worried about you being here."

"Exactly." An'gel's expression turned fierce. "And exactly the wrong tactic to use on me. It's really childish, when you think about it."

"Yes, and it was definitely a risk," Dickce said. "Anyone might have come along — besides you and me, that is — and spotted the perpetrator going in or coming out of your room."

An'gel nodded. "We're not going to say a word about this to anyone."

"Why not?" Dickce asked.

"I think it will be interesting to act like nothing happened," An'gel replied.

"Do you think someone in the house did it? Or someone who got into the house?"

"Could be either," An'gel said. "I don't think it was a spirit, though. A human being did this."

"I agree," Dickce said. "Though I suppose we can't rule out a ghost completely."

An'gel snorted. "Maybe you can't, but I'm

going to, until we get strong evidence to the contrary." She pushed up from the chair. "I'm going to see about my hair, then I need to visit the bathroom. Are you ready to go downstairs?"

"Yes, but what's the plan?"

"I want to look over the house," An'gel said. "It's been a few years since we last visited, and it won't hurt to refresh our memories."

"Good idea. I'll meet you downstairs, then, in the hall." Dickce got up from the bed and left the room, shutting the door behind her.

An'gel attended to her hair and spent several minutes fussing with it until she was happy with the result. She checked her lipstick and decided it needed to be refreshed. Finally satisfied with her appearance, she started for the door. Her glance fell on her luggage, and she stopped for a moment. She really should unpack, but right now she wanted to explore the house. Unpacking could wait, she decided. She headed for the door. She could deal with wrinkles later. *Curiosity over fashion,* she thought with a smile and shut the door behind her.

The upstairs hall was lit only by the afternoon sun that found its way through the half-closed blinds over the west-facing windows near her room. The floor creaked in spots as she walked down the hall toward the stairs. The creaks were not loud enough to be heard in her room, she reckoned, unless she left her door open. She didn't like her bedroom door open at night, even at home, and she didn't think it would be a good idea to leave it open here.

As she neared the head of the stairs, she felt in her pocket for her phone. No luck. It was probably still in her purse. She turned back to retrieve it. She didn't expect any calls, but she might want to take pictures as they looked through the house.

She swung her door open into the room and paused. What was that sound? A click perhaps? She swung the door back and forth.

No repetition of the sound, yet she would have sworn she heard something when she opened her door. *Maybe you're starting to imagine things. This house is getting on your nerves.*

"No, it's not," she said aloud to reassure herself. She found her purse and retrieved the cell phone. She checked the battery to be sure she had enough of a charge to last for a couple of hours, and she did.

She glanced at the bed before she turned

back toward the door. She stopped and turned slowly back to the bed. Her mind focused on what she saw; she laid her purse down again and moved closer to the bed.

Her nightgown — the nightgown she had folded and placed under her pillow — lay unfolded across the foot of the bed.

CHAPTER 7

An'gel stared at her nightgown for a moment. She felt strangely calm. The attempts to frighten her were having the opposite effect. The person behind this — she still refused to believe that a supernatural hand had moved her dress and nightgown — had miscalculated. Badly. An'gel wasn't going to throw her hands up in the air and scream bloody murder. No, An'gel was going to get to the bottom of this and take great satisfaction in telling the miscreant exactly what she thought of his — or her — juvenile behavior.

She remembered the odd click she had heard just as she opened the bedroom door. The sound hadn't emanated from the door, she was sure of that. It had come from somewhere inside the bedroom.

But where?

She glanced around the room. There was no closet in the room, only the wardrobe and the clothes press for storage of clothing. The room had a large window on each outside wall, one facing west and the other north. One could open the window and step out onto the gallery that ran around three sides of the second floor. Had someone come in through the window from the gallery to move her clothes?

An'gel checked each window in turn, and both were locked on the inside. The click she had heard wasn't the sound of a window latch, then. She would have to examine the room further, but now she had better meet Dickce downstairs and look over the first floor of the house. She wanted to question Mary Turner about the possibilities of a hidden passage or secret rooms in the house. She had never heard of the existence of either at Cliffwood, but that didn't mean the house had none.

Downstairs she found Dickce looking a bit irritated.

"What took you so long?" Dickce asked. "I was about to come back up and get you."

"I was on my way but realized I hadn't brought my phone," An'gel said. "I wanted it in case we needed to take pictures." She paused to glance around. They appeared to be alone. She stepped close to her sister and lowered her voice. "There was another incident."

Dickce's eyes grew wide. "What happened?"

An'gel told her about the click she'd heard and the moving of the nightgown.

"This is getting creepier by the minute," Dickce said. "Why on earth is someone doing this? Are they trying to drive Mary Turner and Henry Howard out of the house?"

"That's what I'm thinking," An'gel said. "But I can't see Mary Turner ever selling this house and leaving her family heritage behind, can you?"

Dickce shook her head. "No, this house is her legacy from her father, and I don't believe she would ever willingly leave it."

"There may be something else going on that we don't know about," An'gel said. "I have the distinct feeling that Mary Turner and Henry Howard haven't told us the whole story yet."

"You're probably right," Dickce said. "Why would they invite us here to help figure out what's going on, though, and not tell us everything?"

"I don't know," An'gel said, "and that worries me. Back to the nightgown incident again for a moment. This time I thought to check the windows because that click I heard could have been the closing of a window."

"You mean someone getting into the room from the gallery?" Dickce grimaced. "I certainly don't like the idea of that."

"Both windows were locked. Be sure to check yours next time you're there," An'gel said. "While we go through the house, keep an eye out for any kind of spatial oddity."

"What kind of spatial oddity?"

"Think of it like a blueprint," An'gel replied. "Look for places where there could be a false wall, for example, with a crawl space between rooms. Where the inside of a room doesn't seem to match with the outside."

"I think I see what you mean. You're looking for a secret passage, aren't you?" Dickce's eyes sparkled. "Just like in my favorite Nancy Drew book, *The Hidden Staircase*. Oh, how I loved that book as a girl."

An'gel smiled briefly. "I did, too, and that's exactly what I'm talking about. There could be a secret room or two, small spaces, I'd say."

"Maybe there's a secret tunnel from the house to one of the outbuildings," Dickce said in what An'gel considered a hopeful tone.

"Possibly," An'gel said. "But I'm not planning to go through any secret tunnels, especially one that could be one hundred and fifty years old or more."

"Chicken." Dickce grinned. "But I know what you mean. At our age, the last thing we need to do is go exploring underground passageways."

"If there ever was one," An'gel said. "Let's start with the front parlor."

"Okay." Dickce followed her sister to the room in question.

"Have you seen anyone since you've been downstairs?" An'gel asked as she opened the parlor door.

"Not a soul," Dickce said. "Oh, this is such a lovely room. It reminds me of home."

"It should," An'gel said tartly. "It's furnished with the same period of furniture, and the carpet is nearly like ours, too." She regarded the Aubusson with a critical eye. She spotted a few nearly threadbare sections. "This one needs some restoration work, however. Remind me to give Mary Turner the name of the company that did ours."

"They might not be able to afford to have it done," Dickce said. "You need to keep that in mind."

"True," An'gel said. "I'll have to think of a way to mention it tactfully."

"You do that," Dickce said. "I don't see any spatial oddities in here, do you?"

"No, can't say as I do," An'gel replied.

The spacious front parlor at Cliffwood formed a large rectangle. The longest walls were the north and south ones, with the east and west walls perhaps three or four feet shorter. The west and north walls each had two windows that opened onto the porch.

An'gel thought, *This is a room where you could comfortably entertain twenty to thirty people, although you'd have to bring in extra chairs.*

"Weren't this room and the one next door all one room at some point?" Dickce said. "I seem to recall that there was a large great room where they could hold balls and dancing parties."

"Yes, don't you remember that Mary Turner's father had that wall put in to divide the rooms? He also had that fireplace installed in the center of the new wall." An'gel gestured toward the ornately carved oak mantel and the stone hearth.

"This room and the next are under our bedrooms," Dickce said. "If there's a secret room with stairs up to the second floor, perhaps it's near the fireplace."

"Excellent point," An'gel said. "Let's have a closer look."

They approached the fireplace. An'gel estimated the mantel was about eight feet wide and perhaps seven feet high. She wouldn't have to stoop much to get inside the fireplace, she reckoned. At the moment, however, she wasn't about to, because the detritus of a fire covered the bottom.

"If there's a secret room here, and the fireplace is connected to it," An'gel said, "there has to be a mechanism of some kind to open the entrance."

"Maybe it's somewhere in all this carving," Dickce said. "It's really elaborate. Trees on the sides, with various creatures hiding in the leaves and branches. And that's some kind of vine across the front over the fireplace."

"Something just occurred to me," An'gel said, annoyed with herself for not having thought of it sooner. "Remember that Mary Turner's father had all this work done. Why would he have a secret room with a staircase to the second floor put in? There wouldn't have been one already here, since it was one large room. Does that seem reasonable?"

Dickce frowned. "When you put it like that, no, it doesn't. Should we bother to look any further here?"

"I'm inclined to think not," An'gel said. "Marshal Turner Junior was a good man, but not a particularly imaginative one. I simply can't see him wanting a secret passage."

"You're right," Dickce said. "I guess we'll have to look elsewhere in the house, then." She traced the pattern of the upper part of the tree on the left side of the mantel. She pushed on various carved figures and several leaves but without result. "Nothing," she said.

"Before we abandon the fireplace altogether," An'gel said, "let's try an experiment." She headed toward the door, and Dickce followed after a moment.

"What are we going to do?" Dickce asked.

"I'm going to stand in the doorway in a position where I can see both sides of the wall. You will walk along the wall out here" — she indicated the hallway — "slowly, until it seems to me that you are even with the dividing wall. I will tell you to stop."

"Then you'll go to the doorway in the next room and look to see if where I'm standing is even with the wall on that side." Dickce nodded. "Yes, let's do it. If there seems to be a discrepancy, we can get a tape measure and do it more exactly."

An'gel got in place, and Dickce walked at a slow pace down the hallway next to the wall. An'gel watched carefully, and when she thought her sister had reached the point where the dividing wall crossed, she called out, "Stop."

Dickce stood in place, and An'gel hurried past her to the doorway of the next room, the library. The door was shut, and An'gel knocked three times. Hearing no sound from within, she opened the door and got in position. She thought Dickce's position was roughly equivalent to the dividing wall on the library side. She shook her head.

"No spatial oddity?" Dickce asked.

"None that I can see," An'gel replied as she began to move toward her sister. "We ought to move on."

A voice from above somewhere startled both An'gel and Dickce.

"What *are* you doing?"

An'gel glanced up to see Primrose Pace peering over the banister rail about halfway down the stairs. "Conducting an experiment," she said. Should they tell this woman what they were doing? she wondered.

Mrs. Pace saved her the trouble. "Looking for a secret passage, I'll bet." She laughed. "That would sure make things even more interesting, but I think you'll find that what's going on in this house has nothing to do with any secret rooms or staircases."

"You're convinced, then," An'gel said, her

tone cool, "that the spirits are the cause?"

"I am, sure as I'm standing here." Mrs. Pace laughed again, then started down the stairs. After three steps she paused, and as An'gel watched, the woman's eyes grew large and her expression turned to one of sheer terror. Her knees gave way, and she sat on the stair tread with a loud thump.

CHAPTER 8

For a moment An'gel feared that Mrs. Pace might tumble forward down the stairs, but the woman grabbed one of the spindles of the banister and steadied herself. An'gel followed Dickce up the stairs to proffer assistance.

They stood side by side on a stair that put them at eye level with the medium. Mrs. Pace's eyes remained closed, and her skin had an ashy cast to it, but when An'gel started to ask the woman what they could do to help, Mrs. Pace held up a hand to silence her.

Is this part of an act? An'gel couldn't be certain. Had the medium really experienced a supernatural episode, or was this a stunt geared to encourage their belief in her abilities? An'gel exchanged a look with her sister, and she could tell Dickce felt some of the same skepticism she did.

An'gel decided to speak even if the medium wanted her to remain silent awhile longer. "Mrs. Pace, are you all right? Do you need anything? A doctor? Something to drink?"

The medium's eyelids fluttered open, and she appeared to be having trouble focusing on An'gel and Dickce. Then her eyes cleared, and a slow smile replaced the dazed expression.

"That was amazing," she said. "Did either of you feel it?" She glanced from one sister to the other and back again.

"Feel what?" Dickce asked.

"The cold," Mrs. Pace replied. "It passed right through me, though it did seem to linger a moment. I wasn't expecting to encounter a spirit so soon." She shivered suddenly. "The cold of the grave. That's what it felt like." She pulled herself upright and looked down upon An'gel and Dickce.

"I hoped the spirit would remain and try to communicate with me." The medium motioned for the sisters to precede her down the stairs, and An'gel and Dickce turned and walked down. Mrs. Pace said, "She did not, despite that momentary hesitation. I feel sure she will eventually."

Once they'd reached the first floor, An'gel turned to face the medium and asked, "You believe the spirit is female?"

Mrs. Pace nodded. "Yes, I do. That was definitely a feminine energy that passed through me. Now, if you will excuse me, ladies, I really must find the kitchen. After that experience, I need food and drink to renew my energy."

Dickce pointed the way to the kitchen, and Mrs. Pace strode purposefully down the hall. An'gel waited until the medium was out of earshot before she turned to her sister. "What did you think of that? Performance? Or an actual supernatural episode?"

"At first I thought it had to be real." Dickce shrugged. "Her expression when she stopped and then suddenly sat down hard on the stairs, well, she seemed utterly surprised. But if this is her business, then I figure she must be quite an accomplished actress."

"You were standing nearer the stairs than I was," An'gel said. "Did you feel any cold?"

"No." Dickce frowned. "I was several feet away from where Mrs. Pace was on the staircase, so I don't suppose there's a reason I would have felt anything."

An'gel wasn't so sure. Could the spirit — if indeed it was a spirit — hold its essence so close as not to be felt more than a few inches away from the person it enveloped? If only they had a trustworthy authority on these things that they could consult. She dredged her memories to come up with a name but couldn't.

Maybe there was an expert in Natchez. Mary Turner might know, An'gel thought, and decided to ask her soon. Surely, given the fact that Natchez was alleged to be so haunted, there had to be someone around who was knowledgeable.

An'gel shared these thoughts with her sister, and Dickce nodded. "Excellent idea. The only things I know about the occult are what I've read in fiction."

"Yes," An'gel said. "Me, too, since we read many of the same authors. Too bad we can't call up Carolyn Haines or Charlaine Harris to ask them their opinions."

"Or Carolyn Hart," Dickce added. "I love her ghost series, and at least her ghost is nice."

An'gel laughed. "They'd probably think we were crazy if we did manage to find their phone numbers and called them up out of the blue, asking for advice."

Dickce giggled in response. "I'm sure they'd be nice to us, but you're right, they might wonder how we got loose long enough to get to a phone."

An'gel felt better after this brief interlude of humor. She had begun to feel somewhat oppressed by the burden of the task they had agreed to take on. *Chasing ghosts, at my age.* She almost snorted at the thought, but when a friend needed help, what could you do?

"What next?" Dickce pulled An'gel out of her reverie. "Keep looking through the house?"

"Yes," An'gel replied, though she had already begun to tire of the search.

The front doorbell interrupted them before they could continue their survey.

"Should we answer it, do you think?" Dickce asked.

"Probably best to let Mary Turner or Henry Howard do it," An'gel said, "in case it's someone looking for a room. Let's go back in the library and look further."

She turned to head toward the library, with Dickce behind her, and the doorbell sounded again. "Certainly impatient, whoever it is." An'gel paused. "Maybe we should answer it. I don't think anyone else is coming."

The caller began knocking on the door, sounding louder and louder with every strike. An'gel frowned, annoyed at the person. She strode toward the door and swung it open to confront the caller.

A young woman, her hand raised to strike

again, pulled back in time to avoid hitting An'gel, who noted the woman's petulant expression without sympathy. There had been no reason she could see for this person to bang on the door like a drunken sailor.

"Good afternoon," An'gel said, her tone barely civil to her own ears. "May I help you?"

The young woman, who An'gel judged to be in her mid-twenties, had attractive features, though at present marred by a scowl.

"You can stand aside and let us come in," the young woman said, her tone haughty. "You look a little old to be the housekeeper, you know."

"I am not the housekeeper," An'gel said over the sounds of her sister's smothered laughter somewhere behind her. "I'm a guest of the owners, if you must know." She continued to block the rude young woman from entry.

The stranger shrugged. "Well, how nice for you. You're still standing in the way."

"So I am," An'gel replied. "You haven't stated your business here, and until I know why you're here, I'm not going to move."

"Get this old biddy," the stranger said over her shoulder.

For the first time An'gel noticed a handsome blond man, probably twenty years older than the woman, standing a few feet behind his companion. He stepped forward.

"Our apologies, ma'am," he said, his voice husky. He smelled faintly of cigars and brandy, and An'gel decided he was well on his way to being fully lit. "My client happens to be under considerable stress at the moment. Normally she's not this discourteous." He stared hard at the young woman, as if willing her to apologize.

She did not comply. Instead she tossed her head. "Truss, don't be such a weenie. We have every right to come into this house. Part of it belongs to my family anyway."

The man took a breath, held it for a moment, then slowly expelled it. He smiled at An'gel. He was quite handsome, she decided, but had begun to run to seed. Probably because of his fondness for brandy and cigars. *And younger women,* she thought.

"Ma'am, again I beg your pardon. I am Truscott Anderson Wilbanks, the fourth of that name. Perhaps you have heard of my family, who have been in Natchez for generations." He didn't wait for An'gel to reply, which was just as well because she had never heard of him or his family. "This young lady is Serenity Foster. She and her brother, Nathan Gamble, are distant cousins of Mary Turner Catlin."

"Thank you for introducing yourself and your client, Mr. Wilbanks." An'gel then introduced herself and Dickce, who had hovered behind her impatiently the whole time. Once her introductions were acknowledged, she stood aside and let Ms. Foster and Mr. Wilbanks enter the house.

"I thought I heard the front door," Mary Turner called out as she came down the hallway from the back of the house. An'gel and Dickce moved aside to let her see the newcomers, and Mary Turner's progress faltered. An'gel saw a grimace, quickly erased, as her hostess stepped forward.

"Hello, Serenity, Truss. What brings you here today?" Mary Turner said, her arms now crossed over her chest. Not a welcoming stance, An'gel thought.

Wilbanks started to speak, but Serenity Foster interrupted him. "Nathan said he was coming here this afternoon, and I've got to talk to him. He's going to have to change his mind about the trust fund."

Mary Turner frowned. "Nathan? He's not here now, and this is the first I've heard he was planning to show up here today." From the young woman's tone, An'gel deduced that Nathan would be no more welcome than Ms. Foster and Mr. Wilbanks.

"This isn't a good time for him to come bothering me yet again with the same old crazy story," Mary Turner said, her tone becoming increasingly heated. "He's got to get it through his head that he has no legal rights here. No one in the Gamble family does. That will probably never existed, but if it did, it's long gone by now. Henry Howard and I are sick and tired of dealing with Nathan."

The name *Gamble* struck a chord. An'gel remembered then that her friend Jessy, Mary Turner's grandmother, had often mentioned the Gambles — offshoots of a younger sister of a Turner sometime in the nineteenth century — but never in a friendly or complimentary manner.

Serenity Foster shrugged. "That's Nathan's gig, not mine. He's obsessed with finding that will, and I don't care what he does. What I do care about is him trying to cheat me out of rights to the trust fund."

An'gel knew that she and Dickce should politely withdraw, but she had the odd feeling that Nathan Gamble might have something to do with the problems at Cliffwood. If he had a claim against the estate, perhaps he was trying to drive Mary Turner and Henry Howard out of the house. The pertinent question was, of course, what kind of claim did Nathan Gamble have against the Turner family and their possession of Cliffwood? An'gel decided she and Dickce needed to know everything they could about this. She stood where she was and indicated to Dickce that she should as well.

"You've got no call to bring your dispute with your brother here," Mary Turner said. "This is my home, but it's also a place of business. I can't have the two of you screaming and carrying on with each other while we have guests here."

Wilbanks stepped forward and laid a hand on Mary Turner's arm in a placatory gesture. "Serenity has no intention of creating that kind of disturbance here, Mary Turner. She simply wants to talk to her brother, who has refused recently to let her in his house." He smiled briefly. "As her advisor, I suggested that meeting with him on neutral ground was the best approach. Cliffwood is her best chance, and she has to talk to him soon. He's got to see sense, or she is going to lose her case for joint custody of the twins. All she needs is money to catch up on her mortgage and show the court she has a good home for the boys."

At these words, Serenity Foster started to cry quietly, her expression full of tragedy and loss.

This was sounding more and more like a soap opera, An'gel thought, and Serenity Foster was now behaving like the downtrodden heroine looking desperately for help. An'gel had never trusted women who could cry on cue like that, and she was convinced that was exactly what Serenity Foster was doing.

Mary Turner looked stricken. "I had no idea the situation had gotten that bad with your ex-husband, Serenity." She paused, then continued in a rush, "I guess you might as well wait here and see if Nathan shows up. Y'all go into the front parlor, and I'll go talk to Marcelline about coffee or something." She turned and hurried down the hall without waiting for a response.

Wilbanks took his client by the arm and turned her toward the parlor. He flashed a smile at An'gel and Dickce. "If you'll excuse us, ladies."

As he led Serenity Foster away, An'gel heard the young woman mutter to her companion, "If Nathan doesn't come through with the money, I swear I'll kill him this time."

CHAPTER 9

An'gel stared at the retreating backs of Serenity Foster and her lawyer. If she had been Mary Turner, she would have not-so-politely shown the two of them the door, custody battle or no custody battle.

Dickce's elbow dug into her side. "Did you hear that?"

An'gel regarded her sister with a frown. "The threat, you mean? Yes, I heard it. What of it?"

"Doesn't it worry you a little?" Dickce asked. "The last thing we need is to be involved in another murder."

An'gel resisted the temptation to roll her eyes at Dickce. "I seriously doubt that petulant young woman is going to do anything of the kind. Don't let your imagination run away with you, Sister."

"We'll see." Dickce shook her head. "I'm getting a bad feeling about all this."

"That's probably the extra piece of carrot

cake you ate at lunch." An'gel was in no mood to deal with Dickce's *feelings.* She had them far too often, and most of the time they were wrong. Just figments of Dickce's frequently overactive imagination.

"Do you have any idea, *Sister,* how often I long to slap your smug face?" Dickce looked annoyed.

An'gel paid no attention to this little sally. She badly wanted to talk to Mary Turner in private, but at the moment she didn't see much hope of that. Mary Turner would be bound to engage in conversation with her cousin and her lawyer. She certainly wouldn't leave them alone in the parlor if she were their hostess, and not necessarily because of good manners. That lawyer looked more than a little seedy to her.

Mary Turner returned pushing a tea cart. She paused a moment to speak to An'gel and Dickce. "I'm so sorry about all this," she said. "I'm sure you don't want to have anything to do with this mess, but would you come in with me? I have a hard time dealing with Serenity."

"Certainly, my dear," An'gel said. "You shouldn't have to face this by yourself. Where is Henry Howard?" She thought it odd that he wasn't here during a situation of this kind, when his wife obviously needed support.

Mary Turner frowned. "He's gone into town to the library to do some research, and then he's meeting later on with his critique group."

"I didn't know he was a writer," Dickce said.

"Yes," Mary Turner replied. "He's been working on an epic fantasy novel for several years now."

"I hope he's successful with it," Dickce said. "I mostly read mysteries and nonfiction, but I'd read his fantasy novel since I know him."

"He really wants to be able to write full-time," Mary Turner said, "but of course, we can't afford for him to. I can't run this place by myself, and we don't have the money to hire someone full-time to do all the things he does. If he ever manages to sell this thing and it takes off, well, that would be different." She shrugged. "I'd better take this into my guests before the coffee gets cold."

"Of course," An'gel said. "We'll be right behind you."

Mary Turner resumed her progress with the tea cart, and the sisters followed. When An'gel entered the room, she caught a glimpse of Serenity Foster and Wilbanks, apparently oblivious to the fact that they had company, engaged in making out on one of the sofas. An'gel cleared her throat loudly, and the two sprang apart. Wilbanks got hastily to his feet, his face red.

"Here's the coffee," Mary Turner said. "Plus some of Marcelline's wonderful oatmeal raisin cookies." She placed the cart near the end of the sofa where Serenity Foster still sat.

She didn't look in the least embarrassed at having been caught in a clinch, An'gel thought. At least the lawyer had the grace to look abashed. Girls these days simply had no sense of proper behavior. Carrying on like that with a man who looked to be old enough to be her father, or almost. And her lawyer to boot. An'gel's opinion of the girl, not high to begin with, sank even lower.

While she and Dickce found seats on the other sofa, facing Serenity Foster and Wilbanks, Mary Turner served the coffee as if she had not observed the behavior of her two most recent guests. After passing around plates and then the cookies, Mary Turner took a seat in a chair placed perpendicular to the sofas.

"Did Nathan give you any idea of what time he planned to arrive here?" Mary Turner took a sip of her coffee while she waited for an answer.

Serenity Foster put down the cookie she had been about to sample and frowned at her cousin. "Not exactly," she said. "He said midafternoon, but the way he keeps track of time, who knows? Could be ten o'clock tonight before he shows up."

Mary Turner did not reply to this, and a brief silence ensued. Wilbanks ended it. "These are great cookies," he said. "I'd forgotten how good a cook Marcelline is."

"I'll be sure to tell her that," Mary Turner said. "Tell me, Truss, when did you become Serenity's lawyer? I didn't realize you two knew each other."

"A couple of months ago," he said. "Actually we've known each other for several years, but only recently did Serenity ask me to take over her case. Her previous attorney couldn't seem to make any headway on the custody issue, and she thought a fresh approach might make a difference."

An'gel followed the conversation with interest, and she knew Dickce was an intrigued as she was. Wilbanks had a smooth manner, and he had an excellent voice, though roughened by his smoking. She could imagine him addressing a jury or a judge. She did wonder how successful he was, however, because the suit he had on looked at least ten years old and rather worn in places, like the cuffs of the jacket. There appeared to be a button missing from one sleeve as well.

Or maybe he spends all his money on liquor and cigars, she thought.

"I hope you'll be able to help her," Mary Turner said. "I can only imagine how you must feel, Serenity, not being able to see the children as much as you'd like."

"It's horrible," Serenity responded. "That jerk is doing his best to turn them against me." She stared at An'gel and Dickce. "Don't you think that's a terrible thing to do to a mother?"

Depends on the mother, An'gel thought but did not express this aloud. Instead she said, "I'm sure it must be trying for you."

"Yes, it must be," Dickce said.

"My brother knows all this, and he's too cheap to help me out." Serenity stuffed half a cookie into her mouth and chewed. She hadn't quite finished it when she spoke again. "He keeps going on about depleting my capital and crap like that, when I know there's more than enough money for me to pay what I owe on the mortgage if only he'd turn loose some of it."

An'gel did not care to see people talking while they chewed their food, and she glanced away until Serenity finished speaking. When the words ceased, she looked back again.

Mary Turner said, "For your sake, I hope you can come to some sort of compromise. Would anyone like more coffee?"

Everyone declined, and conversation lagged again. An'gel did not feel impelled to contribute, because she and Dickce didn't know these people. An'gel remained curious, however, to see whether there was any connection between the Gambles and the goings-on at Cliffwood. The more she and Dickce learned about the family and their claims on the Turner estate, the better.

"I don't know what Nathan thinks he can accomplish by coming here," Mary Turner said. "Nothing's going to change the fact that the alleged will has never turned up. There's no written documentation, in fact, that the story is true. That's all it is, a story."

"A story passed down through several generations, as I understand it," Wilbanks said. "Isn't that right?"

Serenity nodded. "Yes, it is, and I don't care what you say, Mary Turner, it all really happened."

Mary Turner glanced at An'gel and Dickce. "I know this is confusing for you, because you have no idea what we're talking about."

"No, we don't," An'gel said, "but we don't have to know, if you think it's none of our business."

"You might as well hear the whole thing," Mary Turner said. "Once Nathan gets here, that's all he will talk about. He's obsessed with it."

"What is the story that's been handed down?" Dickce asked.

"It goes all the way back to my fourth great-grandfather." Mary Turner paused and counted silently on her fingers. "Yes, that's right, fourth great-grandfather on the Turner side. He was the one who rebuilt Cliffwood after it was destroyed in that fire. Once the house was rebuilt, he and his wife started to refurnish it because they had lost almost everything in the fire. At the time his youngest sister, another Mary, lived here, and she evidently loved everything French. So he imported all the furniture for her room from France and decorated it with mostly French things like those Baccarat vases."

"So that's how the French room got its name," An'gel said. "Now that you've told us, I remember your grandmother telling us this story years ago."

"Yes, that's it," Serenity said. "But the important part is that this baby sister of his was my fourth great-grandmother. She married a man from Vicksburg named Jedediah Gamble. Her brother had told her she could take everything in the room with her, but his wife pitched a fit because she was horribly jealous of my great-grandmother. So he backed out on his promise but he swore he would leave it all to her in his will, and if she died before him, to her heirs."

Mary Turner took up the story once again.

"She lived to be quite old and outlived him, as it turned out, but this will — if it ever existed — never turned up. The will that he did leave made no mention of any legacy to his sister. He hadn't wanted her to marry Jedediah Gamble." She stared hard at Serenity. "You left out that part."

"Because it doesn't really matter," Serenity said.

"Why did your great-grandfather not want his sister to marry Mr. Gamble?" Dickce asked. "Was he a poor man?"

"No, he was not," Serenity said. "His family lost a lot during the war, like most people did, but he was smart and ended up restoring the family's wealth before he married my great-grandmother."

"Then what was the issue about the marriage?" An'gel asked. "Is it really pertinent to the story?"

"Yes," Mary Turner said. "I think it explains why there was no will leaving the contents of the French room to my four times great-aunt. I know this will probably sound ridiculous to you, but it was because he was from Vicksburg. After the war, there was a lot of dissension between the people of Natchez and the people of Vicksburg."

"Whatever for?" An'gel asked. "I suppose it had something to do with the war."

"It sure did," Serenity said, her tone becoming increasingly heated as she talked. "The people of Vicksburg stood up to the Union Army. They refused to give in, but the traitors in Natchez let them in. They didn't want anyone to hurt their precious houses."

"Seriously?" Dickce asked.

"I'm afraid so," Mary Turner replied. "Families, particularly in Vicksburg, refused to have anything to do with their relations in Natchez for years afterwards. There was a tremendous amount of resentment. Naturally, people in Natchez didn't like the attitudes of the people in Vicksburg." She paused for a moment. "Supposedly, Jedediah Gamble had been pretty outspoken about all this because his family lost their home while Cliffwood wasn't really harmed. But he fell in love with Great-Aunt Mary and was determined to have her."

"If I understand all this correctly," An'gel said, "the reason that your great-grandfather didn't leave his sister the contents of the room in his will is because he disliked his brother-in-law so much, he didn't want even his sister's children to have it."

"Basically, that's it," Mary Turner said. "And that's why the Turners are sure there never was a will leaving anything to Great-Aunt Mary."

A voice from the doorway startled them all. "That's a damn filthy lie, and you know it."

CHAPTER 10

Given the aggressive attitude and the contents of his statement, this had to be Nathan Gamble, An'gel thought.

Mary Turner quickly confirmed it. "Why do you always have to sneak into my house, Nathan? And then behave like a crazy person, I might add." She rose from her chair to confront her cousin. "Why are you here?"

Nathan seemed not to have heard her. An'gel could see that his attention now appeared to be focused on his sister. "Why are *you* here, Serenity? If you think you're going to badger me into giving you that money, you might as well save yourself the effort. I'm not going to let you have it."

Serenity jumped to her feet and let loose a string of profanities directed at her brother and his stinginess and other unpleasant qualities. Wilbanks put out a hand to get her attention but she brushed him aside.

An'gel and Dickce exchanged glances of distaste and disapproval. This young woman was downright nasty, An'gel thought, debasing herself this way. She was screaming now but her brother didn't appear to be affected by it, other than by continuing to shake his head at her.

An'gel had had enough. No one else seemed willing to stop this tirade. She might as well do it. She got up and positioned herself practically in the young woman's face and glared at her. Serenity appeared startled by An'gel's actions and sputtered to a halt.

"You sit down right this moment, young woman," An'gel said, "and close that nasty mouth. I don't want to hear another vulgar word out of you, or I will slap you so hard you'll think it's next week. Do you understand me?"

Serenity shrank against the back of the sofa and nodded in a jerky fashion. "Yes, ma'am," she whispered.

Nathan Gamble grinned at An'gel. "I don't know who you are, lady, but you're the first person since my mama died who's ever been able to shut her up once she gets going in one of her hissy fits. Thank you."

"You need to learn to control your temper and your language, young woman," An'gel said. "No one is going to move an inch to assist you when you behave like a deranged lunatic." She turned to Nathan Gamble. "I realize this is really none of my business or my sister's, but I will not be forced to listen to such carrying-on." After one last glare at Serenity, she resumed her seat.

Dickce laughed. "An'gel the Terminator at your service." She introduced herself and her sister to Nathan Gamble, and he responded with the traditional, "Nice to meet you."

"You still haven't answered my question, Nathan," Mary Turner said. "Why are you here? I know it's not a social call."

"I'm having some work done at my house, and I need a place to stay for a few nights until they're done," Nathan replied. "I figured here was as good as any. Do you have a family rate?"

Now that relative calm once more reigned, An'gel had a more thorough look at Nathan Gamble. Late thirties, she thought, rather short, probably no more than five foot six, and scrawny. He had thick, curly dark hair that could use a good trim, and he wore dark-framed glasses. His clothes appeared to be clean, but they were old and worn in places. Was he that poor, to go around looking like he wore charity-bin rejects? An'gel wondered. Or was he too cheap to buy newer clothing?

"If he's going to stay here," Serenity said, suddenly assertive again, "then I'm going to stay here too. He's going to talk to me one way or another."

Mary Turner closed her eyes for a moment and drew a deep breath. After releasing it, she spoke. "We already have other guests staying here, and it's supposed to be vacation time for Henry Howard and me. Marcelline isn't expecting to have to provide meals for a lot of extra people, only those who were invited to be here."

That was pointed enough, An'gel thought, but would Nathan Gamble and his sister be deterred? She doubted they would.

"Marcelline doesn't have to cook most meals for me, maybe just breakfast," Nathan said, "as long as you knock the price down. I can go out and get my other meals."

"We can do the same thing." Serenity poked Wilbanks. "Can't we?"

The lawyer did not appear pleased by this appeal. An'gel was surprised he had been quiet through the recent ruckus, not doing a thing to curb his client's intemperate behavior. "If you say so, I guess we can."

Mary Turner glanced at An'gel as if she were asking for advice. An'gel thought it would be better not to have these people around while they were trying to work out what was behind the odd happenings at Cliffwood, but she didn't feel it was her place to tell Mary Turner this in front of Nathan, Serenity, and Wilbanks.

After a moment Mary Turner nodded. "Okay, then, I guess you can stay for a few days. The rooms in the annex are clean, so you can all stay there."

"No, I want to stay in the house," Nathan said. "I want to stay in my great-grandmother's room. The contents belong to me by right, no matter what you say."

"Miss An'gel has the French room," Mary Turner said, "so you will have to stay in another room."

An'gel foresaw a prolonged argument over the room, and she decided that, peeved as she was over Gamble's behavior, the simplest thing to do would be to let him have the room. There was another bedroom upstairs unoccupied that she could take.

When Nathan started to object, An'gel interrupted him. "Mary Turner, it's quite all right with me. I haven't unpacked, so it's easy for me to move to another room. I did, however, take a short rest in the bed, so it will need to be remade with fresh linen."

Mary Turner looked as if she wanted to

override An'gel's offer, but a stern glance from An'gel quelled her. Instead she said, "Very well, Miss An'gel. If you'll come up with me now, I'll help you move your things to the room on the other side of Miss Dickce."

An'gel rose to go with Mary Turner, and Dickce rose also. "I'm coming with you," she said with a bright smile to the others. "I'm sure y'all will excuse us while we take care of this."

Gamble said, "Sure thing," and Wilbanks and Serenity nodded.

Mary Turner shut the door to the parlor behind them once An'gel and Dickce had followed her into the hallway. She leaned against the door for a moment. "I'm so sorry about this, Miss An'gel," she said. "It's very kind of you to give up your room this way. Nathan is always determined to get his way, and he's got an obsession with that room. He's convinced the will is somewhere in the room, despite the fact that it's been gone over many times and nothing has ever turned up."

"The problem with an obsession," An'gel said, "is that the person obsessed tends to lose his sense of proportion and his ability to see things objectively. Nathan apparently is desperate to believe the will still exists, so therefore he is sure it will be found."

"Sounds a bit like Heinrich Schliemann," Dickce said.

"I'd hardly equate this with the discovery of Troy or Mycenae," An'gel said.

"Of course not," Dickce retorted. "It was simply an observation."

Mary Turner smiled. "The French room contains some valuable antiques, though. Maybe we ought to sell them and redo the room to match the others. Get rid of the reason for the obsession once and for all." She headed to the stairs and began to climb.

An'gel said, "Now that would be a shame, though you're correct about the value of pieces in that room. There's a small fortune in there, and if you ever really needed the money, I don't think anyone could blame you for selling the things."

"Nathan would blame me," Mary Turner said, "but he has no legal claim on anything in this house, no matter what he thinks."

"Do you think he wants the contents of the room in order to sell them?" Dickce asked as they stepped onto the upstairs landing. "Or does he want them because he thinks they're rightfully his?"

"Nathan loves money more than any-thing," Mary Turner replied. "I'm sure you saw the clothes he's wearing. He can afford

112

new clothes, but he wears things until they're practically in tatters because he can't bear to part with the money."

"You mean he would probably put the things from the French room in his home so he could sit there and gloat over them?" An'gel asked.

"Yes," Mary Turner said. "Silas Marner, but without many of the redeeming qualities." She opened the door to the French room but stood aside to let the sisters enter first.

An'gel had been apprehensive over what they might see, but a quick survey assured her that everything was as she had left it.

"Everything looks fine to me," Dickce said.

"Yes, thank goodness," An'gel replied.

"What made you think it might not be?" Mary Turner asked.

An'gel told her young hostess about the items that seemed to have moved on their own, and Mary Turner grimaced.

"I hope you weren't frightened by this," she said. "Frankly, though, I'm almost glad it happened, so you don't think I've been imagining things. It's a relief to know that someone besides me has seen it."

"What about Henry Howard?" An'gel asked. "Surely he has witnessed this, too."

Mary Turner shook her head. "Not in this room. He never — well, almost never — comes in here. I'm the one who has been treated to the moving objects show."

"And this only started recently?" Dickce asked.

"Well, no," Mary Turner said, then seemed reluctant to continue.

"My dear, both Sister and I suspect that you haven't told us quite everything yet," An'gel said kindly. "We do want to help you, but you have to tell us the whole story if we're going to accomplish anything."

Mary Turner sank into the armchair near the window. She threw up her hands in a gesture that was half surrender, half apology. She let her hands fall into her lap.

"Okay, then, the whole story is that weird things have been happening in this room for years. I didn't become aware of it, though, until about a year after Henry Howard and I got married and came here to take over running the bed-and-breakfast after my parents died."

"Did your parents ever say anything about strange activities in here?" Dickce asked.

"Not that I can recall," Mary Turner said. "But Daddy and Mother were always the kind of parents who thought their little girl shouldn't know about anything bad that was going on." Her eyes suddenly pooled with tears. "Like Mother's cancer or Daddy's heart problems. By the time I found out how sick they both were, it was too late for me to do anything but come home to make the funeral arrangements."

"Oh, my dear," An'gel said, "I had no idea. I'm so sorry."

"Thank you," Mary Turner said. She wiped away her tears with the back of one hand. "I'm sorry to go on like this, but sometimes it just hits me all over again."

"We understand," Dickce said.

"You were telling us that you didn't notice anything odd in this room until after you had been back here a year," An'gel said gently.

Mary Turner nodded. "That's right. At first I thought I was just imagining it, and I put it down to one of the maids doing it while she dusted. It didn't happen that often at first, and I didn't come in here every day either. But the maids didn't like dusting or cleaning in here, and I could never get a clear answer as to why. They simply told me they didn't feel comfortable.

"It turned out that they had noticed things being moved around but were afraid to tell me," Mary Turner said. "I decided to take over cleaning and dusting in here myself rather than make a fuss about it. And of course, with me being in here more often, I began to notice things more."

"Were you ever truly frightened by it?" An'gel asked. She herself had not really felt afraid for her life, but she had been a bit spooked by what had happened to her.

"No, and that's the strange thing," Mary Turner said slowly. "It's spooky, of course, but I've never felt it was intended to scare me or warn me. Whoever or whatever is doing it doesn't seem to mind me being in the room. We never let guests stay in here, you see, because of the value of the contents. It's just safer in the long run to keep them off-limits to guests."

"But you were going to let An'gel sleep here," Dickce said.

Mary Turner looked slightly abashed. "Yes. For one thing, I knew we could trust her not to damage anything because you live with valuable furniture and objects like this every day. Then I figured you wouldn't be scared out of your wits, maybe only spooked a little, like I was at first."

"You were correct on both counts," An'gel said, her tone rather dry. "It's just as well that I don't frighten easily, however."

"But now you're going to let Nathan Gamble stay in this room," Dickce said.

"He's never stayed in it before, I gather?"

"No, he hasn't." Mary Turner grinned suddenly. "Frankly, I hope something happens while he's in this room that will spook the life out of him."

CHAPTER 11

Benjy thought the ghost looked an awful lot like his stepfather.

But what was his stepfather doing here? He ought to be in California.

Am I in California?

The ghost didn't look like his stepfather now. It didn't look like anyone Benjy knew. It also looked really angry about something. Its arms shot out, and its hands grabbed for Benjy's throat.

Benjy screamed and backed away, but there was a wall behind him. Nowhere to go as the hands kept grabbing at his throat.

Somewhere a dog barked, and Benjy banged his head against the headboard and woke up.

He rubbed the back of his head and tried to orient himself. Where was he? Oh, yeah, the haunted house in Natchez.

His eyes fully open now, Benjy saw Peanut on the bed beside him, looking anxious.

Peanut woofed at him again, and Benjy patted the dog's head to reassure him.

"I'm okay, boy," Benjy said. "Thanks for waking me up. That was some creepy dream I was having."

He yawned. Where was Endora?

As if she had read his mind, the Abyssinian jumped down from atop the headboard and landed in his lap. He stroked her soft fur, and Endora stretched and yawned.

Benjy checked his watch and was surprised to see that it was nearly four o'clock. That meant he had been asleep for about two hours.

"Man, I didn't think I was that tired," he told the dog and the cat. He rubbed the back of his neck. "My headache's gone, but I must have been sweating like crazy." His neck felt a little clammy, and he realized his head was also damp.

Peanut suddenly licked his face, and Benjy grinned. "Thanks, but I think a shower is what I need. Let me take one and get dressed, then I'll take you out. How does that sound?"

Peanut barked happily. He understood the word *out*. Endora did, too, Benjy knew, though she was not always as keen on going outside as the dog was.

Ten minutes later, freshly showered and

back in his clothes, Benjy found Peanut's leash and attached it to the dog's collar. "I know you don't like this leash much," Benjy said in response to loud whining, "but we're not at home, and I can't let you just run around outside here. Next thing I know, you and Endora will be digging up a flower bed."

Or a dead body, he thought, like the one they'd found not that long ago after a big storm back in Athena.

While he walked Peanut and Endora in a grassy area surrounded by trees behind the annex with the guest rooms, Benjy thought about his dream.

He figured he knew why he dreamed about ghosts. All the talk about haunted houses the last couple of days before they came to Natchez had kept the subject firmly in his mind. At first, he thought it would be pretty cool to see a real ghost. Then, the more he thought about it, he wondered how he would really react. Would he stand his ground and face the ghost? Or would he scream and run away, terrified, like people in the old horror movies he used to watch on television? He wasn't sure at the moment whether he wanted to put himself to the test, not after that creepy dream about his stepfather.

But why had he dreamed about his stepfather? The man hadn't been in touch with him after the events of a few months ago, when Benjy's mother died. As far as Benjy knew, Miss An'gel and Miss Dickce hadn't heard anything from him either. Benjy didn't particularly *want* to hear from him. He had never liked the man all that much, and his stepfather hadn't cared for Benjy either.

Benjy was nineteen, an adult, with no legal ties to his stepfather, but he realized that secretly he was afraid the man would come to Mississippi and try to make him move back to California. Benjy didn't want that. There was nothing for him in California anymore.

Besides, he thought, he was really fond of Miss Dickce and Miss An'gel. They cared about him, had taken him in and given him a home. They had allowed him to adopt Peanut and Endora — well, really, they had all adopted the cat and the dog. But the animals were in his care most of the time, and he couldn't ever give them up, no matter what. He wanted to stay with the Ducote sisters, he realized. They were the only family he had now, along with Clementine, Peanut, and Endora.

He hadn't thought much about it before — hadn't allowed himself to, really —

because it was all like a wonderful dream. If he thought about it too much, something might happen to make it all go away. Make the dream into a reality, and his reality in California hadn't been happy or pleasant.

He had found a home, and he wanted to keep it. The sisters seemed like they truly cared about him, and he cared about them. Miss Dickce was like the grandmother he had never known, and Miss An'gel was like an aunt, he thought.

Now he didn't feel so spooked by the dream, he realized. Feeling unburdened, he came out of his reverie to see Peanut and Endora digging a hole near the roots of a tree.

"Stop that," he told them. They recognized the tone of voice and immediately stopped digging. Endora looked annoyed with him, but then she always did when he stopped her from creating a mess.

He caught them before they had dug much up, and he patted the dirt and grass back into place. He didn't want to know what lay underground there, and he would have to watch to be sure they didn't try to dig there again.

Thwarted from digging, Peanut concentrated on sniffing around and doing his business. Benjy picked up the poop in the plastic bag he had brought and dropped it in a large garbage can at the side of the annex.

"How about some water and a treat or two?"

Both Peanut and Endora looked happier once they heard the word *treat,* and he opened the door to their room and let them in. He was about to close the door behind him when he heard voices outside. He stuck his head out the door and saw Mary Turner walking toward the building, and she had two people with her. A guy and a woman. The guy looked kind of old, Benjy thought, over forty at least, but the woman looked okay. Younger than Mary Turner, but nowhere near as beautiful. Maybe the guy was the woman's father.

They hadn't spotted him, and he didn't want to be caught gawking at Mary Turner. His face reddened slightly as he drew his head back inside and shut the door. He couldn't help himself somehow when she was around. She was so nice and sweet and beautiful. His heart thumped a little harder whenever he thought about her.

Peanut barked to remind him that he had promised treats. Benjy went to the bag that contained the animals' food and dug around until he found the small bags of treats for each one. He had a couple in each hand before he turned around to give them out. He had quickly learned one would sulk if the other one got a treat first.

Peanut gobbled his down immediately and looked up at him hopefully. Endora picked her small bites up in her mouth and jumped on the bathroom counter away from Peanut. Sometimes the Labradoodle managed to steal hers before she could eat them, but not this time. Peanut knew better than to try to climb or jump on the counter.

"That's all you get for now," Benjy told him. He picked up their water bowls, dumped the contents, and refilled them. While Peanut lapped thirstily at his, Benjy retrieved a bottle of water for himself from the small fridge in the room and drained half of it in one go. He hadn't realized how thirsty he was.

He checked his phone to see if he had missed a text or a call from the sisters, but there was no message. He decided he ought to go over to the house and find them, see whether they needed him for anything.

"You two are going to stay here for a little while by yourselves." Benjy gave each a couple of rubs on the head. "Now be good, and don't make a racket. As soon as I can, I'll come back and get you, and you can visit in the house, okay? I need to see if everything is okay over there first."

Peanut woofed, but Endora, true to form, simply yawned at him and began washing a paw.

Making sure the door was securely locked behind him, Benjy headed across the wide courtyard toward the back door that led into the kitchen. Halfway across the courtyard that separated the house from the annex, he stopped for a moment to look at the back of the house.

Was it *really* haunted? He figured a house this old had seen its share of deaths. Remnants of those dead souls might linger on because of unfinished business. He had read that recently. What was the word the author had used? *Revenant.* Something that had returned from the dead. Despite the late afternoon sunshine, he shivered. That *returned from the dead* bit bothered him.

Miss Dickce and Miss An'gel didn't appear to be frightened by the thought of ghosts, so he decided he shouldn't be either. Besides, it was still daytime, and ghosts really didn't come out until nighttime. He was okay going into the house now, he decided, and continued his progress.

He knocked on the back door but received no answer. After a moment he opened the door and stepped inside. "Hello, anyone here? Miss Marcelline, are you here?"

There was no answer, so he pulled the door closed behind him and advanced into the kitchen. He sniffed appreciatively at the scent of a roast emanating from the Crock-Pot he espied on the counter. He wasn't sure if they would be dining here tonight, but he sure hoped so. Based on the food at lunch, he thought Miss Marcelline was in the same class as Clementine back home. Clementine cooked the best food he had ever eaten. He patted his stomach ruefully. He had gained at least ten pounds since he'd come to live with the Ducote sisters.

Benjy passed through the kitchen and out into the hallway, where he paused briefly to listen. He didn't hear any voices. Where were Miss Dickce and Miss An'gel? He wandered down the hallway and glanced into the open doors.

The first floor appeared to be empty. He walked back to the staircase and looked up. He remembered what Miss Dickce had said about the cold she had felt on the stairs. He hesitated a moment. What would he do if he felt it, too?

Might as well find out. He climbed the stairs to the second floor without feeling any change in temperature. He felt almost disappointed by that, but a little relieved as well. He paused at the top. He wasn't sure which room either of the sisters was occupying. He recalled a mention of the French room, where Miss An'gel was going to stay, but he had no idea which room it was.

He didn't want to knock on any doors and disturb anyone unnecessarily, so he pulled out his cell phone to call Miss Dickce. The phone began to ring, and he waited for her to answer. After a moment, he heard her say, "Hello, Benjy. Where are you?"

Before he could answer, he felt a soft touch on his shoulder, yelled in fright, and dropped the phone.

CHAPTER 12

While she unpacked in her new bedroom, An'gel kept pondering Mary Turner's remark about Nathan Gamble. How she hoped something would happen while he was in the French room that would scare the life out of him. Had Mary Turner told the man anything about the strange events in that room? She would have to ask Mary Turner when she saw her next. It didn't seem fair to let the man spend the night there without some kind of warning.

Of course, Nathan Gamble might not believe his cousin. He might think she was simply trying to get him out of the room so Miss An'gel could have it back. An'gel and Dickce could certainly vouch for Mary Turner, after the two incidents that An'gel had experienced. If the man didn't believe them after that, he could look out for himself.

A scream from outside her door startled An'gel into dropping the dress she was in the act of hanging in the wardrobe. Whoever screamed sounded terrified, and An'gel stood rooted to the spot for a moment. Then she hurried to the door and yanked it open, only to behold Benjy, hands clapped over his eyes, bent slightly forward, trembling.

Mary Turner, who stood behind him, said, "Benjy, I'm so sorry. I didn't mean to frighten you. I thought you heard me coming up the stairs not far behind you."

An'gel relaxed against the door frame and felt the pounding in her chest begin to ease. They were all on edge, and poor Benjy had evidently had a real fright. She watched as he dropped his hands, straightened his back, and turned to face his hostess. The poor boy's face was beet red, and An'gel knew he was terribly embarrassed. Bad enough that he had yelled like a scared child, but worse that it was in front of Mary Turner, whom he admired. An'gel felt bad for him.

Benjy offered Mary Turner a sheepish grin. "Sorry to yell like that. I guess I've been thinking too much about ghosts, and since I didn't think anyone was in the hall with me, I overreacted." The red began to recede from his complexion.

"There's no need to apologize to me," Mary Turner said firmly. "I'm the one who is apologizing. I should have called out to let you know I was behind you."

"The main thing is," Benjy said with a shaky laugh, "you're not a ghost. No telling what I might have done if I'd looked around and nobody was there."

Dickce hurried into the hallway from her room. "What's going on? Who screamed? Is everyone all right?" She stooped to pick up Benjy's cell phone from the carpet runner. "Isn't this yours?" She held it out to Benjy.

"Yes, ma'am, thank you." Benjy accepted the phone and then explained to Dickce that he was the one who'd yelled and why.

"My goodness, no wonder you reacted that way," Dickce said. "An'gel and I are both a little jumpy after what we've experienced today."

"What happened to you?" Benjy asked. His eyes widened in alarm, and An'gel hastened to assure him that she and Dickce were fine.

"There were two incidents of my clothing being moved from one place to another in the French room." An'gel related the details to Benjy.

Dickce said, "The only thing I've experienced so far is that cold sensation on the stairs. Did you feel it when you came up here?"

Benjy shook his head. "No, ma'am. Thank goodness. I was kind of expecting to, but it didn't happen." He indicated the doorway where An'gel stood. "Can I see inside the French room? I'm really curious to see what it's like."

"This isn't the French room," An'gel said. "I've switched to this one so that Mary Turner's cousin can have that room."

"My distant cousin, Nathan Gamble. My fifth cousin, I think. At least that's what my grandmother always told me," Mary Turner explained. "Anyway, he's having work done at his house — or so he says — and needed a place to stay for a couple of nights. He thinks the French room is his by right."

"What does that mean, *his by right*?" Benjy asked, obviously confused by Mary Turner's explanation.

"Tell you what," An'gel said before Mary Turner could respond. "Instead of standing out here in the hall, why don't we all go back downstairs to the parlor, where we can sit down and be comfortable. Then we'll explain." She pulled her door shut and headed around Mary Turner and Benjy to the stairs.

They all followed her into the parlor. Dickce and An'gel chose one sofa while Mary Turner and Benjy took the other. Now that they were seated comfortably, An'gel looked at Mary Turner. "Do you want to explain, or shall I?"

"You go ahead," Mary Turner said. "You'll do it more succinctly than I will because I usually get annoyed over the stupidity of it all and start digressing."

An'gel nodded. "Very well." She proceeded to give Benjy a précis of the story of fourth great-grandfather Turner and his young sister. When she'd finished, she rested against the back of the sofa and waited to hear what Benjy might say.

"This cousin of yours reminds me a little of my stepfather's mother." He glanced at An'gel and Dickce. "She was a friend of Miss Dickce's and Miss An'gel's. Anyway, she had an obsession, too, so I kinda know what you mean when you say your cousin is obsessed with the room."

"He's talking about our friend Rosabelle Sultan," Dickce explained. "You might have heard your grandmother talking about her. They knew each other at one time."

"Vaguely," Mary Turner said. "What was her obsession, Benjy?"

"Herself," he responded promptly. "I found out later, after reading about it in a psychology book, that she was a narcissist. Do you know what that means?"

Mary Turner nodded. "Yes, I do. Nathan is somewhat like that. He's really only concerned about himself and his bank account."

"Even if it is an obsession, and maybe he can't help himself," Benjy said, "the whole thing seems useless to me. Why would anyone in that family think the stuff in that room really belongs to them after all this time?"

"That's what comes from nursing a grudge, generation after generation," An'gel said. "I agree the whole thing is pointless on Nathan Gamble's part. But that doesn't mean people still don't feel that way. Dickce and I know two families in Athena that haven't spoken to each other if they can help it for over sixty years."

"I don't get it," Benjy said, "but I don't have to." He turned to his hostess. "Does he know about the weird things that happen in that room?"

"No, I don't think so," Mary Turner said. "I've certainly never told him, and I don't intend to." She glanced quickly at An'gel and Dickce. "I'd rather no one else did either. Let him experience it for himself." She shrugged. "Who knows? Maybe nothing at all will happen while he's in the room. He has little imagination that I've ever seen,

133

so he probably won't even notice if something gets moved."

An'gel felt that Mary Turner was wrong not to tell her cousin but she figured it would do no good to argue with her about it. "Very well," she said. "We won't say anything, but I think you should be prepared for the backlash if anything does happen and he is injured, for example."

"I really don't think anything serious is going to happen," Mary Turner said. "Nothing really terrible has happened so far, after all. It's been annoying and occasionally creepy, but neither Henry Howard nor I has been physically hurt."

"That's reassuring to hear," An'gel said. "Until we know what or who is behind all this, however, we can't take it for granted that no one will be hurt. It depends on the motive, I think. If the person responsible doesn't get what he or she wants, then the incidents could escalate."

"Now you're making it sound like one of those horror movies where the family moves into a house and starts getting attacked." Dickce shivered.

"I'm sorry if I frightened you, Sister," An'gel said, more irritated with Dickce than she cared to show. "The point is still valid. I don't think this is a house of horrors, but what's going on here isn't normal. Now, Mary Turner, there's a question I've been wanting to ask you."

"Yes, ma'am," Mary Turner said. "What is it?"

"Do you know whether there is a secret room or a hidden passageway in the house?" An'gel asked.

"Like in that Nancy Drew book?" Mary Turner asked. "I loved that book. My grandmother gave me her copy when I was nine years old." She shook her head. "No, there isn't that I know of. Daddy never said anything about one, and neither did Granny. I tried to find one after I read that book, but I never found anything."

"I see. It would certainly go a ways toward helping explain things if there were," An'gel said. "I'm not convinced there is one, mind you, but we have to keep our minds open to all possibilities."

"Naturally," Dickce said. "Does this mean you want to continue going through the house looking for those spatial oddities of yours?"

"We might as well," An'gel replied. "We need to observe everything we can about the house, and everyone in it as well. The answer could be anywhere. Anyone."

An'gel thought she heard the stairs creak

a couple of times. She wondered who was going up or down. Where was that medium, for example?s

"Have you seen Mrs. Pace recently?" An'gel directed her question to Mary Turner.

"No, as far as I know, she is still upstairs in her room. I had just come back from showing Serenity and Truss to their rooms when I startled Benjy in the hall. I was actually on my way to see you, Miss An'gel and Miss Dickce, to talk to you about dinner tonight. I'd forgotten all about that in the excitement." She winked at Benjy, who reddened a little.

"We'll be happy to go out to dinner," An'gel said. "We don't want to place any additional burden on Marcelline or you. I imagine Marcelline was looking forward to a little time off herself."

"That's kind of you," Mary Turner said, "but Marcelline has already put a roast on for dinner, and there's enough for all of us." She paused a moment. "Not for the other guests, though. I don't intend to feed them anything other than breakfast."

"I smelled the roast when I came in through the kitchen," Benjy said. "Smelled great. I vote for eating here, if that's okay."

Dickce laughed. "Of course it's okay. As

long as Marcelline has already cooked for us, I vote we stay here, too. We can help clean up in the kitchen afterwards."

"Yes," An'gel said. "That's a good idea."

"I'll tell Marcelline," Mary Turner said. "She might take you up on that, but don't be surprised if she doesn't. That kitchen is her domain." She grinned as she rose from the sofa. "If there's nothing else you need to ask me right now, I'd better go and talk to her about breakfast for the next few days and a few other things."

"Go right ahead," An'gel said. "If I think of anything else, I'll let you know."

Mary Turner nodded and smiled at them before she left the room.

"What shall we do now?" Dickce asked.

"For the moment, y'all can sit right here," An'gel said. "I'm going up to my room to retrieve my phone before we do anything else. I'll be back in a minute."

An'gel left Dickce and Benjy chatting about his room in the annex. She paused at the foot of the stairs and steeled herself for the potential aura of cold but felt nothing when she climbed the stairs other than her own exertions.

She found her cell phone right away and was about to head downstairs again when she decided she might as well use the bathroom before she did so. She walked past the doorway to Dickce's room and tapped on the bathroom door. The bathroom, which she was having to share with both her sister and Nathan Gamble, was between Dickce's room and the French room. Hearing no response from within, she opened the door and entered.

While she was drying her hands, she heard the sound of raised voices coming from next door in the French room. She paused to listen for a moment. She couldn't distinguish the words but thought that both voices sounded male. She wondered who might be arguing with Nathan Gamble. Had Henry Howard come back early from his trip into town?

An'gel replaced the towel on the rack and moved to the door. She opened it a crack and listened. The voices next door had stopped. She opened the door farther and peered to the right, toward the French room. She wanted to avoid the quarreling men if at all possible.

The hall was clear. She was about to step out and shut the door when she heard the French room door open. She stepped back in and peered around the edge of the door frame.

The lawyer Wilbanks stumbled into the

hall as if he had been pushed out the door. He was in the act of fastening his pants. He glared toward the door. He sounded hoarse when he yelled, "That's the last time I let you . . ."

An'gel pushed the door shut at the vulgar verb. She had heard and seen enough to know what had been going on next door.

CHAPTER 13

An'gel hastily shut the door and listened to judge when it might be okay for her to leave her room and head back downstairs. She didn't want to encounter the lawyer or Nathan Gamble at the moment.

She heard Wilbanks stomp by, cursing briefly. Then silence. Her face felt heated as she recalled Wilbanks's parting shot to Nathan Gamble. She thought it had been pretty clear earlier that the lawyer had more than a lawyer-client relationship with Serenity Foster. The fact that he had obviously been having an intimate relationship with Serenity's brother shocked her. She could be wrong, though. She might have misinterpreted what Wilbanks had meant by the use of a vulgar term.

On further reflection, she decided she was correct. Given the state of the lawyer's clothing when he was ejected from the room, there was really only one conclusion.

She waited a minute, timed on her cell phone, before she opened the door again. A quick glance assured her that the hallway was empty, and she closed the door and hurried toward the stairs. She debated whether to share what she had seen with Mary Turner. *Is the young woman aware of an intimate relationship between her cousin and the lawyer?* she wondered.

A few delicate questions might resolve that issue. Once she could think of the right delicate questions to ask, of course. She would share with Dickce and Benjy, though. The incident might have no bearing at all on the strange incidents here at Cliffwood, but An'gel knew better than to rule anything out, no matter how far-fetched it might seem now.

When she walked into the front parlor, she found Benjy and Dickce sharing a sofa. Primrose Pace occupied the other, and from what An'gel heard as she entered, the medium was regaling the others with tales of her exploits with the spiritual world.

"The house was absolutely chock-full of restless spirits," Mrs. Pace said. "I thought I'd never manage to deal with every single one of them. It took me two months, but by the time I was finished, the house was quiet and empty of spirits."

"That's amazing," Benjy said. "How many ghosts were actually in the house?"

"Thirteen," Mrs. Pace answered. "The house had been built partially on an old burial ground for plantation slaves. They were angry spirits, naturally, but I was able to help them find their way onto the next plane of existence."

"I'm sure you felt great satisfaction, knowing that you'd helped all those tortured souls." Dickce looked toward An'gel. "Have a seat, Sister. Benjy and I are absolutely enthralled by Mrs. Pace's adventures."

"Thank you, I will." An'gel chose the armchair Mary Turner had occupied earlier. "Please continue, Mrs. Pace. Don't mind my interruption."

Mrs. Pace inclined her head to acknowledge An'gel's remark. "Yes, I was happy to help the family. They were terrified and on the point of moving out, even though they couldn't afford anywhere else to live. I was their last resort, or so they said. If only they had come to me sooner, they might have saved themselves two years of torment." She shook her head.

"Where was this house?" Benjy asked. "I wonder if it's in one of the books on haunted houses I was looking at."

"I really can't say," Mrs. Pace responded.

"I have to respect the family's privacy, you understand."

And protect yourself from anyone trying to check up on your bona fides, An'gel thought. Such a sensational story was bound to have been known about. Perhaps Benjy could do some research and see if he could come up with anything on it. That would be one way to check Mrs. Pace's authenticity.

"That story reminds me so much of that really scary movie." Dickce turned her head toward An'gel, away from Mrs. Pace, and winked. "What was the name of it, An'gel? You know, the one where that family lived in a house on top of a Native American burial ground, and their little girl began acting so strange."

"*Poltergeist,* is that the one you mean?" An'gel replied.

"Yes, that's it," Dickce said. "Have you ever seen that movie, Mrs. Pace?"

"When it first came out, but not since. I tend to avoid films like that because so many of them really aren't accurate," Mrs. Pace said. "Yes, there are similarities between the movie and the house I cleared of ghosts. Poltergeists, if you prefer." She smiled briefly.

"Do you think that's what we have here at Cliffwood?" An'gel asked. "A poltergeist?"

143

"It's very likely," Mrs. Pace replied, "although poltergeists most often tend to appear when there are children or teenagers present in the house. Perhaps because much of what the poltergeists are said to do usually turn out to be pranks played by the children involved."

"There are no children here," Dickce said.

"No, and the activity that Mrs. Catlin has observed isn't the noisy kind that poltergeists are generally known for."

"The word comes from German, doesn't it?" An'gel said. "It translates roughly as *rumbling spirit* or *noisy spirit,* I believe."

Mrs. Pace nodded approvingly. "Yes, Miss Ducote, that's correct. The spirit or spirits here aren't noisy. They move things around, but they don't hurl things or behave maliciously."

"That's certainly a relief to me," Dickce said. "The last thing I want is a noisy spirit throwing things at me."

"I don't want to mislead you," Mrs. Pace said. "The behavior could escalate. That happens sometimes, so you have to be prepared in case it does."

"What is your plan to deal with any spirits you find here at Cliffwood?" An'gel asked.

"Oh, there are definitely spirits here," Mrs. Pace said. "The first step is to let them get used to my presence, you see. Only then will I be able to establish trust with them. Then I will show them the way on to the next plane of existence, and they can leave this world behind forever."

The woman certainly sounded plausible, An'gel thought. Most of what Mrs. Pace had said jibed with what An'gel herself had read over the years, both in nonfiction and in fiction. There were common threads to it all, and Mrs. Pace obviously knew that.

An'gel wanted to ask the woman what she charged for her services, but since she wouldn't be paying the bill, it wasn't really any of her business. She hoped that Mary Turner and Henry Howard would be able to afford it, because she doubted that Mrs. Pace worked cheap.

Of course, if she and Dickce, with Benjy's help, were able to expose the truth without the aid of Mrs. Pace, the woman would go away empty-handed. An'gel wasn't going to underestimate her. She figured Mrs. Pace was shrewd enough to realize that An'gel and Dickce weren't necessarily her allies in this situation. What Mrs. Pace had shared with them so far was nothing really concrete, at least in terms of Cliffwood's so-called ghosts. It was the standard line for these situations. An'gel intended to keep an

145

eye on Mrs. Pace, and no doubt Mrs. Pace intended to do the same with her.

Now An'gel wished the woman would leave so she could share her latest interesting bit of news with Dickce and Benjy. She wanted their take on what she had observed.

Perhaps sensing that her presence was no longer desired, Mrs. Pace rose from the sofa. "I have enjoyed chatting with you, but it's time I resumed my attempts to converse with the spirits here. I am going into the library. Perhaps the spirit who turns the pages in the dictionary will be there and willing to talk to me." She moved in a stately fashion from the room. A few moments later An'gel heard a door close, and she thought Mrs. Pace had shut herself up in the library.

"Thank goodness," An'gel said. "I've been about to burst to tell you what I saw and heard upstairs right before I came back down. I want to know if you agree with my interpretation of it."

"Go ahead, then," Dickce said when An'gel failed to continue straightaway. "I'm dying to hear about it."

An'gel glanced toward the hall. Perhaps she should go close the door in case anyone happened by. The house was quiet around them. She heard no sounds of activity from anywhere else, and she decided the door could stay open.

She did lean forward in her chair, however, and lower her voice while she related the story to her sister and Benjy. She stumbled a bit over the vulgar word Wilbanks had used but thought that she had managed to convey it well enough without actually repeating it. When she'd finished, she sat back and waited for their reactions.

Benjy appeared briefly shocked, perhaps more by An'gel's euphemism than by the act itself, she thought. Dickce didn't appear to be fazed by any of it. She chuckled when An'gel finished.

"That does add some spice to the mix," she said.

"I'll say." Benjy nodded.

"I can't tell Mary Turner," An'gel said. "Unless it turns out to have a bearing on the situation here."

"No, you can't, not yet," Dickce replied. "Right now, I have to say, Nathan Gamble is my chief suspect in all this. If the contents of that room are the object of these shenanigans, I figure he's trying to spook Mary Turner so badly that she'll agree to let him have everything, will or no will."

"I would say the same," An'gel said. "I'm glad to know we're working on the same assumption here. So far I haven't been able to come up with any other reason for all this."

"What if it really turns out to be a ghost, and not some person pretending to be one?" Benjy asked. "What then?"

"Despite what has happened since we've been here," An'gel said after a moment's thought, "I don't think I really believe that a ghost is responsible. I don't have any explanation yet how my dress and my nightgown were moved around in my room. I also don't have any explanation for what I saw on the staircase this morning. But until I'm convinced there's absolutely no other explanation possible, I don't believe the answer is a spirit."

Benjy nodded. "I agree with you, but I haven't experienced anything weird yet." He grinned suddenly. "Who knows what I'd think afterwards?"

"I'm more open-minded than you, An'gel," Dickce said. "I believe there are sometimes things that we can't explain in any rational way. We've never been able to explain the odd things that happen at Riverhill, you know."

"Yes, I know." An'gel grimaced. "But then we haven't really had anyone in to look at the house. An engineer, I mean, or an architect. There's probably a perfectly rational explanation for what we've experienced."

An'gel became aware that neither Dickce nor Benjy was paying attention to her. They had identical expressions, a mixture of fear and awe. "What on earth is the matter with you two?"

Dickce swallowed hard. "Look behind you."

An'gel turned in her chair to see the parlor door closing slowly.

All by itself.

CHAPTER 14

For a few seconds An'gel couldn't breathe. The sight of the door closing on its own felt threatening in a way that none of the other incidents had done. Were they being shut in?

Benjy jumped up from the sofa and scrambled to get to the door without knocking anything over. An'gel, her breath back, marveled at how light on his feet he was. Within seconds he reached the door, perhaps an inch from being closed, and grabbed the knob. He jerked the door open and stepped into the hall.

An'gel and Dickce waited for him to come back into the parlor. When he did, perhaps thirty seconds later, he was shaking his head.

"There was nobody out there that I could see," Benjy said. "This is the creepiest thing I've ever seen." He stood about a foot from the door, now still, and stared at it. Then he began to examine every section of the door and the door frame.

An'gel and Dickce, after a quick glance at each other to make sure they were both all right, sat in silence until Benjy finished his examination of the door. They watched as he felt along all the edges and then ran his hands carefully over the surface of the door and the frame. After a couple of minutes, he stepped away and shook his head.

"I don't see anything attached to it or any kind of device that could make it close automatically. I guess maybe the ghost was trying to make us believe it's real." He came back to the sofa and dropped down, looking troubled.

"It certainly looks that way," An'gel said. "Thank you for being so quick to check it out. I confess I don't think I could have moved even if the ceiling had started to cave in on us."

"Me either." Dickce shivered. "Part of me wants to go upstairs right now and pack as fast as I can so we can drive home."

"I know how you feel," An'gel said, "but I'm not going. You can go if you want, but I'm staying here. I'm not going to be intimidated by little tricks like closing the door on us." She stood up and turned around, glancing all over the room. She raised her voice as she continued, "Do you hear me?

I'm not going anywhere."

An'gel braced herself for a response of some kind, but although she waited nearly a minute, nothing happened. She glanced at Dickce and Benjy. "Are you staying? Or are you going to pack up and leave?"

"I'll stay if you and Miss Dickce are going to," Benjy said.

"Oh, I'm not going anywhere, Sister," Dickce said crossly. "You know I'd never go off and leave you to face anything like this on your own."

"I didn't think so," An'gel said. "Thank you both." She walked over to the door and stood there, staring at it, for perhaps half a minute. She wasn't convinced that the door had been moved by a spirit. Benjy was a clever young man, but there might be something he missed. For the life of her, however, she couldn't see what it might be.

An idea occurred to her. "I wonder what is beneath us. Is there a basement?"

"I don't ever remember hearing talk of one," Dickce said. "That doesn't mean there isn't one, though."

"I haven't heard any mention either," An'gel said. "Another thing to ask Mary Turner."

"What made you think of a basement?" Benjy asked.

An'gel walked back to her chair and resumed her seat. "It suddenly occurred to me that if there's open space beneath this room, a clever person could figure out a way to manipulate the door from beneath the floor."

"Like with magnets?" Benjy's face lit up. "I hadn't thought of that."

"Yes, exactly," An'gel said. "There's enough metal in the door that a strong enough magnet could move it from under the floor, I think."

"You really don't want to believe in ghosts, do you?" Dickce laughed.

"As long as there's a rational explanation, no, I don't," An'gel retorted.

"Since Mary Turner isn't here, why don't we ask Marcelline?" Dickce said. "She probably knows as much about this house as anyone, she's been here so long."

"Good idea," An'gel said.

Benjy rose from the sofa. "I'll go. She wasn't in the kitchen when I came in a little while ago, but she might be back now."

"Thank you," An'gel said.

Benjy departed the parlor, and An'gel turned to her sister. "Did you bring any old clothes with you? If we're going to go grubbing around in a basement, I don't want to get my dress filthy."

"You're assuming that, if there is a base-ment, it hasn't been cleaned in decades." Dickce laughed. "I didn't bring any old clothes because I didn't think they'd be needed. Let's wait to hear what Benjy finds out, and we'll worry about clothes later."

"Very well," An'gel said. "I suppose I always think of attics and basements as dirty places. And that reminds me, it's probably time we gave ours a good turnout. They could both use a good cleaning, and good-ness knows there are things stored in both that we could probably part with."

"I agree with you," Dickce said. "At our age, though, I don't really think we need to be doing all the cleaning and organizing. We can get help for that."

"I'd already thought of that," An'gel said. "Give me credit for some sense. I'm no more keen on clambering around over things and risking a fall than you are. I'd like to keep my bones intact."

"With you, I'm never completely sure," Dickce said. "You're inclined to forget your age sometimes and get into things that you shouldn't."

"I could say the same thing about you," An'gel retorted. "Let's face it, Sister, we're exactly alike in that regard." She paused for a moment. "I suppose I simply don't want

154

to admit I'm an old woman, with more time behind me than I've got ahead of me."

Dickce winced. "Don't go getting morbid on me, for heaven's sake. After all, I'm only about four years behind you."

"As you remind me quite often," An'gel said.

Dickce did not reply, and An'gel did not say anything further. They waited in silence for Benjy's return.

An'gel checked her watch, and though it seemed an eternity until Benjy reentered the front parlor, it was probably no longer than six or seven minutes.

"Marcelline was back in the kitchen." He paused near An'gel's chair. "She told me that there is a basement, used mostly for storage. She keeps some canned goods down there, old furniture, things like that. She thinks it runs under most of the house, too."

An'gel smiled. "Excellent. I think an investigation of the basement is in order."

"That will have to wait," Benjy said. "Marcelline looked for the key. It's usually kept there in the butler's pantry. The door to the basement is there. The key was missing, though, and she doesn't know where it is."

"That's interesting," Dickce said. "Someone has taken the key to keep others out of it. No investigation."

"We'll have to ask Mary Turner about it," An'gel said. "Did you happen to ask Marcelline where Mary Turner is?"

"She told me Mary Turner has gone into town to pick up more food," Benjy said. "Because of the additional people who will be needing breakfast the next few days. She hadn't left long before I talked to Marcelline in the kitchen, according to her, so it will be a while before she gets back."

"And Henry Howard is gone until sometime this evening," An'gel said. "Then we have no choice but to wait." She felt thwarted. She really wanted to get into the basement and dig around in it and didn't want to have to wait.

"I need to go check on Peanut and Endora," Benjy said. "They've been alone in the room for probably half an hour now. They'll be getting restless. Do you think it would be okay to bring them into the house?"

"I think so," An'gel said. "Mary Turner and Henry Howard are both fond of animals."

"I think as long as we keep an eye on them and don't let them scratch up anything, it should be fine," Dickce added. "Besides, I'd

156

like to take them through the house and see how they react."

Benjy frowned. "I don't want to frighten them."

"No, I don't either," An'gel said. "Dickce has this idea that animals are supposed to be sensitive to otherworldly presences and thinks they'll react if there is one present."

"I've read that, too," Benjy said.

"If they act like they're afraid of anything," Dickce said, "of course we won't force them to stay. It would be a shame for them not to be able to come in the house, though."

"I'll go get them, and then we'll see how they react," Benjy said. "Back in a few minutes."

Moments after Benjy left the parlor, Marcelline came in.

"Beg pardon, Miss An'gel, Miss Dickce. I was wondering if y'all would like something to drink, like tea or coffee? And maybe a little something to nibble on? I just baked a lemon loaf cake."

Dickce smiled. "That sounds wonderful, Marcelline. I sure would love to try your lemon loaf cake. How about coffee to go with it, An'gel? Or would you rather have tea?"

"Coffee is fine," An'gel said. "Thank you, Marcelline. It's thoughtful of you to offer."

157

"My pleasure, ma'am," Marcelline said. "I'll be back in a jiffy. Coffee's almost ready, and I'll slice up the cake." She hurried from the room.

"I don't know what Mary Turner will do when Marcelline decides to retire," An'gel said.

"The same thing we'll do when Clementine decides to retire," Dickce said. "Feel like we've lost our rudder."

"What a depressing thought," An'gel said. "I will feel really old then, because she's younger than we are."

Peanut rushed into the room, woofing happily at the sight of An'gel, who never failed to make a fuss over him. She did so now, and Peanut rested his head on her knee. He gazed adoringly up at her while she stroked his head and told him how handsome and clever he was.

Benjy, carrying Endora, walked into the room moments later. He resumed his seat near Dickce, and Endora jumped from his arms to climb into Dickce's lap. She accepted Dickce's stroking as her due and meowed to encourage its continuance.

"Did they show any signs of hesitation or fear when you came by the stairs?" Dickce asked.

"No, ma'am," Benjy said. "They've been

fine since the moment we walked into the kitchen."

"I think the true test will be when we take them upstairs," An'gel said. "Other than the business with the door, we haven't experienced anything except on the stairs and on the second floor."

"So you're admitting that animals might be able to sense spirits?" Dickce said.

"Not necessarily," An'gel said. "We'll have to see what, if anything, happens."

Marcelline interrupted the discussion by rolling in the tea cart. "Here we go," she said as she brought the cart to a halt near An'gel's chair. "Would you like me to serve?"

"Thank you," An'gel said, "but we'll do that."

Marcelline nodded and turned to go. Then she turned back, her expression hesitant. "Miss An'gel, I couldn't help overhearing what y'all were talking about." She gestured toward Peanut, sniffing at the cake slices atop the tea cart, and Endora, resting in Dickce's lap.

"That's all right," Dickce said. "Do you have something to tell us? Please do."

"Well, it's about Miss Mary's little dog," the housekeeper said. "He died a few months ago. He was old, and Miss Mary'd had him since he was a pup, before she and Mr. Henry got married. Anyway, that little dog, there were times when he wouldn't go up or down those stairs to save his life." She shook her head. "Miss Mary'd have to carry him, and he'd whimper the whole time."

"Other times he was fine?" An'gel asked.

"Sure was." Marcelline nodded. "He'd run up and down the stairs without a care in the world. Until he got too old and crippled, that is. It always gave me the chills when he wouldn't go near those stairs without being afraid of whatever was there the rest of us couldn't see." She shivered suddenly. "I felt it myself. Coldest feeling I ever had."

An'gel took hold of Peanut's collar to keep him from investigating the enticing smells from the cart any closer. "When did this start? The cold on the stairs, I mean."

Marcelline shrugged. "I don't rightly know. Ever since I've been working here, and that's a mighty long time. There's somebody else occupying this house besides us living folks, that's all I can tell you." She turned and walked out of the parlor.

Chapter 15

Dickce felt both chilled and excited by Marcelline's parting words. Her own experiences with the unexplaine at Riverhill notwithstanding, Dickce had tried to maintain a stance of intelligent inquiry about the whole business. Granted, she and An'gel had not personally encountered another situation like the one at Cliffwood before, though friends of theirs in Athena and other places had occasionally owned up to odd goings-on in their old houses. An'gel had always been the one who refused to give much credence to the existence of lingering spirits while Dickce was more willing to believe that some things couldn't be easily explained away. Dickce did not doubt the housekeeper firmly believed that a spirit or a revenant of some sort remained at Cliffwood from a time in the distant past.

Now Dickce looked at her sister and wondered what An'gel was thinking about

Marcelline's statements. She doubted An'gel was ready to commit fully to the fact of a resident ghost, but perhaps she might be less inclined to dismiss the possibility as they continued to investigate. She decided to ask her sister, knowing that An'gel likely wouldn't say anything unless pressed to do so.

"What do you think of what Marcelline just told us?" Dickce asked.

An'gel shrugged before she picked up the coffeepot and began to pour. She didn't say anything until she had filled all three cups and set the pot down again. "I'm sure Marcelline isn't making things up to frighten or titillate us. She sounded completely sincere, I thought."

Peanut woofed and looked hopefully again at the lemon cake slices on dessert plates atop the tea cart. "No, Peanut, that isn't for you," An'gel said. "Or for Endora." She glanced at the cat, apparently asleep in Dickce's lap.

Benjy waited until An'gel finished with the cream and sugar for her coffee before he doctored his own and Dickce's. He placed Dickce's cup and saucer on the coffee table in front of her, then picked up a dessert plate and fork and set them beside the coffee. Then he helped himself.

"I thought she sounded sincere, too," Benjy said. "I think she really believes there's a ghost here." He took a bite of lemon cake, chewed for a moment, swallowed, and smiled. "That's wonderful."

"I agree," Dickce said. "I also agree with her that there is another presence here along with us. Not necessarily at this moment, but there was certainly something on the stairs with me earlier." She adjusted the sleeping cat in order to lean forward, pick up her cup, and sip from it. "Excellent coffee."

"Have a bite of the cake," An'gel said. "We ought to ask Marcelline for the recipe, if she'll share it. This is one thing I wish Clementine would bake."

"The only thing I've seen — so far — is the door closing on its own," Benjy said. "That could have been rigged somehow, though it's not clear yet how it was done, if it was. This cold thing on the stairs sounds really creepy to me."

Dickce caught a movement in her peripheral vision as she leaned forward to get a bite of her lemon cake. She looked up to see Nathan Gamble advancing toward them from the doorway.

"Are y'all talking about the Terrible Specter of Cliffwood?" He laughed. "That's a bunch of hooey, you know that, right? I've been in and out of this house for years, and I've never seen one weird thing."

"Because you haven't experienced it doesn't mean it hasn't happened to someone else, young man," An'gel said tartly.

Gamble shrugged and dropped down on the sofa across from Dickce and Benjy. "Have it your way, ma'am. I think it's all part of the plot to keep me from my rightful inheritance. Mary Turner thinks if I think the house is haunted, and especially the French room, then I'll stop asking for my rights and leave her with that fortune in antiques. Marcelline would do anything or say anything to help her precious Mary Turner, believe you me." He folded his arms across his chest and shrugged again.

Dickce itched to point out to Gamble that his boorish behavior was hardly an aid to his cause, but she doubted he cared in the least. He seemed obsessed with owning the contents of that room, and nothing apparently would deflect him.

"You can scoff all you like," Dickce told him, trying to keep her tone mild, "but odd things have happened here since we arrived this morning. More could happen while you're here."

"Have you ever stayed here?" Benjy asked.

"In the French room?" He ate another bite of lemon cake.

Gamble got up from the sofa and went to the fireplace, where he rang the bell on the wall near it for Marcelline. Dickce hadn't noticed it earlier. She was surprised it was in working order. Theirs at home wasn't because they had never bothered with keeping the wiring up-to-date.

Gamble leaned against the mantel and regarded Benjy. "No, I've never been allowed to spend the night in that room. In fact, I've never spent a night here before in any room. This is a first." He looked thoughtful for a moment. "Not sure why Mary Turner finally let me. Her parents never would."

Dickce exchanged a quick glance with An'gel. She knew they both recalled Mary Turner's jest earlier about Gamble's being frightened. She wasn't about to tell Gamble about that, however, and neither was An'gel, she knew.

Marcelline appeared in the doorway, and when she spotted Nathan Gamble, she frowned but quickly suppressed it, Dickce noticed. She wasn't surprised he hadn't endeared himself to the housekeeper. Had he ever endeared himself to anyone?

"Yes, Nathan? Did you ring?" Marcelline

asked, her tone flat. She waited in the doorway.

"Yes, I did, Marcelline." Gamble pointed
to the tea cart. "How about another coffee
cup? And some of that cake they're having?
I could use a snack about now."

"I'll see if there's any of the cake left."
Marcelline turned and disappeared.

Gamble snorted. "Thank you very much."
He walked back to the sofa and dropped
down.

Dickce winced. Gamble wasn't a heavy
man, but the sofas were antiques and
shouldn't be treated so roughly. She had to
bite her tongue to keep from admonishing
him. She was surprised An'gel didn't, but
her sister didn't speak, only glared at the
man.

Gamble seemed impervious to their response to him. For the first time, he paid
attention to the fact that there were four-
legged creatures in the room. "Hello, there,
doggie. What's your name?" He held out a
hand toward Peanut.

The dog growled, and Gamble snatched
back his hand. An'gel placed a hand on
Peanut's head to quiet him and keep him
by her side.

Benjy said, "His name is Peanut. He can
be shy around strangers."

Dickce wondered what it was about Gamble that put Peanut off. Normally the dog was friendly, almost to a fault, with everyone. There was obviously something about the man that Peanut didn't like, however.

Gamble shrugged, then shifted his attention to Endora. "I don't think I've ever seen a cat that color. What is he?"

"*She* is an Abyssinian," Dickce said. "They're usually brown or reddish brown in color."

"Never heard of them before," Gamble said.

Endora paid no attention to Gamble. She seemed more interested in sniffing, then licking, the fork that Dickce had forgotten to move out of reach.

"Naughty girl." Dickce laid the fork aside and pinched off a small bite of the cake. When she held it close to the cat's face, Endora sniffed for a moment before she grabbed it and started chewing.

Peanut whined, upset that Endora had been given a treat and he hadn't. An'gel still had a little cake on her plate, and she pinched some off and let the dog have it.

"That's all," An'gel said. "Marcelline doesn't spend her time baking for dogs and cats, you know."

Peanut whined again.

"I said no more, and I meant it," An'gel said, even as she reached for another small piece of cake. "This is absolutely the last bite, you hear me?"

The dog gulped down the cake and waited for more. This time, however, An'gel held firm.

"That's enough, Peanut," Benjy told him. "Quiet now."

Dickce almost laughed at the piteous look that Peanut gave Benjy, but the dog did not whine again. Dickce did laugh when Endora batted her hand with a paw. Evidently Endora decided that if Peanut could have a second bite of cake, so could she. Dickce obliged with a bite that was a bit larger than the first one.

Marcelline returned with a cup and saucer for Gamble, and she also carried a dessert plate and fork. Dickce noticed that the slice of lemon cake she brought was almost half the size of the pieces she had given them.

The housekeeper set the cup and saucer on the coffee table and handed the plate to Gamble. He frowned as he took it. He started to speak but Marcelline cut him off.

"That's all that was left." She turned to An'gel. "Dinner will be at seven, if that's all right."

"That's fine," An'gel said. "Thank you."

"What are we having?" Gamble asked around a mouthful of cake.

Marcelline regarded him with obvious distaste for a moment before she replied. "*They* are having pot roast and vegetables. You'll have to find dinner on your own."

Gamble scowled and swallowed his cake. "How come they get dinner and I don't?"

"*They* were invited." Marcelline glared at him briefly before she marched out of the room.

Gamble's face reddened, and Dickce thought he might retort. He did not. Instead he scowled again and picked up the pot to pour himself coffee.

Dickce felt embarrassed for the man, and she suspected the housekeeper had informed them about dinner in order to give Gamble a snub. He might have deserved it, because he had forced himself on Mary Turner's hospitality. Dickce nevertheless pitied him.

An'gel surprised her by saying, "You'll have to excuse us now, Mr. Gamble. We have business to attend to, and I'm afraid we can't put it off any longer." She started to rise from her chair, and Dickce and Benjy followed suit.

Gamble remained seated. "Sure. Whatever." He stared into his coffee cup.

Dickce could see that Gamble's lack of civility annoyed An'gel. The man was rather graceless. She and An'gel were used to better behavior from the men they knew. The fact that Gamble did not stand when they did was further evidence of his lack of couth.

"Come along, Peanut," An'gel said. "We're going upstairs." The dog followed her toward the door.

Dickce, still holding Endora, followed An'gel, and Benjy brought up the rear.

An'gel paused in front of the stairs to look first at Benjy, then at Dickce. "Shall we give this a try?"

Benjy nodded, then tensed in anticipation.

"Yes," Dickce said. "You go up first and call Peanut to come with you."

An'gel put her right foot on the first tread, then stepped up to the second, then the third. Peanut sat, watching, his tail swishing back and forth over the floor.

"Come along, Peanut," An'gel said in a calm tone. "Let's go upstairs." She moved up another couple of steps.

Peanut didn't hesitate. He trotted up the stairs past An'gel to the second-floor landing. An'gel shrugged before she turned and followed him. Dickce mounted the stairs with Endora, Benjy on her heels. They gained the landing and stepped a few paces into the hallway.

"I didn't feel anything," Benjy said.

"I didn't either," Dickce replied.

"Nor I." An'gel looked thoughtful. "Of course we can't expect it to happen every time one of us goes up or down. We'll remain upstairs for a little while, then take them down again."

"If they don't react this time, will you want to try it again?" Dickce asked as Endora yawned and stretched in her arms.

"Perhaps," An'gel said. "Let's try one other thing, since Mr. Gamble is still downstairs. Come along, Peanut, let's walk to the end of the hall."

An'gel headed toward the front of the house, and Peanut went obediently along with her. Dickce and Benjy waited where they stood with Endora to see what happened.

Dickce watched Peanut carefully. The dog behaved normally until he and An'gel neared the bathroom between her bedroom and the French room. Suddenly he stopped and stared at the bathroom door. He emitted a low growl, then barked sharply, three times.

CHAPTER 16

An'gel awoke refreshed and relaxed the next morning. Not what she would have predicted after the strange and somewhat unsettling events of the day before. She had lain awake for nearly an hour when she first went to bed, tense, waiting for another weird thing to happen. Perhaps a repetition of the moving of her clothing from yesterday during her short tenure in the French room. She was actually relieved that Nathan Gamble had made a fuss over staying in the room. As night had drawn closer, An'gel had felt uneasy enough over sleeping in the room she was now in.

As the minutes had passed and nothing had occurred to disturb her, however, she had gradually relaxed enough to fall asleep. She had slept untroubled by either dreams or ghostly visitations.

She pushed aside the covers and sat up on the side of the bed. After a couple of yawns, she picked up her watch from the bedside table and checked the time. Nearly six thirty. *Heavens, I slept almost nine hours.* She laid the watch aside, found her robe and slippers, collected her toiletries bag, and went down the hall to see if the bathroom was free.

Some half hour later, dressed and ready to go downstairs, An'gel tapped on her sister's door. After a moment, Dickce opened it and greeted An'gel with a yawn, quickly covered by a hand. "Sorry about that," she mumbled. "I haven't been up long. Slept okay but I still feel a little tired."

"And obviously not dressed for breakfast," An'gel said. "I'm going on down, I think. I'm ready for coffee."

"I won't be long," Dickce said. "Leave some in the pot for me." She yawned again as she closed the door.

An'gel heard another door open nearby. She turned to see Primrose Pace stick her head out her door across the hall. Mrs. Pace ducked back inside her room the moment she spotted An'gel looking at her. The door shut firmly but quietly.

An'gel smiled on her way downstairs as she recalled the scene late yesterday afternoon at the bathroom door. Peanut's barking at the closed door made her wary, and when the door opened to reveal the medium behind it, An'gel had felt mighty relieved. Peanut hadn't taken to the medium, nor she to the dog. Mrs. Pace had to be assured that Peanut wouldn't shed all over her clothing, nor would he get in her room and chew up her shoes. An'gel had to wonder how many pairs the woman had brought with her and how many she had ever lost to a bored canine. The way the woman talked, she must travel with one large bag full of nothing but footwear.

They had all been on edge by the evening, thanks to the odd happenings in the house and the tensions among various persons. Mary Turner had seemed distracted during dinner, twice pulling out her cell phone and texting on it. She apologized for doing so, An'gel remembered, but offered no explanation as to whom she was texting or why. The messages appeared to have unsettled Mary Turner, but An'gel did not probe to find out why.

Serenity Foster and her lawyer, Wilbanks, had shown up at the dinner table, and Marcelline told them tartly that they would not be served. Wilbanks started to bluster, but Marcelline shut him down with words similar to those she had used earlier with Nathan Gamble. "You were not invited to dinner, Mr. Wilbanks," Marcelline told him, "and neither were you or your brother, Mrs. Foster. Miss Mary made that clear, I thought. You'll have to go find your dinner elsewhere." After that, Serenity Foster had wisely retreated, urging her lawyer to come away and not make any further fuss.

Henry Howard had made no appearance, nor had An'gel spotted either Nathan Gamble or Primrose Pace leaving the house. She was not eager to encounter them that evening and was relieved not to have to engage in conversation with either of them.

She felt better able to face all of them after a good night's rest. When she walked into the dining room this morning, she saw that the table was laid for six. Another, smaller table near the back of the dining room was laid for four.

An'gel helped herself to coffee from the sideboard, chose a seat, and in a moment Marcelline appeared.

"Good morning, Miss An'gel. You're the first one down this morning," she said. "There's scrambled eggs, biscuits, gravy, and sausage for breakfast. If you want something lighter, I can make you some oatmeal, or there's cereal and fruit. You just tell me what you'd like."

An'gel had a weakness for biscuits and

gravy, and she had no doubt Marcelline's would be heaven on the tongue. Heavy on the stomach, however, and An'gel decided to opt for a breakfast lower in calories.

"Thank you," An'gel said. "I'll have a scrambled egg, a biscuit, and a little fruit."

"Yes, ma'am," Marcelline said. "There's always seconds if you want them." She left the room but returned promptly with An'gel's breakfast.

An'gel had finished her egg and biscuit and was eating her fruit — slices of pineapple and melon, along with a handful of red grapes — when Henry Howard joined her in the dining room.

"Good morning, Miss An'gel," he said. "How are you? Did you sleep all right?"

An'gel returned the greeting and said, "I slept just fine. How about you?" She thought he looked tired, perhaps even a little hungover. He hadn't returned home last night before she retired for the night at nine thirty, as far as she knew. She wondered how late his writing group met and how much drinking they did. A fair amount, she suspected, to judge by the dark circles around the young man's eyes.

Henry Howard stifled a yawn. He looked at her oddly, An'gel thought, before he replied that he'd had a restless night.

176

"Do you suffer from insomnia?" she asked.

He shrugged. "Sometimes. Especially after my meetings. They're really energizing, you see, and I always come home brimming with ideas and eager to write. But of course, by then it's late, and I'm also tired and have to go to bed." He grimaced. "Because I always have to be up early to tend to something around the house or out in the annex."

"Do you get much time to write?" An'gel speared her last bite of pineapple and ate it while she waited for a response.

Henry Howard finished pouring himself coffee and chose a seat across the table from her before he replied. "A little," he said. "Usually in bits and pieces. It's hard to find time to sit down for more than an hour around here, though."

"I'm sure that's frustrating for you," An'gel said. The poor young man was obviously not happy, and she wondered whether this caused any friction between him and his wife.

"It is," Henry Howard replied shortly, "but there's not much I can do about it. We could close the house to guests, and I could concentrate on writing, but then we wouldn't have any money coming in and we'd have to sell the house to survive. Mary Turner is never going to sell the house." He shrugged.

"It's been in her family a long time," An'gel said in what she hoped was a neutral tone. She knew there had not been much money to inherit when Mary Turner's parents died. Everything they made basically went into maintaining the house and keeping their business going. The house had proven popular over the years with tourists, particularly around the time of the annual Natchez pilgrimage every spring when thousands came to tour the antebellum homes and enjoy various festivities. An'gel figured the Turners had made a decent living with the bed-and-breakfast scheme, but they hadn't become wealthy with it.

"Yes, I know," Henry Howard said. "I understand that. The Catlins lost their home in the war" — An'gel knew which war he meant — "and never got it back, unlike the Turners. I don't have the same kind of attachment to the place that she does, because her roots run so deep here. It's all she has left of her close family, and I couldn't take that away from her." He stared into his coffee cup for a moment before picking it up and draining the contents. He got up to refill his cup.

Before An'gel could reply, Primrose Pace and Dickce entered the room.

"Good morning, everybody," Mrs. Pace said.

Dickce nodded a greeting to Henry Howard and followed the medium to the sideboard, where they both helped themselves to coffee. Primrose Pace sat down near An'gel, leaving an empty chair between them. Dickce took it.

Mary Turner came into the room with Marcelline and Benjy. Marcelline checked to see what everyone wanted and departed for the kitchen. Mary Turner and Benjy settled themselves at the table, one on either side of Henry Howard.

"I hope everyone slept well," Mary Turner said. After she received assurances from everyone that they had indeed slept well, she glanced around the table. "Where is Nathan? I thought for sure he would already be down here. It's not like him to be late for a meal."

"I haven't seen him," An'gel said, and the other guests agreed with her. "Nor Mrs. Foster and Mr. Wilbanks."

Mary Turner pushed her chair back. "I'd better go remind Nathan that Marcelline isn't going to stay in the kitchen cooking breakfast for much longer. Serenity and Truss said they would be here on time. I told Marcelline we would be done by eight or eight thirty at the latest. She wants to get ready for church."

"I'll go remind him," Henry Howard said. "He might not be dressed or still in bed, and he might not like having a woman in his room." He exchanged a knowing glance with his wife.

Mary Turner shrugged. "You're probably right. Thanks, honey, I appreciate it."

Henry Howard pushed his chair back and left the room. Mary Turner picked up her orange juice but then set it down quickly. She got up from her chair. "I forgot to tell Henry Howard that you and Nathan switched rooms, Miss An'gel. I was asleep before he came home last night, and I just now remembered. I'll go tell him." She hurried out.

Marcelline brought in the remaining breakfast orders on the tea cart. She served Dickce, Mrs. Pace, and Benjy. "Where'd Miss Mary and Mr. Henry go?"

"They went up to check on Mr. Gamble," An'gel said.

Marcelline frowned. "He'd better get up and get his carcass down here if he wants a hot breakfast. I'm not standing over that stove all morning for him or for his sister and that so-called lawyer." She left the room.

"I take it that the housekeeper isn't fond of Mr. Gamble or those other people," Primrose Pace said. "They don't seem all that welcome here. Who are they?"

"Mr. Gamble is Mrs. Catlin's distant cousin," Dickce said. "Mrs. Foster is his sister, and she has her lawyer, a Mr. Wilbanks, with her. They're staying in the annex with Benjy."

"Ah, yes, family," Mrs. Pace said. "They can be a trial sometimes, can't they?" She chuckled. "Actually, I think I may have heard of Mr. Gamble's family before. Is he from Vicksburg?"

"Yes, he is," An'gel said. "What have you heard?"

"He's a realtor, I think," Mrs. Pace said. "Or maybe he does renovations? Can't remember exactly. I think maybe his father or his grandfather was in the construction business in Vicksburg."

"I don't know," An'gel said. "We really know nothing about him except that he and his sister are Mrs. Catlin's distant cousins."

"The more distant the better," Mrs. Pace said. "I seem to remember that old Mr. Gamble, whichever one it was, father or son, didn't have a good reputation in business."

"Word does get around in the South, doesn't it?" Dickce said lightly.

181

"Something terrible has happened."

Mary Turner surprised them all. An'gel looked up to see the young woman in the doorway, arms across her chest, pale and shivering. She got up immediately and went to Mary Turner.

"Come sit down, my dear, and have some coffee." An'gel guided her to the table and nearly pushed her into the chair before Mary Turner's shaky legs gave way.

"What happened?" Dickce asked. "Is something wrong with your cousin?"

Mary Turner nodded, her hands clasped around her coffee. "He's dead."

CHAPTER 17

"Here, sip some coffee," An'gel said to Mary Turner. "You look like you're about to pass out."

The young woman obediently drank from her cup, and An'gel was happy to see color returning to her face. Mary Turner seemed a bit steadier after another couple of sips.

"Tell us what happened," An'gel said gently.

"Henry Howard was about to go into your room, Miss An'gel, when I got upstairs," Mary Turner said. "I told him about the switch, and it took him a moment to understand. Then he went down the hall to the French room. I went with him, I'm not sure why." She paused for a final sip of coffee, set down the cup, and pushed it away.

"He knocked on the door but he didn't get a response," Mary Turner said. "By that time I'd caught up with him. He knocked again and waited, but there still wasn't any answer. So he opened the door and went in. I hesitated to follow him, but then I heard him cry out." She flushed suddenly. "I can't repeat what he said. It wasn't a nice expression. Anyway, I did go in then. Henry Howard was standing over the bed, staring down at Nathan." She shuddered and closed her eyes.

"My dear, I'm so sorry, I know it must have been a shock to you," An'gel said. "You don't have to tell us any more if you don't feel up to it."

Mary Turner nodded. "It was a shock, I don't mind telling you. Poor Nathan. I never liked him, but now he's dead." She shuddered again. "He had the most horrible expression on his face. I don't think I'll ever be able to forget it."

"Do you think he suffered a great deal?" Dickce asked. "Perhaps he had heart trouble and didn't know it."

"He looked terrified," Mary Turner said. "Like he had been scared to death."

An'gel exchanged a glance with her sister. She knew they were thinking the same thing. Had a malign spirit appeared in the French room during the night and frightened Nathan Gamble into having a heart attack?

An'gel didn't want to believe that. She

patted Mary Turner's hand. "Many people are fearful when they realize they are dying, child. Don't place too much emphasis on his expression." She looked at Dickce again, and her sister picked up the cue.

"Heavens, no," Dickce said. "The poor man may have had a seizure right before he passed away."

"Is there anything I can do to help?" Benjy asked.

An'gel shot him an approving glance. "Yes, we'll all be happy to do whatever you need."

"Henry Howard is in the office calling the doctor," Mary Turner said. "And I guess he'll have to call the police as well, since Nathan died unexpectedly."

"Yes, the authorities have to be notified," An'gel said. "Let's wait here until Henry Howard gets through with his calls. In the meantime, you need some more hot coffee. You're starting to look too pale again."

"I'll get it for her." Benjy reached for the cup and took it to the sideboard.

An'gel glanced across the table at Dickce and then noticed that Primrose Pace had disappeared from the room. Where was she? An'gel wondered. She had no time to ponder the question further, because Serenity Foster and Truss Wilbanks walked into the dining room then.

"Good morning," Serenity said. "I hope we're not too late for breakfast." She looked around the room for a moment, and when she spotted the coffee urn on the sideboard, she made a beeline for it.

"We're here before eight," Wilbanks said as he glanced around the room. "As you told us to be."

Marcelline bustled into the room, and An'gel wondered if the housekeeper had been standing at the kitchen door, watching for the two of them. She started to recite the breakfast menu but broke off when she noticed Mary Turner sitting at the table with An'gel standing by her.

She hurried over. "Miss Mary, what's wrong? Are you sick, honey?"

Mary Turner shook her head. "No, Marcelline, I'll be okay. Something really sad has happened, and I'm a little shaken by it. And now I have to talk to Serenity." She looked across the table toward the sideboard, where her cousin stood sipping coffee.

"What is it?" Serenity asked as she approached the table. "Did Nathan fall down the stairs and break his leg? I warned him about snooping around during the night. He can barely see in the dark." She laughed.

186

An'gel would have found the young woman's remarks in poor taste at any time, but
now they seemed particularly unfortunate.

"Mrs. Foster, I think you'd better sit
down," An'gel told her. "You, too, Mr. Wilbanks. I'm afraid Mary Turner has bad news
for you."

Serenity Foster looked taken aback but
did as An'gel told her to. Wilbanks came to
stand behind her chair and placed his hands
on her shoulders.

"Go ahead, what is it?" Serenity said, her
tone harsh.

"Nathan is dead, Serenity," Mary Turner
said. "We found him, Henry Howard and I
did, I mean, only a few minutes ago. He
must have died in his sleep. He was still in
bed."

Serenity stared across the table at her
cousin. All the color drained from her face,
and An'gel thought the young woman was
going to faint. Wilbanks tightened his grip
on her shoulders, An'gel noticed.

"He can't be dead," Serenity said. "He's
too young, and he was in perfect health as
far as I know. Is this some kind of sick joke
you're trying to play, Mary Turner?"

"No, it's not a joke, Serenity." Henry
Howard spoke from the doorway. He walked
into the room, his own shock still evident in

his expression. "Nathan is dead. I've called for the doctor, well, an ambulance, that is, and I've called the police."

"The police? What the hell for?" Serenity said. "Do you think he was murdered?"

"Calm down, Serenity," Wilbanks said. When Serenity tried to rise from her chair, he kept her in place. "No one is saying he was murdered."

"Why would you think that?" Marcelline demanded. "Why would someone want to kill that brother of yours? He probably had a weak heart, and something scared him to death."

An'gel wished the housekeeper hadn't used those unfortunate words.

"That's crazy talk," Serenity said hotly. "There aren't any ghosts here. That's just Mary Turner trying to scare Nathan away from this place. She's never wanted him to have what was rightly his. Whatever happened to him, I know she did it." She tried again to get out of her chair, and Wilbanks forced her down again.

"Take your hands off me," she told him. "I'm not going to rip her face off, though I sure the hell would like to. I'll wait and tell it all to the police."

"I think you'd better take her out of here, Truss," Henry Howard said, a steely glint in his eye. An'gel was happy to hear him finally speak up and take charge of the situation. "Why don't y'all go out to the kitchen with Marcelline, and she can give you breakfast there if you feel up to eating anything." He held up a hand when Serenity started to protest. "I'll let you know as soon as the police are ready to talk to you, I promise."

"Come on," Wilbanks said. He stepped back to allow Serenity out of her chair. "We'll do that."

An'gel could almost feel the heat pouring off Marcelline. If looks could kill, she thought, Serenity Foster would be joining her brother soon if Marcelline had her way.

"Please, Marcelline," Mary Turner said.

"All right, Miss Mary," the housekeeper said. "For your sake." She marched out of the dining room and didn't look back to see whether Serenity and Wilbanks followed.

Serenity stared hard at Mary Turner. "You're not going to get away with this." She allowed Wilbanks to lead her from the room after that parting shot.

"We never should have let any of them in the house," Henry Howard said in an undertone. "What a nightmare this is going to be."

"I know you're both upset," An'gel said to the couple, "but there isn't much time

189

before the police and the doctor arrive. Henry Howard, how closely did you look at Mr. Gamble?"

Henry Howard stared at An'gel as if he weren't sure he had heard her correctly. "I looked close enough to see that he was dead. I also felt for a pulse, but there wasn't one. He wasn't breathing. What are you getting at, Miss An'gel?"

"Did you notice anything unusual about the body?" she asked. "Other than his expression. Mary Turner said he looked terrified."

Henry Howard frowned. "I didn't notice anything else. He was lying there." He thought a moment. "His hands were clutching the bedclothes, I remember now."

"Tightly?" An'gel asked.

"I don't really remember," Henry Howard replied. "Is it important?"

"It could be," An'gel said. After another look at Mary Turner, she decided to let it drop. The poor girl looked sick, despite having had more coffee, and An'gel couldn't blame her. Gamble's death had come as a great shock. She would only look worse if An'gel started talking about rigor mortis. Depending on what time Nathan Gamble actually died, if his hands were tightly holding the bedclothes, that would indicate he had died most likely less than twelve hours ago. It was barely 8 a.m. now, according to An'gel's watch. She wondered what time he had gone to bed.

The doorbell sounded, and Henry Howard left to answer it. He shut the door behind him.

An'gel heard sirens coming nearer and nearer the house. The police and the emergency responders were arriving.

Mary Turner looked up at An'gel. "What are the police going to think, Miss An'gel? We can hardly tell them that a ghost frightened Nathan to death."

"My dear, don't start thinking things like that," An'gel said. "We don't know that any such thing happened. More than likely, he had a heart condition. He might not even have known about it. That kind of thing happens even to men his age. And to women, too."

"Maybe," Mary Turner said, "but I can't help thinking about what I said to you and Miss Dickce yesterday, about hoping that a ghost scared the life out of him." She started crying. "I didn't want him to die."

"We know you didn't," Dickce said gently. "It's a terrible thing to happen to one so young, but you're not to blame. Even if your cousin did happen to see something spooky in his room during the night, it wasn't anything you did. If there truly is a spirit loose in this house, it's going to do what it wants to. Not what you want or tell it to do. Right, Sister?"

"Right." An'gel spoke with far more assurance than she felt, and she knew Dickce did as well. "All this speculation isn't going to do anything but keep you upset. The doctor will have to sort it out. There will likely be a postmortem if the doctor can't determine the cause of death after examining him. We'll have to wait and see."

Mary Turner seemed calmer after that little speech, An'gel was relieved to see. She urged the young woman to try to eat something. "I'll go ask Marcelline to fix you something," she said.

"No, thank you," Mary Turner said. "I really don't think I could eat anything right now. Coffee is fine for the moment."

"All right," Dickce said. "But if you change your mind, let us know."

"Thank you all for being so kind," Mary Turner said. "I'm so glad you're here. I don't think I could bear any of this otherwise."

An'gel gave her a hug, and she felt the young woman tremble. "Everything will be okay," she said before she released Mary Turner.

Silence ensued in the dining room but An'gel could hear sounds of activity in the hallway. Voices, footsteps, everything muffled by the closed door but still audible. They all sat looking at the door, waiting for someone to come in.

An'gel noticed again that Primrose Pace wasn't with them. Where *had* the woman gone? Had she packed her bags and run off? If she had, An'gel reckoned, that would be a strange thing to do, unless she had something to hide from the authorities.

Even if she hadn't done a bunk, her behavior was still odd. An'gel had a new thought. Had the woman gone up to the French room to see the dead body?

CHAPTER 18

What reason could Primrose Pace have for going to look at Nathan Gamble's corpse?

An'gel considered that question. Simple morbid curiosity was one answer. Or perhaps Mrs. Pace might consider it professional interest? After all, she professed to be a medium, so maybe she went upstairs to try to communicate with the spirit of Nathan Gamble to help him move on to the next plane of existence. Wasn't that what they called it?

That sounded wacky but plausible to An'gel, though she really had no idea how a medium would behave in a situation like this. She felt certain, however, that the reason Mrs. Pace had disappeared from the room had something to do with Nathan Gamble's death. She certainly hadn't acted or looked like she was ill from what An'gel had noticed in the brief moments she was aware of the woman's presence.

The police would not be amused if they caught the medium in the room with the body but somehow An'gel didn't think Mrs. Pace would be caught off guard like that. She suspected that the medium was far too canny.

An'gel remembered what Mrs. Pace told them about Nathan Gamble's family, that his father or grandfather had been in the construction business in some fashion. She looked at Mary Turner, who now appeared calm. She hoped what she was about to ask wouldn't unsettle the young woman any further.

"Mary Turner, Mrs. Pace mentioned earlier that your cousin's family, either his father or grandfather or both, was involved in building or remodeling. Also that your cousin himself was a realtor. Is that true?"

Mary Turner nodded. "Yes, Nathan's grandfather was a builder, and his dad specialized in renovations. Nathan was more interested in selling real estate than in building, but he inherited the construction company from his father."

"What about Serenity?" Dickce asked. "Is she involved with the company?"

"No, she isn't," Mary Turner said. "Their grandfather and their father didn't think women had any business in construction,

195

although I think Serenity's dad did let her help some with redesigns. From what I've heard, though, she doesn't have any real talent for it."

"So she has no financial interest in the company?" An'gel asked.

"Not that I know of," Mary Turner replied. "I believe her father set up a trust fund for her, but that's separate from the business. They were quite successful over the years, although there were a lot of complaints about the quality of their work."

"What will happen to the company now, do you think?" Dickce asked. "Will Serenity inherit?"

"I have no idea," Mary Turner said. "That depended on Nathan, whether he even had a will." She frowned. "There's not really anyone else to leave it to, except for Serenity's boys, but they're really young, under ten, I think."

An'gel exchanged a look with Dickce, sure that they were thinking similar thoughts. If there turned out to be anything funny about Nathan Gamble's death, Serenity Foster might have a strong motive to want her brother dead. An'gel recalled the bitter words the young woman had spouted yesterday about her need for money for setting up a proper home for her children.

You're getting way ahead of yourself, An'gel thought. Most likely Nathan Gamble died of natural causes. The fact that he died in a room allegedly visited by a mischievous spirit probably had nothing to do with it. *Just because you've been involved in several murders recently doesn't mean that this is going to be another.*

The reasonable part of her agreed with this, but there was that niggling little voice that seemed convinced natural causes weren't the answer in this case. An'gel was, like everyone else, curious to hear what the doctor had to say about Nathan Gamble's demise.

"I wish Henry Howard would come back," Mary Turner said. "I want to know what's going on, but I don't want to go out there and find him. Why doesn't someone come and tell us what's happening?"

"There is a lot to do when the authorities first arrive at a scene," An'gel told her. "It might be a while yet before we find out anything. I'll go stick my head out into the hall, though, and see what there is to see." She patted Mary Turner's shoulder before she headed to the door.

An'gel stuck more than her head out because all she could see was a hallway devoid of people. She could hear voices emanating from upstairs. Various sounds floated down the stairs, but she had trouble making out the words. She took a couple of steps out of the dining room toward the stairs, thinking she might actually go up a little way in order to hear more clearly.

"Can I help you, ma'am?"

An'gel had barely put her foot on the first tread when the voice from behind her startled her so badly she nearly stumbled and fell up the stairs. A strong, uniform-clad arm reached out to steady her. She looked up into the face of a young, tall police officer. He had to be at least six foot five, she reckoned, because she had to crane her neck back in order to look him in the eye.

"Are you all right, ma'am?" the young officer asked, his voice a deep baritone. He let go of her arm.

"Yes, Officer, thank you," An'gel replied. "I was only a little startled."

"Was there something you wanted?" the policeman said.

"I was looking to see whether anyone was around," An'gel said. "There are several of us in the dining room, and naturally we're wondering what's going on."

The officer nodded. "I see, ma'am. Some-one will be in to talk to you soon. They're all upstairs at the moment. How many are there in the dining room with you?"

An'gel thought for a moment. "Three others. My sister, our ward, and Mrs. Catlin."

"Thank you. Now, if you wouldn't mind going back to join the others, I'd appreciate it." The officer smiled.

"Certainly." An'gel felt like a guilty child caught out doing something she'd been expressly told not to. She headed to the door and slipped inside, nearly bumping into her sister. Dickce had apparently been at the door watching everything.

"Did you find out anything?" Dickce asked the moment the door closed behind An'gel. "It didn't sound like it."

"No, only that everyone is upstairs now. Someone will be coming to talk to us soon," An'gel said. "Though I wouldn't place any bets on how soon *soon* really is." She shared the news with the others and resumed her place beside Mary Turner.

Soon turned out to be nearly twenty minutes later, when the door opened to admit Henry Howard and the young policeman An'gel had met in the hallway.

"The doctor and the paramedics are still upstairs with the police," Henry Howard said.

"Come sit down," Mary Turner said.

"Right here." She indicated the chair next to her. "You look terrible."

Henry Howard smiled tiredly as he sat next to his wife. "It's a terrible thing. This is the first time we've had a guest die in the house."

An'gel noticed that the policeman did not leave the room. He had stationed himself near the door but well within hearing distance of those in the room. She knew that anything they said might be reported to the officer in charge of the investigation. Dickce and Benjy were aware of that as well, based on their previous experiences with sudden death. She didn't know whether the Catlins would realize it, however.

"Has the doctor seen him yet?" Mary Turner asked. Her anxiety was obvious, although Henry Howard appeared too tired and stressed himself to realize it, An'gel saw.

"Yes, the doctor looked at him, the paramedics looked at him, and the police looked at him." Henry Howard slumped back in his chair and closed his eyes. "Thank the Lord I only had to look at him the one time. I don't like looking at dead people, I can tell you that, especially in that room."

Mary Turner laid a hand on his arm. "I know, none of us do. Did anyone say anything about how he died?"

"Not that I heard," Henry Howard said. "They kept me out in the hall after I showed them to the room."

"Did you happen to notice anyone else upstairs?" An'gel asked. "Other than police and medical personnel?"

Henry Howard sat up. "What do you mean?"

An'gel caught sight of the policeman. She knew he was paying close attention. He had moved a couple of steps away from the door.

"Mrs. Pace left the room abruptly right after you did earlier," An'gel said. "I wondered if she had gone upstairs to her room, that's all."

"I didn't see her," Henry Howard said.

Mary Turner looked at An'gel. "Do you think she might be in the kitchen with Marcelline and the others?"

"It's possible, I suppose." An'gel wondered why she hadn't thought of that. Instead she had immediately come up with much less innocent ideas. *That's what getting involved in murder will do for your thought processes.*

She noticed Dickce and Benjy across the table, their heads together, whispering. Then Benjy looked at her. "Miss An'gel, Peanut and Endora have been alone in the room for over an hour now. I really need to go check on them. They both get bored, and they might tear something up."

"You can bring them in here with us," Henry Howard said. "We don't mind."

"No, of course not," Mary Turner said. "I hate to think of them locked up by themselves all this time."

An'gel rose and approached the policeman. "Officer, we have a dog and a cat with us. They're in the annex in Benjy's room, and as I'm sure you heard, they've been there over an hour. Would it be all right if Benjy goes and gets them and brings them here?"

Benjy had joined her. "Peanut will probably need to do his business," he said to An'gel. "Officer, Peanut is the dog, and he'll need walking for a few minutes."

"I'll ask, if you'll wait a moment." The officer turned and opened the door. He stepped into the hall, leaving the door open, and called up the stairs for someone named Thornton.

An'gel couldn't see who responded but she did hear a voice from the direction of the stairs who asked the officer what he wanted. The policeman explained, and the other voice called out, "I'll get someone."

The officer returned to the dining room. "Someone will be here in a moment to go with you," he told Benjy.

202

Benjy smiled. "Thank you, sir." He and An'gel moved back to the table to wait.

They had to wait several minutes but finally another policeman came into the room. Another youngster, An'gel noted, but perhaps older than the first. Not nearly as tall, though. He beckoned to Benjy. "I'll go with you," he said, and Benjy followed him out.

An'gel resumed her seat. *Thank goodness for Benjy. I'd forgotten all about poor Peanut and Endora.* The pets hadn't been part of the family long, and she was still getting used to them and their needs. She and Dickce hadn't had animals around the house in many years, and she had forgotten what it was like.

A few minutes after Benjy departed the room with the second policeman, the dining room door opened to admit Marcelline, Serenity Foster, Truss Wilbanks, and Primrose Pace. Accompanying them was another police officer, evidently a senior man.

"Please take a seat, everyone." He waited by the head of the table until the newcomers were seated.

An'gel regarded Primrose Pace with a frown. Had the medium been in the kitchen all along?

"Now, I'm sure y'all are wondering what's

been going on," the officer said. "First, I'm going to introduce myself. I'm Lieutenant Steinberg. I appreciate y'all's patience while we've been checking out the situation upstairs. Before I can explain that, though, I'd appreciate if y'all would introduce yourselves and tell me your relationship to the deceased. Mr. Catlin we already know. Are you Mrs. Catlin?" He nodded toward Mary Turner.

"Yes," she said. "The deceased was a distant cousin of mine."

"Thank you," the officer said. "And you?"

An'gel introduced herself, and the others in turn did the same.

Serenity Foster was the last person to answer. "I'm Serenity Foster, and the deceased was my brother. Nathan Gamble." She turned in her chair to point to Mary Turner. "She's the one who killed him, Lieutenant Steinberg."

CHAPTER 19

An'gel would have thought Serenity Foster had more sense than to make a statement like that without even knowing how her brother had died. Evidently her animosity toward Mary Turner overruled her caution and good judgment, had she any.

"I told you to stop saying things like that." Truss Wilbanks fairly hissed the words at his client.

"I don't care," Serenity said hotly. "Lieutenant, you heard me."

"Miz Foster, I can understand you're real upset right now with your brother dying so suddenly and him being a young man," Steinberg said. "But that's a strong accusation you're making. Do you have any reason to believe your brother's death was the result of premeditated murder?"

Before Serenity could answer the officer, Truss Wilbanks spoke up. "As I explained in my introduction, Lieutenant, I am Mrs.

Foster's attorney, and I have to advise her to be careful in making these statements without any facts whatsoever to back them up. They could result, if she persists, in a lawsuit." He glared at Serenity, and An'gel was surprised that the young woman didn't fire back at him. Instead, she seemed to wilt under his glare.

He turned back to Steinberg. "So to answer your question, no, there is no reason to believe this was premeditated in any way."

The lieutenant gazed blandly back at Wilbanks. "I see, Mr. Wilbanks, but I was asking Miz Foster. Do you stand by your earlier statement, ma'am?"

Serenity shook her head. "No, I was just upset."

An'gel hoped that would be the end of it, at least for now. Poor Mary Turner continued to tremble beside her, whether from rage or fear or another emotion altogether, An'gel wasn't certain. She was afraid her young friend might break down if she had to face another onslaught of her cousin's spite. They all felt raw and on edge, she had no doubt, and Serenity's behavior was no help.

She glanced at Primrose Pace and saw that the medium was gazing intently at Serenity. A half smile played around Mrs.

Pace's lips, and she continued to watch Serenity while An'gel watched her. What was the interest? An'gel wondered.

"Very well, then," Steinberg said. "I can't tell you a lot at the moment, and that's because we don't know a lot. The doctor can't sign the death certificate because he's not familiar with the deceased's medical history."

"He wouldn't be," Henry Howard said. "He's a friend of ours and lives nearby. That's why I called him."

Steinberg nodded. "Thank you, Mr. Catlin. Now, Miz Foster, can you tell us who your brother's doctor was, if he had one?"

Serenity shrugged. "He never mentioned one to me. As far as I knew, he was in perfect health. He was too cheap to go to a doctor most of the time, unless he was really, really sick." She named an urgent care clinic, evidently in Vicksburg, where she had known him to go in the past. "He had the flu really bad last year, and for that he went to the doctor."

"Thank you, ma'am, we'll check with the doctors there," the policeman said. "We have no reason to treat this death as anything other than natural at the moment, unless somebody has further information they'd like to share." He looked around the room.

Primrose Pace suddenly pushed back her chair and rose. "I have information, Lieutenant. I communicated with the spirit of the deceased not long after it left his body, and I will be happy to share that communication with you."

An'gel had to admire Steinberg's self-possession after that startling announcement. His bland expression never wavered, though An'gel thought he blinked a couple of times. Then it dawned on her that she had been right about the medium's whereabouts. Mrs. Pace *had* been upstairs, probably in the room with the body, before the authorities arrived. Snooping around, no doubt, but why?

"I see. Mrs. Pace, isn't it?" He waited for the medium to affirm that. "Are you in the habit of communicating with the spirits, ma'am?"

"I am a psychic medium," she responded with a bit of hauteur. "I have helped police in similar cases before."

An'gel wondered what the medium's angle was in this display. She didn't really believe Mrs. Pace had communicated with Nathan Gamble after death. She was making the whole thing up. She had to be, An'gel decided. The question was, why? Maybe the woman was simply delusional and needed medical attention herself.

"What did he tell you? That he was murdered?" Serenity Foster's harsh tones brought everyone's attention back to her.

Wilbanks immediately remonstrated with her, but Serenity ignored him and started repeating her questions to Primrose Pace.

Steinberg's voice rang out. "Quiet, everyone, please." He nodded to the medium. "Go on, ma'am."

"As I was trying to tell you, Lieutenant," Mrs. Pace said with a hostile glance at Serenity, "I have helped the police before. With missing persons mostly, but those cases often entailed suspicious deaths. This death, however, was nothing like that." She paused, and the silence lingered.

An'gel wished the medium would get to the point. She really wanted to hear what the woman would say. She almost felt like speaking up but knew that the lieutenant would not appreciate it.

"Please, go on," Steinberg said after the pause had stretched out uncomfortably long.

"Mr. Gamble died peacefully. His spirit was a bit confused, of course, with the sudden transition. You see, they are often like this, especially when they aren't expecting it." Mrs. Pace shook her head dolefully. "And so often no one is there to encourage them on their way."

"How exactly do you encourage them on their way?" Steinberg asked.

"I tell them that they have to accept the fact that they have passed on," Mrs. Pace replied. "Few souls are ready to accept that right away, you must understand. Most don't want to leave the earthly plane and their loved ones. It's even harder for them if they have a message they want to give their loved ones." She shook her head again in the same doleful manner. "It's truly tragic for some of them, and their loved ones are often desperate for some last word.

"Then once they have begun to accept that they are no longer part of the mortal world," Mrs. Pace continued, "I tell them to look toward the light. Some see it more quickly than others. Some embrace it gladly. Others have to be encouraged to do it."

"Do any of them ever refuse?" Dickce asked.

An'gel frowned at her sister but she was as curious as Dickce, she admitted to herself, to hear the medium's answer.

"Yes," Mrs. Pace replied. "They hang on, refusing to believe that they are dead. They can cause terrible mischief sometimes in their anger and denial. Like the spirit in this house. She is one who refuses to move on. Something has bound her here, but I haven't been able to figure out yet what it is."

"There's a spirit here?" Steinberg asked, his expression still bland. "Where is it now?"

Mrs. Pace shrugged. "She's hidden herself for the moment. I doubt she is happy that there are so many strange persons in her house."

"Let's get back to Mr. Gamble for the moment," Steinberg said. "You assisted his spirit. Did his spirit go willingly?"

"Not at first," Mrs. Pace said. "He needed coaxing, but once he understood that he had died and could not go back, he seemed eager to embrace the light."

"That's good, I guess." For the first time Steinberg's facade slipped, and An'gel thought he was losing patience with the medium. "Now, exactly where were you when all this communicating was taking place, ma'am?"

"In the room with his corporeal self, naturally," Mrs. Pace said. "I would have thought that was obvious. The spirit usually remains quite close to its former shell until it is ready to move on, or the body is removed from where the person died."

An'gel could tell that the lieutenant wasn't happy to find out that Mrs. Pace had been in the room. Even if Nathan Gamble's death had been completely natural, An'gel thought, Mrs. Pace had no business being in there. She wasn't a member of the family, and she had no official standing as a medical or legal person.

"Mrs. Pace, I'd like you to come with me for some further questions," Steinberg said. "Mr. Catlin, is there another room we can use for a little while?"

Henry Howard nodded. "Sure, the front parlor across the hall, or the library. It's the room next to the parlor. Either one."

"Thank you," Steinberg said. "We'll use the parlor. Mrs. Pace, if you please."

The medium inclined her head and moved in a stately fashion toward the door. Steinberg saw her out, then turned to address everyone. "For now, I have no further questions for you, but those of you who are guests, I'd like you to give your home addresses and contact information to my men here in case I need to talk to you further. Miz Foster, I would like to talk to you, however, so if you don't mind waiting." He stated the last as an order, not a request, An'gel thought.

■ ■ ■ ■

Serenity Foster didn't offer any objections, though she immediately ducked her head toward her lawyer and began speaking in a lowered tone to him.

Steinberg left the dining room door open, and the young officer who had been watching them earlier stepped forward, pad and pen to the ready. "I need to get the information the lieutenant wants. Mr. and Mrs. Catlin, we have yours, of course. Miss Ducote, ma'am, if you wouldn't mind."

While An'gel provided the necessary information for herself, Dickce, and Benjy, the latter returned with the older police officer, Peanut, and Endora.

Peanut woofed joyfully at the sight of An'gel and strained against his leash to get to her. Benjy held him back with a quiet command, however, until An'gel finished dictating to the young policeman.

He next took Marcelline's information, and as soon as he finished, the housekeeper turned to Mary Turner. "Now, Miss Mary, I'm taking you upstairs, and you're going to lie down for a while. And don't you try to argue with me, missy."

Mary Turner gave the housekeeper a wan

213

smile. "I'm not going to, Marcelline. I need to be where it's quiet for a while." She turned to her husband. "How about you? Would you like to come with me?"

Henry Howard frowned. "No, you go ahead. I'd better stay here in case the police want anything else. I'll be up to check on you later." He gave her a quick peck on the cheek.

"All right," Mary Turner said. She rose from her chair and followed Marcelline docilely from the room, allowing the house-keeper to put an arm around her as if she were unable to hold herself upright.

Henry Howard looked like he needed rest far more than Mary Turner did, An'gel thought. The circles around his eyes seemed darker, and he moved stiffly. She realized that he had never had much chance to have breakfast.

"You need to eat something," she told him. "You come with me. I'm going to take you to the kitchen, and we'll find some-thing." She turned to Peanut, who had put a paw on her leg. She fondled his head for a moment. "Yes, I'm glad to see you, too, you silly boy. But I need to take care of Henry Howard right now."

Peanut woofed and withdrew his paw. An'gel always marveled at how the dog seemed to understand exactly what she told him. Endora, of course, always ignored her.

An'gel returned her attention to her host and saw him smiling at her. "I miss having a dog," he said.

"Why don't you and Mary Turner adopt one?" An'gel said. "Now, come along with me. Let's get you fed."

"We'll stay here for now, Sister," Dickce told her. An'gel knew Dickce would do her best to find out what was going on between Serenity and Wilbanks. They were still conferring and seemed not to notice what the others in the room were doing.

An'gel repeated her question to Henry Howard on the way down the hall, then added, "There are plenty of animals in shelters who need adopting, after all."

"I know," Henry Howard said. "But dogs need a lot of attention, and sometimes guests don't respond to them well. We have to be really careful, you know. We can't afford to get sued just because some crazy person can't handle a dog or a cat anywhere in the house."

"I hadn't thought of that," An'gel said. "That's a shame, though."

"Yes, it is," Henry Howard replied. "But that's the way it is. The house always comes first, basically, because it's our livelihood."

He walked into the kitchen and went straight to the small table near the back door.

Before An'gel could look for food for Henry Howard, Marcelline came storming in. She walked straight over to Henry Howard, ignoring An'gel.

"You've got to get her out of this house." Marcelline slapped her hands down on the table right in front of Henry Howard. He jerked back in his chair.

"Something has made that spirit angry. It killed Nathan Gamble, I tell you, and now it's going to harm Miss Mary if you don't stop it."

CHAPTER 20

Surely Marcelline couldn't be serious, An'gel thought. A spirit trying to harm Mary Turner? The idea was ridiculous. Primrose Pace hadn't mentioned that a malicious spirit caused Nathan Gamble's death, although she had said that spirits could turn malicious. When she had time to herself later on, An'gel wanted to think about all that the medium had said and try to figure out exactly what was going on here. She wished they knew more about Mrs. Pace's background.

Henry Howard evidently agreed with An'gel about Marcelline's claims of spirit interference. He laughed in the housekeeper's face. "I know you believe there's a ghost in this house, but even if there is, it's never done anything bad before, has it? No one's ever been hurt here, have they?"

Marcelline looked taken aback at Henry Howard's response to her demands. "Well, no, not before now," she said. "But Nathan wanted to take those things from this house, and the spirit didn't want him to. She wants those things left right where they are. They belong here, no matter what Nathan was always saying."

That was an interesting idea, An'gel thought. The spirit was protecting the furnishings of the French room. But why? Was the spirit supposed to belong to the long-dead great-aunt who had once lived in that room, Nathan's great-grandmother four times removed? As far as An'gel was aware, the woman hadn't died in this house. Surely she had died in Vicksburg, where her husband and children lived. That might be something they needed to find out, though.

"You and I are never going to agree on this, Marcelline," Henry Howard said, his tone becoming increasingly testy. "I hope you're not saying all these things in front of Mary Turner."

The housekeeper bridled. "Credit me with some sense, Mr. Henry. I helped raise that child, and I'm not going to frighten her. You're her husband, you're supposed to be looking out for her, and you'd rather be off somewhere writing than looking after her."

"That's enough." Henry Howard pushed back his chair and stood over Marcelline.

"I'm tired of hearing that from you. All you do is criticize me because I'm not a slave to this house the way you and Mary Turner are. I married Mary Turner, not this damn house." He pushed by the housekeeper and stormed out the back door, slamming it shut behind him.

An'gel felt embarrassed to have witnessed this scene. She had never guessed there was such a high level of friction between Henry Howard and Marcelline. She knew the housekeeper was protective of Mary Turner. But why this animosity toward Henry Howard? Was he really that neglectful of Mary Turner?

An'gel figured Marcelline was frightened by the unexplained death and was lashing out in fear for her beloved young mistress. An'gel had already discovered that Henry Howard wasn't truly happy running the bed-and-breakfast, and she could understand that. He apparently wanted to be a writer but his responsibilities to his wife and the family business were frustrating his ambitions and his progress. The situation was rife for discord, and An'gel wondered how far it had developed.

There had been no indication of any kind of rift between Mary Turner and Henry Howard that An'gel could recall. As far as she could tell, Mary Turner loved her husband, and he in turn loved his wife. They seemed devoted to each other. Frustrated ambition could affect even a loving couple in a bad way, though. She couldn't do anything about it unless Mary Turner appealed directly to her for help. She couldn't pry into the young woman's relationship with her husband. That was not her way, although she hated standing by when friends were in need of help of some kind.

Marcelline seemed to notice that An'gel was in the kitchen. Her tone was chilly when she spoke. "Was there something you needed, Miss An'gel?"

"I brought Henry Howard in here because he never really got a chance to have any breakfast," An'gel said. "I thought he needed something to eat. He's under considerable strain at the moment." She intended that last remark to make a point with Marcelline, and she hoped the housekeeper would understand the implicit criticism. An'gel knew it wasn't her place to interfere in matters between employer and employee, but she felt that the housekeeper hadn't been entirely fair with Henry Howard.

"When he comes back, I'll see that he gets something to eat," Marcelline said. "Now, if you'll excuse me, I have work to do."

"Certainly," An'gel said in her best grande dame manner. She might have permanently impaired a previously cordial relationship with the housekeeper with her words, but she wasn't going to back down. She walked out of the kitchen.

In the hallway, the kitchen door shut behind her, An'gel paused to think about what she ought to do next. What she really wanted to do was confront Primrose Pace and find out more about the woman's background. Her turning up at Cliffwood had been suspiciously opportune, and An'gel didn't buy the idea that a spirit had called the woman to the house.

Benjy had a knack for finding things online, An'gel knew, and perhaps it was time to get him to research Primrose Pace. He enjoyed projects like these, and he would be happy to have something to do. An'gel headed to the dining room to discover whether he and Dickce were still there.

The parlor door was closed, and An'gel wondered whether Lieutenant Steinberg still had Mrs. Pace in there. An'gel hoped the policeman questioned the medium thoroughly. She wished she could have overheard their interview, but instead she would have to count on Benjy's ability to dig out what they needed to know about

Mrs. Pace.

Only Serenity Foster and Truss Wilbanks still remained in the dining room. They appeared absorbed in conversation, their positions much the same as they had been when An'gel departed the room only a little while ago.

An'gel was annoyed to discover that, despite what she had said earlier, Dickce and Benjy, along with the pets, had left the room. An'gel hovered in the doorway for a moment, undecided whether to enter and speak to its occupants or steal away, unobserved.

Serenity Foster looked toward the doorway and spotted An'gel. "What do you want?" she said.

An'gel advanced into the room. "I was looking for my sister and our ward," she said. "But I did want to offer you my condolences on the loss of your brother. I know this has been a terrible shock to you."

"Thank you," Serenity said. "I don't understand what could have happened. I'm not going to believe it was natural, and you can tell your friend Miss High-and-Mighty Mary Turner that, too. She's going to pay for what she's done to my brother."

Truss Wilbanks sat back in his chair, apparently exhausted by trying to rein in his client's wild accusations. He did make a token protest. "Serenity, you've got to stop saying those things. The last thing you need right now is another lawsuit."

"Mrs. Foster, you should heed your attorney's advice," An'gel said, enraged by the young woman's continued attack on Mary Turner. "Should it become necessary, I will be happy to serve as a witness for Mary Turner if she decides to sue you. I suggest you look to your own behavior first before you criticize anyone else's. By your own admission, you were enraged by your brother's lack of monetary support for you. It won't take the police long to figure out that you had a far stronger motive to kill him than anyone else did."

An'gel did not wait to see or hear Serenity Foster's reaction to her speech. She turned and walked out of the room and right into her sister, who had evidently been lingering in the hallway.

"That's telling her, Sister." Dickce's eyes danced with mischief. "I get such a kick out of it when you go into terminator mode."

"I wish you wouldn't insist on using that ridiculous phrase," An'gel said, still angry from her confrontation with Serenity. "Come upstairs with me. I need to be somewhere quiet for a little while, and we can talk about this mess in private." She headed up the stairs.

She didn't speak again until she was seated in the armchair in her bedroom. Dickce found a place on the old trunk at the foot of An'gel's bed.

"Where are Benjy and the animals?" An'gel asked.

"They've gone back to their room," Dickce said. "I suggested that Benjy go online and see what he can find out about our mysterious Mrs. Pace."

An'gel nodded approvingly. "Excellent. That's exactly what I wanted him to do. I want to know who — and what — that woman really is."

"What if he doesn't find *any*thing?" Dickce asked.

"That will prove she's a fake," An'gel said. "In that case, I would speak with Lieutenant Steinberg and ask him to investigate. It would be obvious the woman came here to defraud Mary Turner in some fashion, and surely he would look into that if Mary Turner complains to him. I can't see why she wouldn't."

"I don't know," Dickce said. "She might be afraid of the publicity if the story gets out. It's going to be bad enough when the press gets wind of Nathan Gamble's death.

I can see the headlines now. *Ghost Frightens Man to Death. Haunted House Claims Innocent Victim. Death by Ghost.*" She shook her head. "Mary Turner will be upset."

"It will probably triple the reservations to stay here," An'gel said wryly. "There are always thrill-seekers looking for haunted houses, you know."

"Maybe, but I don't think those are the kinds of guests she wants here, do you?"

"No," An'gel said. "I wouldn't want them either, frankly. But this is a business, and they have to have guests if they're going to keep it running."

"Speaking of running the business," Dickce said, "I'm sure you've noticed that Henry Howard isn't all that enthusiastic about it."

"He's not," An'gel said. "He talked to me briefly just now when I took him to the kitchen for breakfast." She relayed the conversation to Dickce and told her about Marcelline's behavior.

"She seemed really fond of him the last time we were here," Dickce said. "Do you think she's actually turned against him? Or was it simply the stress talking?"

"The latter, I think, is more likely." An'gel shrugged. "But the last time we saw them was a few years ago, and they hadn't been

225

married all that long. The three of them spend so much time together, it's no wonder there are sore spots, I suppose."

"Maybe when all this is cleared up and things get back to normal, whatever that may be," Dickce said, "they will all feel happier with one another."

"Maybe they will, Pollyanna." An'gel gave a brief smile. "I would like for them to be happy. We both know what a huge responsibility an old house like this can be."

"At least we're in a better position financially to maintain ours," Dickce said. "We don't have to work the way they do."

"True," An'gel said. "We were incredibly lucky that our father was so astute in business, and we haven't done too badly ourselves."

"Chips off the old block." Dickce smiled.

"Let's get back to the business at hand," An'gel said. "Namely, the unexplained death of Nathan Gamble. You heard what I said to his sister. What do you think?"

"Do I think she has a much stronger motive for getting rid of him than Mary Turner?" Dickce asked. "I do. If Serenity doesn't inherit anything from her brother's estate, though, her motive is pretty weak."

"I've thought about that," An'gel said. "Even if she doesn't inherit directly, she might still benefit from his death."

"How so?" Dickce asked.

"With her brother out of the way," An'gel replied, "she might gain more control over her trust fund."

"We don't know the terms of the trust," Dickce said. "It would be odd if her brother were the only trustee, don't you think? There are usually at least two."

"Yes," An'gel said. "Good point. Still worth considering, though, if her brother's death dissolves the trust."

"I hadn't thought of that," Dickce said.

"And there's another thing," An'gel said. "This time about her lawyer. Remember what I told you I witnessed yesterday between him and Nathan Gamble?"

Dickce nodded. "Do you think their relationship could be the key?"

"Truss Wilbanks wouldn't be the first angry lover to kill his ex."

CHAPTER 21

Benjy walked Peanut and Endora again before he took them back to their room. He wanted to let Peanut play and tire himself out so he would nap while Benjy worked at the task Miss Dickce had set him. Endora needed to play, too, and she always loved chasing the much larger dog.

Once in their room, Benjy opened his laptop and connected to the wireless network. Peanut and Endora snoozed on the bed, and Benjy figured he probably had half an hour before they got restless again and demanded attention.

Benjy entered *Primrose Pace* in the search engine and waited for results. The wireless connection didn't appear to be all that strong because it took longer than Benjy was used to for the results to appear. He groaned. If the connection didn't get any faster than this, he would need twice as long to find anything.

He examined the hits on *Primrose Pace*. The first one, apparently a newspaper article, looked promising, and he clicked on it. The story focused on a kidnapping and murder that had taken place in Louisiana nearly two years ago. A teenager had been abducted, and after months of no results from law enforcement, a psychic had come forward with claims to know the whereabouts of the girl. The psychic was Primrose Pace. There was a photograph accompanying the article. Several law enforcement officers and one woman stood in a small clearing in the woods. They were all staring at a spot under one large tree where the earth had been disturbed. The picture had been shot at enough distance that the faces of the officers and the woman were not clear. Even though Benjy tried enlarging the photograph, he couldn't distinguish enough of the woman's features to identify her.

Benjy skimmed the article. Mrs. Pace's claims had proven helpful, he read. Though the spot pictured in the photograph included with the article had not been a grave, officials did find the remains of the teenager less than half a mile from there. Benjy wondered what had disturbed the earth in the photograph. Probably an animal digging, he thought.

The next two links yielded similar results. No photograph with which he could positively identify Primrose Pace, but otherwise the stories were much like the first one. Mrs. Pace apparently did have some knack for finding areas where human remains had been left or buried, but she never was right about the exact spot, Benjy concluded. Still, it was an impressive feat in itself. The woman either had been involved in the murders, somehow had inside knowledge, or possessed real psychic abilities.

One of the articles contained a brief description of the medium, an attractive black woman in her mid-forties. The Primrose Pace at Cliffwood matched that description, but then so would many other women. Benjy hadn't found anything so far that could positively identify the woman at Cliffwood as the Primrose Pace of the articles.

He continued through the links until he reached the point that he found himself reading through information in which the words *primrose* and *pace* appeared somewhere in the same article. He refined his search to look for the two words together, and his results narrowed immediately to only one screen's worth.

Benjy stopped for a moment to consider

his next move. Mrs. Pace had never mentioned where she came from, but the stories he had read with her in them had all taken place in Louisiana. One of them happened not far across the Mississippi River from Natchez.

He found it odd that the woman didn't have a website to advertise herself. Idly he searched *Louisiana psychics* and after about ten seconds had a result list of over 300,000 hits. He even found a directory of psychics, but there was no listing for Primrose Pace. Idly he clicked on several of the different psychics listed and read their descriptions and scanned some of their testimonials. He found it all fascinating, especially since a few of them listed *missing persons* as a specialty.

Maybe Primrose Pace was one of those people who didn't like the Internet and preferred to find her clients via word of mouth instead of social media. That thought reminded him he needed to check other social media sources, and he proceeded to do so. He didn't find an account anywhere for Primrose Pace on the most popular social media sites or even a mention of her.

Next he tried a genealogical database, but the only hits he got showed the two words in the same entry, usually with the word

Primrose part of a street name and *Pace* as a surname.

Benjy searched every source he could access through the Athena Public Library. He had no access to the library at Athena College, though come spring he would. He was excited about enrolling for his first semester of college and couldn't believe how lucky he was that he had been accepted. Access to a college library would open whole new worlds to him, and he couldn't wait for that to happen.

Before he became too lost in happy thoughts about college, he made himself refocus on the search for information on Primrose Pace. He couldn't think of anywhere further to look. He would report his findings to Miss An'gel and Miss Dickce, and see whether they had any ideas about next steps. He knew they would find it as interesting as he did that there was so little to be found on the mysterious medium.

Benjy shut down the laptop and sat for a moment, watching the sleeping dog and cat. He enjoyed these quiet times with them. They were still so young, and he hated to think of them getting old and suffering from ailments like arthritis or kidney disease. He had read a lot about such things because of his interest in animal welfare, and he was determined to be prepared for their care in old age.

That made him think of Miss Dickce and Miss An'gel. They were already old, but they appeared to be pretty healthy and spry despite their age. He couldn't imagine them any other way and dreaded the thought of their becoming infirm or incapacitated in any way. When the time came, he would do his best to take care of them.

"Enough of the old-age stuff." He hadn't meant to say it aloud, but he needed to get his mind off the subject. Otherwise he'd get depressed, and that wouldn't do anybody any good.

Peanut woke up at the sound of his voice and began to stir. That in turn got Endora awake, and Benjy happily began to give them the attention they now demanded.

"Are you sure about what you overheard?" Dickce asked. "I thought some more about what you told us, and I think there could be a different interpretation for it."

"What would that be?" An'gel asked.

"Maybe it referred to a business relationship, not a sexual or romantic one," Dickce replied. "People use similar terminology with business relationships when things go bad, don't they?"

"I suppose so," An'gel said. "If it weren't for the way he was adjusting his clothing, I would agree that your idea is a more likely answer. Of course, what Wilbanks said to Gamble could refer to both a business and a sexual relationship. The two might have been involved in both ways."

"Double jeopardy, then," Dickce said.

"If you want to put it that way, yes." An'gel thought about it for a moment. "That would certainly add to the bitterness if both had gone sour. And Wilbanks definitely sounded bitter."

"Either way, there is still a strong motive for Wilbanks," Dickce said. "With the two aspects combined, I'd say it becomes even stronger."

"I agree," An'gel said. "I'm beginning to like Wilbanks as the chief suspect myself."

Dickce wagged a finger at her. "You still don't know that Nathan Gamble was murdered. We've spent so much time dealing with murder recently that I swear you're starting to see a murder everywhere you go."

An'gel started to protest but then admitted to herself there was a great deal of truth in what her sister had said. She was being premature in this case, though she had been proven right in the past when she stated that a suspicious death resulted from murder.

"You can't deny it, can you?" Dickce said.

"No," An'gel said. "I can't. But you can't deny that Nathan Gamble's death is odd. The first time he ever spent the night in that room he was so desperate to own. The contents, of course, not the room itself, but you know what I mean. I think it's too great a coincidence myself, and it might have been really convenient for someone."

"Except that we don't know for whom and why it is convenient," Dickce said.

An'gel made a sound of disgust. "We keep going in circles. I wish we knew whether Nathan Gamble was murdered."

"Let's look at the situation from a different angle, then," Dickce said. "Let's look at the *how* instead."

"How he was murdered, if he was murdered, you mean?" An'gel said.

Dickce nodded.

"Mary Turner said he looked frightened," An'gel said. "Maybe someone went into the room and scared him to death."

"If he had a weak heart, I suppose that could have happened," Dickce said. "I wonder if he had locked the door before he retired for the night. I don't think either Henry Howard or Mary Turner said anything about having to unlock his door, did they?"

An'gel thought for a moment, then shook her head. "I don't remember. We can ask Henry Howard."

"It could be important," Dickce said.

"Yes, depending on the method the killer used," An'gel said. "Unless the room is somehow rigged to frighten a person. I suppose I might have found out if I had spent the night there."

"It's a good thing you didn't," Dickce said. "You could have been the one frightened to death instead of Nathan Gamble."

"Don't be ridiculous. I'm not that easily frightened."

"You don't know what Nathan Gamble might have seen. It might have terrified the life out of you."

An'gel rolled her eyes. "I seriously doubt it. My heart is in excellent condition, according to my cardiologist."

"I'm just glad it wasn't put to the test," Dickce said wryly. "You're annoying, but I'd rather be annoyed by you than by anyone else."

An'gel grinned. "Same to you, Sister."

A knock sounded at the door, and An'gel called, "Come in."

The door opened to reveal Mary Turner. She hesitated in the doorway, and An'gel could see that the young woman was upset about something.

An'gel got up and went to her. "Come in, my dear. Tell us what's wrong."

Mary Turner responded with a weak smile. "Thank you, Miss An'gel. I'm sorry to bother you with this, but have you seen my husband recently?"

"The last time I saw him was in the kitchen about an hour ago," An'gel said.

"Marcelline told me about what she said to him. I got so angry with her," Mary Turner said. "She means well but sometimes she isn't fair to him."

"Henry Howard isn't in the house?" Dickce asked.

Mary Turner shook her head. "No, he's not. I've texted him, but I'm not getting any response. I'm worried. He's never gone off like this before without telling me where he was going."

"Did you look to see if his car is in the garage?" An'gel asked.

"It's there," Mary Turner said. "I checked, but when my husband is worried or aggravated about something, he walks. Sometimes for miles, until he's figured out the answer to a problem or he's worn off his aggravation."

"Then that's probably what he's doing now," Dickce said.

"I wouldn't worry, except that he always tells me when he's going for one of these walks. This isn't like him."

"He may have stopped somewhere for a bite to eat," An'gel said. "He never did get breakfast this morning, with all that was going on. He simply forgot to tell you he was going for a walk, and he's too distracted to notice that you've texted. I'm sure it's as simple as that."

"I hope you're right," Mary Turner said.

"Come sit right here by me and stop worrying about Henry Howard for a few minutes." Dickce patted a spot next to her on the trunk. "We need to talk to you about other things, if you're up to it."

"All right." Mary Turner did as Dickce asked. "What do you want to talk about?"

"First let me say that neither Dickce nor I believe you had anything to do with your cousin's death," An'gel said.

"Thank you," Mary Turner replied. "Your support means a great deal to me. Serenity is being hateful. That's the way she is."

"I warned her to be careful about accusing you the way she has," An'gel said. "The threat of a lawsuit got through to her, I think."

"Her ex-husband is looking for anything he can get on her to keep her from having joint custody of their children," Mary Turner said. "She really needs to be careful."

"She seems to be in desperate need of money," Dickce said. "All to do with this custody battle, from what I've heard."

"I think so," Mary Turner said.

"She seems to think her brother had plenty of money," An'gel said. "Do you know whether she would benefit significantly from his death, by any chance?"

"Nathan inherited a lot of money from their parents, I do know that," Mary Turner said, "but all Serenity got was a trust fund. A pretty hefty one, too, I think. Nathan probably had a will. He was careful about things like that. If it hadn't been for his obsession over the French room, I think we would have gotten along fine."

"If Nathan did leave a will," Dickce said, "whom do you think he left his money and property to?"

Mary Turner shrugged. "My guess would be to either Serenity or to Truss Wilbanks. Nathan and Truss were still a couple, as far as I know."

CHAPTER 22

"That's interesting, don't you think, Dickce?" An'gel shot a pointed glance at her sister. She knew she had been right about the sexual component of the men's relationship.

Dickce nodded. "How long had your cousin and Mr. Wilbanks been together?"

"Going on ten years, at least," Mary Turner said. "Mind you, it was a pretty volatile relationship from what I saw of it. Truss lives here in Natchez, and Nathan lived in Vicksburg, although they were always going back and forth, I think."

"Were Mr. Wilbanks and your cousin in business together?" An'gel asked.

"Yes, Truss handled the legal side of Nathan's real estate business, but he also has other clients," Mary Turner said.

"Like Mrs. Foster," Dickce said.

Mary Turner nodded. "Actually, I think Truss started out as their father's lawyer.

He's been involved with the family since not long after he finished law school. That was about twenty years ago, I think. He's ten years older than me." She paused a moment. "If you don't mind my asking, why are y'all so interested in this? Is it because you think Nathan's death wasn't natural?"

"We think it's possible that it wasn't," An'gel said. "We don't want to alarm you, but you have to be prepared for that possibility. If it turns out that he didn't die naturally, then the police will want to know who killed him."

"And people will think it's me or Henry Howard," Mary Turner said. "Serenity will keep pointing the finger at me because she thinks I've always hated her and Nathan. All because of the contents of that stupid room." She shook her head. "Sometimes I wish my father or my grandfather had given the Gambles all that stuff and been done with it."

"You could have done it yourself after you inherited it," An'gel said. "Couldn't you?"

"Yes, I suppose so." Mary Turner sighed. "Although I know my father wouldn't like it. He thought it should stay in our family. If Nathan hadn't been such a gadfly about it, I might have decided to let him have it, despite the loss it would mean for Henry

241

Howard and me. But Nathan was so annoying."

"What about his sister? Would you give it to her?" Dickce asked.

"Never," Mary Turner said. "She's always been hateful and spiteful, and I'll burn the stuff before I let her get *her* hands on it." She laughed, and to An'gel, it was a bitter sound. "I know that sounds terrible, but that's the way it is. I never hated Nathan, despite how irritating he was. Serenity has never done a good thing for anyone in her life, always acting like she was too good to work for a living like the rest of us."

"She has certainly not impressed me," An'gel said. "While I feel sorry for her over her brother's death, I don't think I could ever like her or want to spend time around her."

"I'm glad you told us about Nathan's relationship with Mr. Wilbanks," Dickce said. "Frankly, at first I thought he and Serenity were involved."

Mary Turner appeared amused at the thought. "I think Serenity would like them to be more than friends, but I'm not sure Truss sees it that way. Truss really has put up with a lot for that family."

"Presumably he's been well paid for his legal work," An'gel said.

"Possibly," Mary Turner said. "Nathan wasn't known for being generous about anything much, except giving to his church maybe. I know he helped them buy a new organ. But he had trouble keeping employees in his real estate business. They were always leaving because of low pay. A friend of mine from high school whose husband took a job in Vicksburg worked for him for about a year. That was as long as she could stand it. What he paid didn't cover the cost of child care, according to her."

"Do you believe Nathan was well off? Did he have a significant estate to leave to someone?" An'gel asked.

"I don't know for sure," Mary Turner said. "I would think he was worth a good bit, though. He bought property in other states where the economy was better, particularly in Texas. I heard him mention properties in Dallas and Houston, for example. He went around looking like he could barely afford to buy clothes and he drove a twenty-year-old car, but that was just him."

"Sounds to me, then, that he might have been worth killing," Dickce said.

"When you put it like that," Mary Turner said slowly, "I suppose he was. Serenity and Truss would benefit the most, in that case, unless Nathan didn't leave them anything."

She thought a moment. "But Nathan was big on family and family history; otherwise he wouldn't have been so obsessed with the French room. I can't imagine he would cut his sister off completely."

"This is putting you on the spot, really," An'gel said, "but if you had to point the finger at either Serenity or Truss, which one would you point to?"

"That's a hard question. My first instinct is to say Serenity, but that may be because I loathe her so much." Mary Turner shrugged. "I actually sort of like Truss. He's really not so bad, but he does love money. Could be either one of them, or they might have been in it together."

"That's an interesting thought," An'gel said. "They were both angry with him certainly."

"I didn't realize Truss was angry with Nathan," Mary Turner said. "Why do you say that?"

An'gel told her what she had seen, minus the vulgar language. Mary Turner looked stunned. "Miss An'gel, I'm so sorry you had to see that. How nasty."

"It was unpleasant," An'gel said, "but I've lived a long time, my dear. I've seen far worse."

"Wait till I tell Henry Howard about this."

Mary Turner's face clouded. "If he ever comes back, that is." She pulled out her cell phone. "Still no response from him."

"Don't let yourself get worked up again, my dear," An'gel said. "He'll turn up soon, I'm sure. By now he will have walked off his frustrations and be on his way home."

"Bound to," Dickce said.

"I sure hope so." Mary Turner started to rise. "I really should go talk to Marcelline. I was pretty rough with her."

An'gel privately thought that a little rough talk would do Marcelline good. The housekeeper had been unpleasant to Henry Howard and shouldn't be interfering in her employers' marriage. She had behaved like a mother-in-law instead of a housekeeper.

"Don't go just yet," An'gel said. "I have something else I want to ask you about. It won't take long, I promise."

Mary Turner resumed her seat promptly, and An'gel guessed she wasn't eager to confront Marcelline again.

"What is that?" Mary Turner asked.

"It's about Primrose Pace," An'gel said. "Did she tell you anything at all about her background? Give you any references?"

"References? No, she didn't, but then I didn't ask." Mary Turner frowned. "I probably should have, shouldn't I? I was so

245

excited by the idea of having an experienced medium in the house, I guess I wasn't thinking clearly."

"About her background," An'gel said. "Did she tell you anything?"

"I did ask about that," Mary Turner said. "She told me that she had been involved in solving several missing persons cases. She even pulled out a couple of newspaper clippings to show me. I didn't take time to read every word, but it was pretty obvious she has some kind of ability with spirits."

"What did she tell you about those cases?" Dickce asked. "Did she offer you any details besides what was in the clippings?"

"Let me think about that for a moment," Mary Turner said.

An'gel and Dickce waited semi-patiently while Mary Turner thought. They were both curious about Primrose Pace, although at this point they couldn't see a connection between her and Nathan Gamble that would give her a motive in his murder.

"She said she was from Louisiana," Mary Turner said. "I remember that. Oh, and she also said she was in Natchez visiting a friend. She happened to be driving around looking at old houses, and when she drove into the driveway near the house, she started getting a strong feeling about it. She sat in her car for a few minutes and concentrated, and that's when she realized there was a spirit here that wanted someone it could talk to."

Given the stories about ghosts and antebellum homes and other places in Natchez, An'gel reckoned, Primrose Pace might have simply taken a chance that she could get a few nights' stay and some free meals in turn for her so-called services at Cliffwood. If Mary Turner had looked blankly at her and told her there had never been any supernatural activity at Cliffwood, the medium could have made her excuses and been on her way. Instead, Mary Turner had basically welcomed her with open arms.

"This isn't our business, and you can certainly tell us so without hurting our feelings," An'gel said. "Did Mrs. Pace mention a fee for her services?"

Mary Turner said, "Heavens, Miss An'gel, I don't mind you asking about that. I know Granny and Daddy trusted you and Miss Dickce, and I certainly do. Otherwise I wouldn't have begged you to come and help. In addition to her stay here and her meals, Mrs. Pace asked for five hundred dollars for five days' stay while she worked with the spirit."

An'gel had no experience with psychics,

but five hundred dollars, plus room and board, sounded pretty low to her for what some would consider professional services. She would ask Benjy to research how much psychics charged for their services. Primrose Pace's request made her think the woman was more a scam artist than an actual psychic. She probably thought she could get away with it more easily if she didn't ask for a large fee.

"Do you think I shouldn't have let her stay?" Mary Turner asked. "From your expression, I'll bet you're thinking I made a mistake in doing so."

"Perhaps," An'gel said. "I'm skeptical, frankly, about Mrs. Pace and her psychic abilities. We asked Benjy to see what he could find about her online. She might be who she says she is and be a known psychic. She could also be a con artist who goes around looking for —" She cut herself off when she realized what she had been about to say.

"Looking for gullible victims. That's what you were going to say, wasn't it?" Mary Turner didn't sound upset. "I know I'm a little too trusting sometimes, especially with people I don't know. I take everyone at face value, and to me, Mrs. Pace seemed sincere."

"I'm sorry," An'gel said. "Yes, that's what I was about to say, more or less. I would be happy were Mrs. Pace to prove me wrong. If there really is a spirit lingering here, and she can communicate with it and help it find peace, then all the better. The important thing to me and Sister, of course, is your happiness. If her being here makes you feel better, then Mrs. Pace's services are worth the price."

An'gel could tell by Dickce's expression that she might have been laying it on a bit too thick, but she only wanted to reassure Mary Turner. The poor child had too much on her plate as it was, without An'gel and Dickce worrying her over Mrs. Pace's bona fides.

Mary Turner appeared to accept her words at face value, An'gel was relieved to see. She would be more careful in what she said about Mrs. Pace in front of Mary Turner from now on, until she had proof positive the woman was a fake.

An'gel heard a bell tinkle somewhere in the room, and the sound startled her. Mary Turner, however, appeared delighted. She pulled out her phone and examined it eagerly.

"It's Henry Howard," she said as she jumped up from her seat on the trunk.

"He's home, and he's downstairs." Then her face clouded over. "He says Lieutenant Steinberg is on his way here, and he thinks it's bad news of some kind."

CHAPTER 23

"We'd better go downstairs and find out what this is all about," An'gel said.

Mary Turner was already halfway out the door. An'gel and Dickce moved more slowly. They reached the foot of the stairs in time to see Mary Turner dart into the library. Inside they found her with Henry Howard.

An'gel and Dickce held back discreetly while Henry Howard finished apologizing to Mary Turner for upsetting her. After the apology appeared to be done, they entered the room and joined the couple, who stood, arms around each other, by one of the windows.

An'gel thought Henry Howard looked better than when she had last seen him earlier in the day. Evidently he had at least managed to eat. He confirmed it when she asked him.

"There's a fast-food place about a mile away," he said. "I walked there and had something, and then I came back here and took a nap in one of the rooms in the annex. I slept for about an hour, I guess, and when I woke up, I realized I had left my phone here and hadn't told Mary Turner that I was going for a walk." He hugged her close to him. "I hate it that I worried you, honey."

"He does sometimes lay his phone down and then forgets where he left it," Mary Turner said fondly. "I should have realized that's what he'd done. I never thought of looking for you in the annex, though."

"We're glad you're all right," Dickce said.

"Yes," An'gel said. "Now what's this about Lieutenant Steinberg coming to the house? I gather he must have called you."

Henry Howard nodded. "Yes, that's actually how I found my phone. I heard it ringing and followed the sound. I managed to find it and answer the call before it went to voice mail."

"What did he say?" Dickce asked.

"Did he give you any details?" Mary Turner spoke at the same time.

"Nothing specific, no," Henry Howard said. "Only that there were developments and he wanted to talk to us all again. I thought the fact that he was coming here again to talk about these developments

252

wasn't really a good sign. He didn't sound like it was good news."

"What do you think, Miss An'gel?" Mary Turner asked.

"I think we need to wait and hear what the lieutenant has to tell us." An'gel could see that her young friend was apprehensive, and she didn't want to make her feel any more unsettled than she already was. She speculated that the *developments* were further information about the cause of death. She hoped that they had somehow confirmed it was natural, although they hadn't had time to examine the body much further.

"He ought to be here any minute now," Henry Howard said. "Why don't y'all go into the parlor, and I'll see if I can round up Serenity and Truss. Oh, and Mrs. Pace. She's still here, isn't she?"

"As far as I know," Mary Turner said. "I'll go check her room."

"I'll call Benjy," Dickce said. "Is it okay if he brings Peanut and Endora?"

"Fine with me," Mary Turner said before she hurried out the door.

"Ditto with me." Henry Howard smiled and followed his wife.

"Should we go tell Marcelline?" Dickce asked.

An'gel shook her head. "Henry Howard will probably go through the kitchen to get to the annex. He can tell her. Let's go in the parlor, and you can call Benjy."

To her surprise, she and Dickce found Primrose Pace already in the parlor, standing at the fireplace and evidently examining the mantel. "Hello, Mrs. Pace. Mary Turner just went upstairs to look for you."

The medium smiled. "She won't find me there." She gestured toward the mantel. "Isn't this a beautiful piece? I don't think I've seen one like it in any of the other antebellum homes I've visited."

"Yes, it is beautiful," An'gel said. "Mrs. Pace, Mary Turner is looking for you because Lieutenant Steinberg is on his way here with news of some kind." She watched carefully to note the medium's reaction to this announcement.

"Is he now?" Mrs. Pace murmured as she turned her attention back to the mantel. An'gel thought the woman's back had stiffened slightly before she turned away. Otherwise Mrs. Pace didn't seem affected by the news at all.

"I texted Mary Turner to let her know Mrs. Pace is here," Dickce said.

"Good," An'gel said. "We might as well be comfortable while we wait." She chose one of the sofas and indicated that Dickce should join her. The one she selected afforded a good view of most of the room.

Benjy walked in with Endora on his shoulder and Peanut on a leash. Peanut immediately came to greet An'gel as if he hadn't seen her in months, and she gave him the attention he craved. Benjy seated himself between Dickce and An'gel, and Endora immediately climbed down from his shoulder and into Dickce's lap.

"Any luck?" An'gel asked, keeping her voice low. Mrs. Pace stood only about seven feet away.

"A little. Three articles." Benjy matched his tone to An'gel's. "Nothing conclusive. There's no website, and that surprised me. Must use word of mouth."

Mrs. Pace turned and stared at them, and An'gel felt uncomfortable. Had the woman heard them and figured out that they were talking about her? An'gel smiled in a friendly manner, and Mrs. Pace turned away again.

"Later," she whispered to Benjy, who nodded to let her know he had heard.

Marcelline came into the room with Mary Turner. The housekeeper distanced herself from her employer, however, even though Mary Turner tried to get the woman to sit next to her. Marcelline shook her head and chose a nearby chair instead.

An'gel thought it a shame that the two women were on the outs with each other, but she thought Mary Turner was right to stand up for her husband. Marcelline was no doubt hurt, and An'gel hoped she would get over it. She understood the housekeeper's protectiveness but thought the woman had gone too far. Clementine, her own housekeeper, was protective of her and Dickce but she never spoke to them the way Marcelline had talked to Henry Howard.

Protective. An'gel said the word several times in her mind. Marcelline always watched out for Mary Turner's best interests. What if Marcelline had decided that getting rid of Nathan Gamble once and for all was in Mary Turner's best interests? She wanted to discuss the idea with Dickce and Benjy and felt frustrated that she couldn't do so right away. Depending on what Lieutenant Steinberg had to tell them, however, her new idea could be moot. She wished the man would get to Cliffwood and get it over with.

Henry Howard shepherded Serenity Foster and Truss Wilbanks into the parlor. An'gel was not surprised to note that Serenity's face bore its evidently habitual scowl.

Wilbanks, on the other hand, looked nervous to An'gel. The moment he seated himself on the other sofa, he pulled a handkerchief out of his inner jacket pocket and started mopping his brow. His skin tone was rather gray as well, An'gel decided. What was the man so afraid of?

Serenity Foster chose an armchair several feet away from the one Marcelline occupied. Henry Howard hovered near the parlor door, ready to admit the police when they arrived.

"Mrs. Pace, wouldn't you like to sit down?" Mary Turner asked. "There's room here by me, or I can bring another chair closer if you prefer."

"Thank you, Mrs. Catlin," the medium said. "I'm happy right where I am." She had not strayed more than a foot or two from the north side of the fireplace, An'gel noted. Why wouldn't she sit, though?

The doorbell rang, and An'gel immediately felt the level of tension in the room begin to rise. Even Peanut and Endora were quiet. She glanced at Mrs. Pace. The medium's enigmatic expression interested her. The woman's eyes appeared to rove from face to face. Was she getting vibrations, or whatever they were called, from people in the room? An'gel wondered.

An'gel could see the front door from where she sat, and she watched as Henry Howard admitted Lieutenant Steinberg and two other police officers, one of them female. Then several more people, also in uniform, came in behind them. An'gel began to worry. What was about to happen here?

Henry Howard escorted the lieutenant to the fireplace and then took the spot on the sofa next to his wife. Steinberg waited a moment before he spoke, letting his gaze wander over the assembled group much the same way Mrs. Pace had done not long before. An'gel was about ready to tell the man to get on with it when he finally spoke.

"I appreciate y'all's patience as we have been investigating this case of a sudden death," he began. "I know there's probably been a lot of confusion and wondering what's going on. I'd like to be able to set your minds at rest and tell you we've got an answer." He paused. "Unfortunately, I can't do that. We don't have a definitive answer yet."

Get to the point, An'gel thought. *What answers* do *you have?*

"I'm not at liberty to discuss all the details, pending the outcome of our investigation, you understand," Steinberg said.

258

"We're still in the information-gathering stage, and I have more questions for some of you, those who were either family or close associates."

An'gel glanced quickly at Truss Wilbanks. He had turned even grayer, if that were possible, and his hair was dark with perspiration. He was definitely frightened.

Steinberg reclaimed her attention as he continued. "I'll need to talk to you separately, of course, and Mr. Catlin has suggested that we use the library again for that purpose. I would like for you all to remain in this room while I talk to those I've already mentioned." His glance swept over An'gel, Benjy, and Dickce. "Even the ones who I don't plan to question further today need to remain as well. My men will be examining the scene of the death more closely, and it will be easier if all of you stay here and out of the way. Are we clear on that?"

An'gel fought the temptation to say "Sir, yes, sir!" Instead she merely nodded, as did most of the others. Wilbanks still looked too scared even to nod. He stared like a hypnotized rabbit at Steinberg.

"I appreciate your cooperation in this matter," Steinberg said. "I realize it's getting on for lunchtime, and I plan to finish this round of questioning as soon as possible. I intend to be thorough, however, and so it might take a while. If anyone here has a medical condition that requires meals at certain times, or if you have medication you need to take, please inform the officer who will remain on duty in this room." He paused. "Now, if you'll excuse me, we'll be getting on with our work."

An'gel was thoroughly aggravated with the man. He hadn't given them anything other than that the investigation was continuing. Why make a production out of a simple announcement like that? He could have done it with much less drama. She suspected that there was something more serious going on here, and she was going to challenge him to admit it.

She rose to her feet before Steinberg had taken two steps away from the fireplace. "Lieutenant, before you go, I have a question for you."

Steinberg turned to face her, his expression steely. "Yes, Miss Ducote. What is it?"

An'gel figured some people were intimidated by that clipped tone, but it didn't work with her.

"I don't think you're being completely frank with us, Lieutenant. I think you should tell us whether you are now treating

260

the death of Nathan Gamble as suspicious."

Steinberg held her gaze for a long moment, but An'gel never wavered. She was determined he was going to give her a satisfactory answer.

Finally, he spoke. "Yes, Miss Ducote, we are."

CHAPTER 24

An'gel heard the sounds of indrawn breaths from several people in the room. Her gaze was still locked with that of the policeman. She let it go a beat longer before she said, "Thank you, Lieutenant. I appreciate your candor."

"Ma'am." Steinberg nodded. "I'll be ready to start questioning in a few minutes. One of my officers will let you know." He strode out of the room.

An'gel resumed her seat. The tension seemed to lessen with Steinberg's departure from the room, but not greatly, An'gel felt. She glanced from face to face, trying to discern whether one of them appeared more worried than the others. After her survey she concluded that, whoever was responsible for the death of Nathan Gamble, he or she wasn't giving anything away at the moment.

They sat in silence for several minutes. An'gel saw that the officer in the room with them was the same tall young man from earlier in the day. He stood near the front of the room between the windows. He would have a good view of the assembled suspects, An'gel thought. He wouldn't be able to hear whispered conversations, however.

An officer appeared in the doorway and summoned Henry Howard to the library. Henry Howard gave his wife a quick kiss, squeezed her hand, and then accompanied the officer from the room. A different officer came in to make an announcement.

"Lieutenant Steinberg requires fingerprints from everyone," he said. "We are set up in the dining room, and I will ask you to come one at a time. We'll start with you, ma'am." He nodded toward Marcelline.

The housekeeper started to protest, then evidently thought better of it, and left her chair to head to the dining room. After that, the officer slowly worked his way through the group, escorting them back and forth to the dining room. Henry Howard returned about midway through, and Mary Turner was asked to join the lieutenant.

By the time the fingerprinting was done, Mary Turner was back with them, and Serenity Foster left for the library. An'gel badly wanted to talk to Mary Turner and

Henry Howard. One thing she wanted to know was whether the French room door had been locked when Henry Howard went up to check on Nathan Gamble.

When Serenity returned and the officer called for Truss Wilbanks, An'gel seized the chance. She got up and stood for a moment, then casually moved over to join her hosts on the other sofa. Primrose Pace chose that moment to move from her spot near the mantel to another part of the room. She chose a chair by one of the front windows, An'gel noted.

Now that the police were treating Nathan Gamble's death as suspicious, An'gel wondered briefly about Mrs. Pace's claims about the man's peaceful passing. She intended to ask the medium about that as soon as she had the opportunity.

Now, however, she focused on Henry Howard, who occupied the place between her and Mary Turner. She leaned slightly toward him and said in a low tone, "I have a question for you. When you went up to check on Nathan this morning, was his door locked?"

Henry Howard nodded. "Yes, it was. The lieutenant asked me the same thing. I used my passkey to open it."

"Thank you," An'gel said. She leaned back

and glanced toward the front of the room at the attendant policeman. She realized he had moved a couple of steps closer to the group. He seemed intent on her. No doubt he was curious about her conversation with Henry Howard. She had more questions for her young host but decided she would wait until they were no longer under police scrutiny to pose them.

She focused her gaze on the wall across from her, over her sister's head. She began to consider the importance of the locked bedroom door. How significant was it?

The lieutenant was treating this as a suspicious death. To An'gel, that meant murder. So, did the murderer need to be in the room to kill Nathan Gamble? If, for example, Gamble had been poisoned, the killer could have been anywhere else in the house, depending on the action of the poison and the method of administration. She wondered if Gamble took any medications. Perhaps it had been done that way. The point was, with poison, the locked door was likely less significant.

If Gamble had been murdered by some other method, the killer would have needed access to the room while the door was locked. The killer might have a passkey. The locks on the bedrooms weren't sophisticated ones, An'gel knew. They had been updated at some point in the recent past but were definitely not state-of-the-art. Could they be easily manipulated? Another question for Henry Howard.

The killer could have come in through one of the windows from the gallery. An'gel glanced casually toward the young policeman. At the moment his attention seemed focused on Serenity Foster. An'gel leaned toward Henry Howard again. "Were the windows in the French room locked, do you know?"

"They usually are," Henry Howard whispered. "But I didn't check them this morning. I'm sure the police did, but they didn't say."

An'gel wanted to groan with frustration. Too many variables, too many questions for which she had no answers. She had no hope of being able to get those answers from Lieutenant Steinberg. An'gel was pretty sure he wouldn't welcome any assistance from her quarter. *If only Kanesha Berry was investigating this.* Kanesha, the chief deputy in the sheriff's department in Athena County, knew and respected An'gel. Though Kanesha didn't precisely welcome An'gel's and Dickce's assistance, she didn't disdain it either.

An'gel refocused her thoughts on the question of access to Nathan Gamble. If the door and the windows were locked and the killer needed to be able to get into the room, was there another way in? An'gel hadn't quite given up on her notion of a secret passage or a hidden door.

If such a passage or a door existed, where was it? An'gel reluctantly had to rule out the secret passage after a few moments' thought. The architecture simply didn't support that idea. There was no unaccounted-for space between the French room and the bathroom next to it that she had been able to discern.

If there was a secret door into the French room, then it had to be through the bathroom, the only contiguous space other than the hallway and the gallery outside. An'gel decided that the moment the police released them from the parlor, she would head upstairs and examine the wall between the two rooms as minutely as possible. Benjy could help her. His young eyes might spot something more easily and quickly, and his young knees could stand crawling along the floorboards far more easily than her elderly ones. He would enjoy the experience, she knew. By now the police would have sealed off the bedroom, of course. She would have to rely on her memory for now for the way the room was arranged. What was along the mutual wall?

Truss Wilbanks lumbered into her line of vision, and his reentry distracted her from her speculations. The man looked dreadful, she thought as she moved from his former place back to her spot next to Benjy on the other sofa. His time with the lieutenant had not eased his mind. That much was obvious. His hands and arms trembled, his legs looked shaky, and he was still perspiring. The man actually looked ill. She wondered if he suffered from any particular medical condition that could account for any of this. If he needed help, though, surely he would ask for it.

Was guilt the reason for his obvious terror? If not guilt, then perhaps it had something to do with the nature of his relationship with the deceased. Was Wilbanks worried that the police would focus all their efforts on him because of that relationship?

An'gel leaned forward and caught the man's eye. "Mr. Wilbanks, you don't look well at all. Are you ill? Should we call a doctor for you?"

Wilbanks shook his head. "No, I'm just upset, and I have a bad headache. Thank you, though. This is all a bit overwhelming."

"If you change your mind, I'll see that you get medical attention," An'gel said.

The man had to be dehydrated by now because he had perspired so heavily, An'gel realized. The least she could do was to see that he had water to drink. She called out to the young policeman. "Officer, I'm sure that everyone here is as thirsty as I am by now. Couldn't one of us go to the kitchen and get water for everyone?"

"I'll see to that, ma'am," the young man said. "Just a moment." He walked to the door and conferred with someone in the hall, then turned back into the room. "One of the officers will bring water in a minute."

Marcelline stood and advanced toward the policeman. "No one is going to be rooting around in my kitchen except me. I won't have someone making a mess that I have to clean up later, young man. Let *me* go, and I'll take care of it."

The officer nodded. "All right, ma'am. If you'll go with the officer there." He indicated the female officer An'gel had noticed before. Marcelline moved briskly to the door and disappeared into the hallway.

"Thank you, Miss An'gel," Mary Turner said. "I'm about parched myself." She cast a sideways glance at Truss Wilbanks. "I'm sure we could all use some water."

269

Wilbanks nodded. "Thank you, ma'am."

An'gel smiled in return. Then she looked at Serenity Foster. The young woman didn't appear upset or grieving, An'gel thought. If anything, she looked bored. Was that because she was too stupid to understand the gravity of the situation? An'gel didn't give the woman high marks for intelligence. Or maybe she was innocent and thus not worried about the police investigation? Either was possible to An'gel's way of thinking.

Now that Wilbanks was back in the room, An'gel wondered, had the lieutenant finished with his questioning? She was getting hungry. According to her watch, it was nearly one thirty, well past her usual lunchtime. She glanced around and realized that Primrose Pace was no longer in the room. She must have been called in to speak with Steinberg again, An'gel decided.

Either that, or she had slipped out the front window near her chair while everyone's attention was directed elsewhere.

Like when you asked the policeman for water.

That would have been the perfect time for Primrose Pace to act. An'gel looked where Mrs. Pace had been sitting.

The window was open. Mrs. Pace was gone.

CHAPTER 25

An'gel got immediately to her feet. "Officer, did anyone escort Mrs. Pace to talk to Lieutenant Steinberg?"

The young man shook his head. "No, ma'am, he hasn't asked for her yet."

"Then she's gone," An'gel said. "Look at the window. She was sitting right there a few minutes ago."

The policeman whirled around to stare at the window. He stood frozen for a moment. Then he shouted for backup as he ran for the window and climbed through it. Another officer ran in, spotted the open window, and followed behind the first man.

Marcelline and the woman officer who had accompanied her to the kitchen returned amid the excitement. Marcelline had the rolling tea cart, and atop it sat two large pitchers of ice water and numerous glasses.

"What's all the fuss about?" Marcelline asked, seeing everyone standing and staring toward the front windows.

"Mrs. Pace made a run for it," Henry Howard said. "She must be the one who killed Nathan." He glanced at Mary Turner. "I thought it was a bad idea to have that woman in the house. She's nothing but a fraud."

"How was I to know that, Henry Howard Catlin?" Mary Turner said, obviously stung by her husband's words. "She seemed like a nice person to me, not some con artist."

Her husband's reply was acid-tinged. "That's how they work, honey."

"Don't start getting all superior on me because I thought she was a nice woman." Mary Turner suddenly burst into tears. "Oh, dear Lord, what if she really did kill Nathan?"

An'gel felt she had to get the situation under control. The police officer wasn't making any effort to, and An'gel didn't want Mary Turner and Henry Howard's argument to escalate any further.

"Marcelline, please see that everyone has water, and start with Mr. Wilbanks." An'gel spoke in a tone that brooked no argument. Marcelline went to work immediately and handed Wilbanks a glass.

An'gel turned her attention to Mary Turner and Henry Howard. "Now is not the time for recriminations. We don't know for sure that Mrs. Pace had anything to do with Nathan Gamble's death. I agree it looks highly suspicious, her sneaking away like this, but there could be other reasons." *Like because she's a fake and a con artist,* she thought, but didn't say aloud. She didn't want to injure Mary Turner's feelings any further.

"I don't care what you say." Serenity Foster was on her feet, looking furious. "Why would that woman disappear like that if she wasn't guilty? The sooner they catch her and throw her in jail, the better." She stared hard at Mary Turner. "And you're the one who let her stay here. I'll bet you were in on the whole thing with her, maybe even asked her to come here."

For a moment An'gel thought Mary Turner would launch herself from her position near the sofa to attack her cousin ten or more feet away. She had never seen the young woman so angry before. "You sit down and shut up, Serenity," Mary Turner said, "or I swear to God I will take you to court and sue you for everything you've got. I have not had anything to do with that woman, other than make the mistake of letting her stay here. Whatever she did to Nathan, she did on her own."

An'gel figured she had better back up Mary Turner yet again, because Serenity didn't appear cowed by what her cousin said.

"I will remind you, young woman, that I have already offered to serve as a witness for Mary Turner against you, and I know my sister and our ward will do the same. You had better shut that mouth of yours and try to get control of your temper. These wild accusations aren't doing anything to improve the situation." She didn't bother to look at Truss Wilbanks. The poor man was in no shape now to rein in his client.

Serenity opened her mouth to speak but Marcelline gave her no chance. She marched over to within a few inches of the young woman and got right up in her face.

"You'd better listen to Miss An'gel, girl, if you have any brains at all. I don't reckon you have many, but you'd better use 'em. Miss An'gel is too much a lady to come slap your face, but I'm not. I'm not putting up with you calling Miss Mary a murderer, no way, no how."

An'gel hoped Serenity wasn't going to be stupid enough to ignore Marcelline's warning.

She wasn't, An'gel saw. Serenity backed away from the housekeeper, never taking her eyes off Marcelline's face. She put the chair between them and nodded.

"That's the last I want to hear out of you," Marcelline said. "Now sit down in that chair, and keep your mouth shut till somebody asks you to open it."

Serenity slowly complied with the housekeeper's command. Her legs shook, and she dropped quickly into the chair. Marcelline stood over her for a moment, then moved away to stand by her employer.

"Thank you, Marcelline." Mary Turner stared hard at her cousin. "Once this is all done, I never want to see you in this house again or anywhere near it. As far as I'm concerned, you're no family of mine."

By this time An'gel had had enough of the drama. Her head had begun to ache, partly from the need for food, but mostly from the tension and the shouting. She used her sternest tone. "Everyone, sit down. Right now. Enough of this carrying-on."

Even the police officer started to sit, evidently realized she wasn't supposed to, and straightened up again. An'gel surveyed the results of her command with satisfaction. She heard light clapping and knew without turning her head that Dickce was applauding. She ignored her sister for the moment.

"Officer, I would like to speak to Lieutenant Steinberg," An'gel said. "Please get word to him right away."

The policewoman nodded. "Yes, ma'am." She hurried from the room. An'gel hoped she wouldn't get in trouble for leaving them alone, but the officer returned in less than twenty seconds at An'gel's estimation.

"He's ready for you, ma'am," the officer told her.

"Thank you." An'gel did not relish the thought of the conversation she was about to have with the taciturn Steinberg. He was not going to be happy with her when she had her say, but she had faced worse.

Another officer opened the library door for her, and An'gel walked in. Steinberg stood before the fireplace, his back to it. "You wanted to speak to me, Miss Ducote?" He gestured to a nearby chair, about seven feet away from where he stood.

"Thank you, Lieutenant." An'gel approached the chair, but instead of seating herself, she took her position beside it. She let her right arm rest on the back of the chair.

"I have two things to discuss with you, although the first is more in the nature of a confession." An'gel paused to gauge the effect of her words. The lieutenant did not

276

react in any way that she could detect. "I'm not confessing to causing the death of Nathan Gamble, mind you. I believe it was my fault that Mrs. Pace had the opportunity to exit the house without being seen."

Steinberg frowned. "Would you care to explain that, ma'am?"

"I plan to," An'gel replied, a little more tartly than she'd intended. "I could see that Mr. Wilbanks appeared to be in distress. He had been perspiring heavily, and I was afraid he was becoming dehydrated. I asked the young officer in the room if we could have water brought to us. I believe that while he was distracted by my request and trying to get water for us, Mrs. Pace seized her chance and went out the window. I didn't notice it for at least two or three minutes after she must have done it. I alerted the officer as soon as I realized what must have happened."

"I appreciate your candor, Miss Ducote," the lieutenant said.

Was that a none-too-subtle payback for her question earlier about Nathan Gamble's death? An'gel wondered. If so, she decided to ignore it. She simply nodded.

"It's unfortunate that Mrs. Pace chose to take such action," Steinberg said, "but she will soon be in our custody. I'll see that she doesn't escape again. Now what is the second thing you wish to discuss?"

"Food," An'gel said. "It's nearly two o'clock now, and I don't believe any of us has had anything to eat since around eight this morning. I request that you allow us to feed ourselves, either from the kitchen here, or I will be happy to call and have food delivered. Enough food for everyone, including you and your officers."

"That's kind of you," Steinberg said. "My officers and I have to decline your offer, but I see no reason that you and everyone else can't eat now. Except for Mrs. Pace, of course. I will need to talk with her first."

"Thank you, Lieutenant," An'gel said. "I know everyone will be grateful." Did she dare push her luck and ask another question? She had many, of course, but figured the most she could hope to get away with was one. But which one?

"Was there anything else, ma'am?" Steinberg asked.

"Yes, there is." *Might as well try,* she thought. "Was Nathan Gamble murdered? He didn't seem the type to commit suicide."

Steinberg regarded her in silence, probably only for ten seconds, but those ten seconds felt like a hundred when she thought about it later.

"Suicide seems unlikely," the lieutenant said. "That's all I can tell you. I trust it will go no further at the moment, although I'm sure you will want to tell your sister."

"Yes, I will." An'gel wondered why he had answered. She really hadn't expected him to.

"I know who you are, you see," Steinberg said.

"I beg your pardon," An'gel said, confused.

"I know Kanesha Berry," Steinberg said. "We recently served on a state law enforcement task force together. She had several interesting stories about the Ducote sisters."

"I see," An'gel said. She might have a little talk with Kanesha when they were home again. She wanted to know exactly what the deputy had been telling her colleagues.

"Kanesha assured me that if I ever encountered you in the course of an investigation, I might as well resign myself to being helped." Steinberg quirked an eyebrow. "She also told me that you wouldn't overstep and that I should listen to you if you had something to tell me."

"That was kind of her," An'gel said, now feeling embarrassed. Was the lieutenant about to confide in her? Give her more details of the case?

"I would appreciate it, Miss Ducote, if you and your sister did not try to help me," Steinberg said. "Now, if there's nothing else, I have to get on with this investigation."

"Very well, Lieutenant," An'gel said. He hadn't been rude. His tone had been respectful, but nevertheless her pride was smarting. She turned to walk out of the room, but before she could leave, two of Steinberg's officers escorted Primrose Pace into the room.

An'gel moved around the trio but contrived to remain by the door in hopes that Steinberg might forget about her momentarily.

"That was not a smart thing to do, Mrs. Pace," Steinberg said. "Or would you rather I address you by your real name?"

CHAPTER 26

An'gel slipped a little farther out the door and pressed herself against the wall right outside, her head slightly cocked.

"All right," the lieutenant said. "Alesha Jackson. Have a seat, Ms. Jackson." Then there was a pause until Steinberg barked out an order. "Shut that door."

An'gel sidled away by the wall as quickly as she could. No one left the room before the door closed. Belatedly she realized that she had forgotten to look in the hallway to see whether there was an officer observing her. She turned and looked toward the parlor door. The hallway was empty of cops at the moment. Suppressing a huge sigh of relief, she hurried into the parlor.

She almost knocked right into the female officer.

An'gel caught herself in time, and the officer neatly sidestepped her. "So sorry," An'gel said.

"No harm done, ma'am," the officer replied.

"Officer, Lieutenant Steinberg said it would be okay for us to have something to eat." An'gel smiled. "Breakfast was around six hours ago, and I for one am famished. I'm sure the others are, too." She raised her voice as she turned to address the group. "Aren't you?"

"Hungry?" Benjy piped up. "I certainly am." Peanut woofed to let everyone know he would be happy to eat as well. An'gel thought he and Endora both deserved treats because they had been so well behaved the past hour or so.

Mary Turner stood. "Marcelline, let's go to the kitchen and see what we can put together for everyone. Will that be okay, Officer?"

"Just a moment, ma'am," the policewoman replied. "There needs to be an officer with you, if you don't mind. I'll call for someone." She stepped away toward the door, and An'gel took this as her cue to resume her seat.

In a couple of minutes another uniformed cop appeared to accompany Marcelline and Mary Turner to the kitchen. The latter waved away Dickce's offer of assistance.

"Thank you, Miss Dickce, but we'll manage. Why don't y'all go ahead and move into the dining room, though, and we'll bring the food in there."

"Excellent idea," An'gel said, getting to her feet once again. She grabbed a glass of water for herself from the tea cart and carried it with her. Her throat was feeling parched, but the water soothed her and eased her headache a little.

Henry Howard made sure there were enough places at the table for everyone and encouraged them to sit. An'gel, Dickce, and Benjy, with Peanut and Endora with him, sat at one end of the table. Truss Wilbanks took the seat next to Dickce. Serenity Foster chose a place at the other end, away from the others. Henry Howard sat next to Benjy. Their minder, as An'gel thought of the officer, stood in the doorway watching them.

An'gel kept glancing at her watch and saw that it was a full twenty minutes before Marcelline and Mary Turner brought in two large trays, cold roast beef and sliced chicken on one, bread and cheese on the other. Marcelline, along with her escort, went back to the kitchen to fetch in the drinks and the condiments. Henry Howard found utensils from the sideboard, and soon they were all making and eating sandwiches and drinking cans of cold soda.

An'gel hadn't yet had a chance to share with Dickce and Benjy the fact that *Primrose Pace* was an alias. She glanced around the table. Henry Howard moved next to Serenity so that Mary Turner wouldn't have to, but Marcelline had no choice. Marcelline didn't look at the woman. Everyone seemed intent on eating, and An'gel wondered whether she dared risk talking to Benjy and Dickce.

No, she decided, others would overhear, and she didn't want the lieutenant to find out she had let something slip in front of all of them. Instead, she pulled out her cell phone and composed a brief text to her sister and Benjy. They both observed her with her phone, and neither one reacted when their own phones registered receipt of her text. Dickce waited for at least a minute before she pulled out her phone to look at it, and Benjy not long after. From what An'gel could tell, no one else was paying any particular attention. In fact, both Serenity and Truss had their own cell phones out, fiddling with them.

An'gel had kept her message brief: Primrose Pace is really Alicia (? Alesha? Alisha?) Jackson. Benjy looked up and nodded. An'gel knew that as soon as he was able, he would see what he could dig up on Ms.

Jackson. She put her phone aside.

She continued to observe the others as discreetly as possible. Truss Wilbanks looked considerably better now, and An'gel was glad to see that. She had really been afraid he might collapse on them earlier. Had he played any role in Nathan Gamble's death? Had his near-collapse been symptomatic of guilt or simply sheer nerves?

Henry Howard and Mary Turner continued to whisper to each other. Henry Howard met An'gel's glance from across the table but immediately dropped his eyes.

How long would they all have to remain together like this? An'gel was eager to go upstairs and start examining the bathroom for signs of a hidden door. Surely Lieutenant Steinberg would release them soon, maybe once he had finished dealing with Alesha Jackson, alias Primrose Pace. She must have a police record, An'gel thought. Her fingerprints had given her away. If Ms. Jackson had nothing to do with the death of Nathan Gamble, she'd had a mighty unlucky break when she chose Cliffwood to try her scam on a trusting Mary Turner Catlin.

Let that be a lesson to her.

Mary Turner might not press charges, An'gel figured. After all, what had the woman taken? One night's stay here at Cliffwood and two meals. Two hundred dollars, maximum. Unless she was wanted in connection with another crime, Ms. Jackson might go free.

The entrance of Lieutenant Steinberg into the dining room surprised everyone, An'gel thought, even her. They had all relaxed, thanks to the food and drink, but with Steinberg in their midst, An'gel felt the level of tension begin to rise again.

"If I could have your attention, please," Steinberg said, although no one was talking and all eyes were gazing at him. "I wanted to bring you up-to-date and also tell you that you will be free to move about the house. The French room, as I understand it is called, is off-limits at the moment and is sealed. I must warn you that any attempts to tamper with the seal will not be treated lightly, and you could face charges if you do make an attempt." He paused to glance around the room.

"We have apprehended Alesha Jackson, who was presenting herself to you under the name *Primrose Pace*. I'll be talking with Mr. and Mrs. Catlin to discuss whether they want to file any charges against her for fraud. And maybe for theft of room and board as well. As I told you before, we are treating the death of Nathan Gamble as suspicious. For the moment I must ask you all to remain in the house until we have made further progress with the investigation. If you have any problems because of that, I will be happy to discuss the situation with you. Now, are there any questions?"

Marcelline spoke up immediately. "Am I allowed to go to the grocery store? We're going to run out of food before much longer. I had no idea all these people would be here for more than a couple of days."

"I will see that you're able to go to the grocery store," the lieutenant said. "Just let one of the officers on duty know when you need to go."

At least we won't be on starvation rations, An'gel thought. She had no pressing need to go anywhere outside the house at the moment, but knowing that she couldn't, at least not without a police escort, was annoying. The sooner this situation was resolved, the better. Despite the lieutenant's words during their last interview, An'gel wasn't going to sit idly and wait for him to wrap everything up. Not, that is, if she happened to discover anything pertinent that could move things along.

"Lieutenant, I have a question," Mary Turner said.

"Yes, ma'am?" the lieutenant prompted when she didn't immediately continue.

Mary Turner cast a quick glance at Henry Howard before she addressed the policeman again. "It's about Mrs. Pace, or rather Mrs. Jackson. Will she be remaining here as well?"

"That depends on you and your husband, Mrs. Catlin," Steinberg replied. "If you press charges, then we will escort her to jail. If you don't, then yes, I would like her to remain here with everyone else."

"I don't intend to press charges," Mary Turner said.

Henry Howard started to protest, but Mary Turner shook her head. "No, we're not going to press charges, Henry Howard."

Her husband grunted in frustration and crossed his arms over his chest. "Have it your way, then." He leaned back in his chair and shut his eyes.

"If you're sure about that, ma'am," the lieutenant said, "then I'll hold off for the moment on any charges we might want to make."

"I'm sure," Mary Turner said.

While An'gel couldn't help but admire her young friend's generosity of spirit, she had to wonder whether it was wise to let Ms. Jackson off completely. Of course, An'gel

288

realized, having the woman remain in the house with them meant that she would be available to question. An'gel intended to do that because she wanted to know more about the so-called medium.

"Then if there are no further questions," Steinberg said, "I will get back to work. I will be working out of the library here for the rest of the day, if anyone wants to talk to me." He turned and walked out of the room.

Serenity stood and dropped the napkin she had been clutching on the table. "I'm going to my room." She left immediately.

"I think I'll do the same," Truss Wilbanks said. "If y'all will excuse me." He nodded at An'gel and then at Mary Turner before he left.

Marcelline got up and started clearing the table. Henry Howard, without a word to anyone, stalked out of the room, obviously still upset over Mary Turner's insistence not to press charges against Alesha Jackson. Mary Turner gazed after his retreating back, but when he disappeared from view, she turned to face her remaining guests with a determined smile.

"Miss An'gel, if y'all need anything, please let me or Marcelline know. I'll be helping her in the kitchen, since we're going to need to plan meals for everyone. If you have any special requests, we'll do what we can to fulfill them."

"We'll be fine, my dear," An'gel said. "You let *us* know if there's anything we can do to help you and Marcelline."

"Yes, indeed," Dickce said. "We'll all pitch in."

"Whatever you need," Benjy added shyly.

Mary Turner smiled and thanked them. "I'll do that, I promise. For now, though, why don't y'all relax and rest. We've had a stressful morning."

The sound of a throat clearing focused all their attention on the doorway, where Alesha Jackson now stood. She gazed at them for a moment before she stepped into the room.

"I'm sorry if you feel I have deceived you, Mrs. Catlin," she said. "The lieutenant told me you declined to press charges, and I want you to know how grateful I am."

Marcelline snorted. "You don't deserve it, playing tricks on good people. Why don't you go out and get a real job instead of trying to cheat people out of money? Running around telling people you can talk to ghosts. You ought to be ashamed of yourself."

Alesha Jackson flinched briefly at the onslaught of words, then her expression hardened. She stared defiantly at the house-keeper.

"I do have a real job," she said heatedly. "I am a psychic." Her eyes narrowed as she focused intently on the housekeeper. "If I wasn't, how would I know that you've lied all these years about never being married?"

CHAPTER 27

Marcelline gasped and dropped the dishes she was carrying, to An'gel's surprise. Alesha Jackson's words had obviously struck home.

"How . . . how did you know that?" Marcelline said, her voice hoarse, before she collapsed into the closest chair.

Alesha Jackson smiled enigmatically but did not answer.

"Marcelline, is this really true?" Mary Turner asked. "When were you ever married?" An'gel could tell she was shocked by this revelation.

"A long time ago," the housekeeper responded dully. "When I was a young girl, only seventeen. It just lasted a year. Then he ran off with another woman, and I never saw him again."

"Are you still married to him?" Mary Turner asked.

"I don't know," the housekeeper said. "He

never came back, and I never divorced him. The church wouldn't approve."

An'gel recalled then that Marcelline was Catholic, obviously one who didn't believe in divorce.

"My goodness." Mary Turner shook her head. "Did you ever tell Granny about this? Or Mother and Daddy?"

"Your granny knew," Marcelline said. "She knew what it was like to be married to a faithless man. Sorry, honey, but your grandfather was a bad man."

"I know," Mary Turner replied. "Daddy told me all about him, and so did Granny."

"Your granny never told anyone about me," Marcelline said. "I didn't have no other family, and Miz Turner felt sorry for me and took me in, gave me a job and a home. I thought no one would ever find out, as long as he never turned up again."

An'gel had been watching Alesha Jackson during this conversation. The woman must have some kind of intuitive ability, she decided, or else she was a gambler who had taken a shot in the dark and watched it pay off beautifully. She didn't appear to be gloating at her success, however.

Mary Turner went to the housekeeper and bent to give her a hug. "Why don't you go lie down for a little while?" she said. "You've had a bad shock. I'll take care of clearing up and everything."

"I think I will." Marcelline smiled uncertainly at her young mistress. "You don't think badly of me, do you?"

"Of course not," Mary Turner said firmly. "Now go get some rest. You can tell me about it later if you want to." She helped Marcelline to her feet, and the housekeeper headed from the room, her shoulders slumped and her head down.

An'gel started to speak but Mary Turner spoke first, her words directed at Alesha Jackson.

"That was cruel of you to expose her secret like that," she said. "Although I suppose I understand why you did it. I wish you hadn't done it, though."

"I had to prove myself," Ms. Jackson said, her tone not in the least apologetic. "You need to understand I am who I say I am, and that I can do what I told you I could. I didn't come here under false pretenses. I used my professional name like I always do in these situations. I keep my personal and my professional lives separate that way."

"Then why did you try to run away?" An'gel asked. "If you weren't here under false pretenses, there was no need to escape, surely?"

"A lapse in judgment," the psychic said with a shrug. "I have a fair amount of experience with the police, and I didn't want any further involvement in this situation."

The woman could still be lying. An'gel was convinced there was something else she was hiding, but what was it?

"I'm hungry," Ms. Jackson said. "If you have no objection, I'd like to eat." She pointed to the uneaten meat and bread on the table.

"Help yourself," Mary Turner said. "I'll find you a clean plate after I check on Marcelline." She left the room.

Alesha Jackson shrugged and seated herself. She pulled the two platters close to her and began to eat directly from them. She ate neatly and efficiently as An'gel watched.

Dickce nudged her, then whispered close to her ear, "Are we going to sit here and watch her eat? Or are we going to do something productive?"

An'gel frowned. She wanted to question the psychic but had been trying to decide whether the time was right. Would the woman even talk to her?

An'gel whispered back to her sister. "I want to get her to talk to me. I want to ask her some questions."

After a moment Dickce responded. "Then tell her you want to hire her when all this is over."

"Hire her?" An'gel asked, incredulous. "Whatever for?"

"To deal with the spirit at Riverhill," Dickce said. "What else?"

An'gel started to argue but then stopped herself. Dickce's idea was actually a good one. Telling the woman she had a job for her gave her an excellent pretext for asking some pointed questions. "Good idea."

"Mrs. Jackson," An'gel said.

"Not Mrs., Ms.," the woman responded.

"Ms. Jackson, then," An'gel said. "Perhaps sometime later today you and I could talk. My sister and I may be interested in hiring you to help us with a problem back home. We live in an old house, too, you see."

Alesha Jackson put down the piece of roast she had been about to eat and regarded An'gel, her expression blank. After a few seconds, she spoke. "If you're serious, I will be happy to speak with you. I'd like some time to rest and refresh myself, however."

"Of course," An'gel replied. "How about four this afternoon, in the parlor?"

The psychic nodded. "That's fine."

An'gel rose. "Thank you. Dickce, Benjy, I

think we ought to leave Ms. Jackson to finish her meal in peace. No, Peanut, you're not going to get any more bites of chicken, or you either, Endora."

Peanut whined and thumped his tail against the floor. "Come on, boy," Benjy said firmly. "I'll give you both some treats in our room, okay?"

Peanut woofed at that, and Endora perked up too. She climbed on Benjy's shoulder and nuzzled his left ear.

"They deserve their treats," Dickce said. "They've been really good, not making a fuss."

"Probably because you and Benjy kept slipping them food under the table," An'gel said. "You might have thought I didn't see you, but I did."

Mary Turner returned with a plate and napkin in hand. She stopped short when she saw Alesha Jackson already eating. She approached the table and set down the plate and napkin. "I'll be back to clear up when you're done. I guess you'll be going up to your room for a while afterwards."

The psychic nodded. "Yes, I will. I must rest before my appointment with Miss Ducote to discuss a job."

Mary Turner looked at An'gel, obviously shocked. "Miss An'gel, is she serious? Are *you* serious?"

"Yes, my dear, I am," An'gel said. "Dickce and I decided to consult with Ms. Jackson about a matter concerning a possible spirit at Riverhill."

"Oh, I see," Mary Turner said. An'gel could tell by her tone, however, that she was only being polite. "I'll finish clearing the table when you're done, Mrs. Pace."

"Call me either Primrose or Alesha." The medium smiled. "I answer to either. I've had enough to eat, thank you. Would you like me to help you finish clearing?"

Mary Turner shrugged. "Sure. Extra hands are always welcome."

"Then I guess we will leave you to it," An'gel said. "Come along, Dickce, Benjy." She gave the other two women a smile before she headed for the door.

In the hallway, Benjy spoke before she started to mount the stairs. "Miss An'gel, if you don't mind, I'll take Peanut and Endora to our room and let them have a t-r-e-a-t. I want to get my laptop anyway so I can do a little more research."

Peanut woofed, despite Benjy spelling the word *treat*.

"I believe he has learned how to spell." Dickce laughed.

"He's so smart," An'gel said, and Benjy

298

nodded.

"You go ahead, Benjy, and reward them for being so good. Dickce and I won't start on the project I have in mind until you're back. We'll be in my room." An'gel mounted the stairs slowly, bracing herself for the cold, but she never felt it. Halfway up the flight she paused and turned back to look at Dickce, three steps below her.

"I haven't felt anything so far," Dickce said. "Have you?"

"No," An'gel said. "I suppose the spirit is taking a rest." She began to climb again.

"Probably hiding because of all the strangers in the house today." Dickce chuckled. "Can't say as I blame her."

"Nor I." An'gel stepped on to the landing. "All those people in the house are exhausting." She started to yawn and covered her mouth.

Dickce followed An'gel to her bedroom. "Are you sure you don't want to lie down and have a short nap? I don't know about you, but I feel like a little quiet time."

"Go ahead and lie down if you want," An'gel said. "I'm going to put my feet up until Benjy gets back. I'll call you when we're ready to see if my idea pans out."

"What idea is that?" Dickce asked.

"I'll tell you later." An'gel opened her door

and stepped into the room. "Go rest." She closed the door on her sister. Seconds later she heard Dickce say, "You know I hate it when you do that."

An'gel paid no attention to that. Instead she focused her attention on the disarray in the bedroom. The police hadn't created a huge mess when they searched the house earlier, but her things were not as she had left them. She knew it was old-fashioned of her, but she hoped the female officer was the one who looked through her clothes. She abhorred the idea of strange men touching her things. *Best not to know.* She would have to push those thoughts completely out of her mind, or she would have to wash or dry-clean everything she had brought before she wore it again. She hoped that whoever had searched her things had worn those disposable gloves she saw on television cop shows.

She decided to leave the straightening up until later. Right now she wanted to relax in the quiet and aloneness. After all the clatter of voices, all the drama, the silence felt good. She made herself comfortable in the armchair and put her feet up on the small ottoman.

Slowly she let the tension drain from her body as she focused on relaxation. As eager as she was to search for a secret door into the French room, she hoped Benjy didn't hurry back from feeding the pets and retrieving his laptop.

She let her gaze wander around the room again, and as she observed the areas that needed tidying, she thought again about strangers handling her things. She reminded herself about the disposable gloves and told herself to let it go.

Focus on where that door might be instead.

She could see herself and Benjy examining the wall between the bathroom and the French room, their hands feeling their way, looking for signs of a mechanism of some sort.

Hands feeling their way.

She sat up suddenly, her feet sliding off the ottoman. *We might destroy fingerprints or other evidence by touching everything,* An'gel realized. Steinberg would not be happy with her for doing so.

But if we have disposable gloves, it wouldn't be that different from the police doing the same thing.

A knock at the door roused her, and she called out, "Come in." She expected Benjy to walk in, but instead it was Marcelline.

"Miss An'gel, I need to talk to you about something." The housekeeper hesitated in the doorway.

An'gel could see that Marcelline was worked up about something. "Please, come on in. Tell me what's troubling you."

Marcelline closed the door slowly behind her. An'gel indicated the room's other chair, and Marcelline sat on the edge, back stiff, hands clasped together.

"Go ahead," An'gel said. "I'm listening." Marcelline seemed to be debating with herself over whether to confide in An'gel, or so the woman's expression led An'gel to believe.

"I've got to tell someone," Marcelline said, "and I don't rightly know how to tell Miss Mary. I know who that woman is. At least, I think I do."

"What woman?" An'gel asked. "Are you talking about Alesha Jackson?"

Marcelline nodded. "Yes, her." She hesitated again. "I think she's Miss Mary's cousin."

CHAPTER 28

Whatever An'gel might have expected Marcelline to tell her, it definitely wasn't that Mary Turner and Alesha Jackson were related to each other. She quickly grasped the situation, however, because of her knowledge of the family history.

"Mary Turner's grandfather, Marshall Turner, is also Alesha Jackson's grandfather. Is that what you think?" An'gel asked.

"Yes, ma'am," the housekeeper said. "You've been knowing this family a long time, Miss An'gel, and you know how Mr. Marshall was. Couldn't keep his hands off a woman he wanted to get ahold of. Thank the Lord he died about nine or ten months after I started working here. By then he was getting sick, and he didn't bother me."

"I know all about Marshall Turner," An'gel said wryly. She wasn't going to tell Marcelline, but she'd had her own run-in with the lecher. He had never made that mistake again, An'gel recalled with great satisfaction. In fact, after she'd gotten through with him, he had stayed away from her like she had the plague. "Who was the woman involved?" An'gel asked.

"A real pretty black lady that worked for Mrs. Turner for a while. I didn't know her because she must have left a couple years before I started working here. Anyway, she came up to the back door one day when I was just coming out to bring in the clothes from the line. She asked to speak to Mr. Marshall. Now, this was when I'd only been here maybe a couple of months, so Mr. Marshall was still around. I asked her into the kitchen, and I went to find him."

"Did she tell you her name?" An'gel asked.

"Oh, yes," Marcelline replied. "She told me she was Arletta Jackson. Mrs. Lonnie Jackson. She stressed that part, that she was married, I mean, but she said to tell Mr. Marshall it was Arletta Kemp asking for him."

"Did Mr. Marshall talk to her?"

"He talked terrible when I told him, bad words I'd never even heard before. He was in the library by himself, and he swore me up and down that I wouldn't tell Mrs. Turner about this. I promised, although I know Mrs. Turner got to know about it later. He wasn't too good with hiding things from her."

"Do you know what Mrs. Jackson wanted to talk to him about?" An'gel suspected she knew exactly what Mrs. Jackson and Marshall Turner talked about, but she needed to hear it from the housekeeper.

"I did, but I didn't do it on purpose," Marcelline said. "I wasn't the type of girl who tried to find out everybody's business, but when you overhear things, it's not your fault."

"No, I suppose not," An'gel said. "Go on."

"Mrs. Jackson had a little boy, she said, just turned two years old, and she was asking Mr. Marshall for the money he promised her for their son. That's exactly what she said, *their son.*" Marcelline shook her head. "That was the first I heard tell of Mr. Marshall getting his women pregnant, but I sure wouldn't be surprised if there's others out there besides that boy and Miss Mary's poor dead father."

An'gel wouldn't be surprised either, although she figured it was more in the late Marshall Turner's style to pay the woman in question to get rid of the baby. Lord, what a nasty man he had been, she thought in distaste.

"What happened after that?" An'gel asked.

"I reckon Mr. Marshall gave her some money," Marcelline replied. "I never saw her again, not even after Mr. Marshall died. I've been trying to remember what she looked like. I kept getting a funny feeling I'd seen this Alesha Jackson somewhere before, and I finally figured it out. She must be that Arletta Jackson's granddaughter. She's not old enough to be her daughter."

"Thank you for telling me about this," An'gel said. "I won't say anything to Mary Turner either. First, of course, the relationship would have to be proven, but a blood test can do that. Ms. Jackson may not want anyone to know she's related. I don't really think it would bother Mary Turner all that much, you know. She heard about her grandfather and his behavior, and she's smart enough to know there could have been consequences, shall we say, of the old goat's philandering."

"Maybe so." Marcelline looked doubtful. "But I had to tell you in case it was this Alesha Jackson who caused Nathan's death."

"At the moment I don't know what her motive might be," An'gel said. "But all the angles need to be considered. This is certainly an unexpected one."

"I reckon her being that lady's granddaughter might account for how she knew about me being married," Marcelline said. "I was still wearing a ring back then, and I remember Mrs. Jackson saying something about it now. Something like it might not protect me. I knew what she meant, of course."

"I wonder if Mrs. Jackson is still living," An'gel said.

"Don't see why not," Marcelline said. "She wasn't all that much older than me at the time. She'd be maybe seventy-five now."

"I'm going to be talking to Alesha Jackson later, and I'll see what I can find out about all this," An'gel said. "You leave it to me."

"Thank you, Miss An'gel." Marcelline rose to go. "I won't say anything to anybody about it."

"Good. Now, I'll have to tell my sister about it," An'gel said. "She and I always discuss things like this."

"Don't matter to me," Marcelline said. "I'll be going now. Got to start working on something for dinner tonight." She left the room, obviously relieved to have shared her burden with someone else.

An'gel was inclined to believe that Marcelline was right, that Alesha Jackson was Arletta Jackson's granddaughter. That fact would certainly explain Alesha Jackson's interest in Cliffwood. An'gel had never really bought into the idea that the so-called psychic had heard the spirit of Cliffwood calling to her. She didn't believe the woman had a psychic bone in her body, now that Marcelline had exposed her. Her grandmother could easily have told her about the people at Cliffwood and about meeting the young Marcelline. It wouldn't have taken much work for Alesha Jackson to find out details about the current inhabitants. The two maids who did most of the heavy cleaning could well be the source.

The forthcoming interview with Ms. Jackson promised to be interesting, and An'gel looked forward to it. She had the advantage now because Ms. Jackson would have no idea that An'gel knew who she really was. Would the woman admit it, though? Perhaps Benjy could dig up information on the family, now that An'gel had the putative grandparents' names.

Benjy ought to be here soon. An'gel decided she had better rouse her sister and fill her in on the fascinating information from Marcelline. She met Benjy in the hall, laptop under his arm, Endora on his shoulder, and Peanut on the leash.

"Go on in," An'gel said. "I'm going to get Dickce."

A few minutes later, the group was comfortably situated in An'gel's room. Dickce occupied the other armchair, Endora in her lap. Peanut lay stretched out beside Benjy, who was sitting on the floor, his computer open on his lap. An'gel related the story of Arletta Jackson, and both Dickce and Benjy were astonished.

Benjy started tapping the keys on the computer and was quickly engrossed in a search for details about the family of Alesha Jackson.

While he worked, An'gel and Dickce talked.

"If all this is true," Dickce said, "what do you think her motive is in coming here? And why didn't she just explain who she really is, do you think?"

"She might have been intending simply to scam Mary Turner for the money she was asking for ridding the house of its ghost," An'gel said. "Or she might want more. If her father really was Marshall's son, Alesha might feel that he should have part ownership in the house and in anything Marshall Junior inherited."

"At the time Marshall Senior died, that would have been a significant amount," Dickce said. "But by the time Marshall Junior and his wife died, basically all they had left was this house."

"And the business they turned it into," An'gel said. "It's a pity that Marshall Junior didn't inherit his father's head for business or his knack for making money."

"No, he was too much like his mother in that regard," Dickce said. "They managed fine on what Marshall Senior left until Junior was grown, at least."

"Alesha Jackson might think there's money somewhere besides the house," An'gel said.

"If Marshall Senior didn't mention his other son in his will, I don't see that Alesha has any legal claim, nor does her father. I wonder if he's still living."

"He isn't," Benjy said. "He died three months ago. I found an obituary, and it mentions the surviving family members. 'Survived by his mother, Mrs. Arletta Jackson; his wife, Laura Ann; and his daughter, Alesha. Preceded in death by his father, Lonnie Jackson, and a sister, Aretha Jackson.'" He looked up from the computer. "They lived in a town called Port Gibson."

"Not far from Natchez," An'gel said.

"Maybe Alesha didn't know about her grandfather until her father died," Dickce said. "Do you think that's possible? And maybe his death set her onto finding about her father's other family?"

"That's possible, I suppose," An'gel said. "I intend to find out when we talk to Ms. Jackson later."

"You think there might be another motive, besides money, I mean?" Benjy said. "Like revenge?"

"Possibly," An'gel said. "I think her motives in coming here are complex. The desire for money, revenge, recognition maybe."

"Would she have any reason to kill Nathan Gamble?" Benjy asked. "Maybe her coming here had nothing to do with him."

"I can't see a connection myself," Dickce said. "Can you, Sister?"

An'gel shook her head. "No, there's no immediate connection that I can see. Of course, Nathan and Serenity are her cousins, too. Same degree of relationship as they are to Mary Turner. Alesha Jackson could very well have known Nathan in another context, though she and Serenity don't appear to know each other."

"No, I don't remember seeing any kind of sign that they knew each other," Dickce said. "They could be pretending not to know each other."

"I can't imagine why, unless they're involved in some sort of conspiracy," An'gel

311

said. "And frankly Serenity doesn't impress me as intelligent enough to handle any kind of responsibility for some sort of undercover scheme."

Dickce snorted with laughter. "No, she doesn't me either."

"I think I found the connection," Benjy said. "The one between Alesha Jackson and Nathan Gamble, that is."

"What is it?" An'gel and Dickce said in unison.

"Lonnie Jackson's obituary says he was an employee of Gamble Construction Company at the time of his death," Benjy said, his eyes focused on the screen of his laptop. He grimaced. "He apparently fell to his death on a construction site."

CHAPTER 29

"There's a potential motive right there," An'gel said slowly. "If the family holds Nathan Gamble responsible for Lonnie Jackson's death, Alesha Jackson could have killed him out of anger. A life for a life."

"Benjy, see if you can find out anything about the accident," Dickce said.

"Already on it," Benjy said.

An'gel and Dickce waited in silence while Benjy searched. They knew it wouldn't take long.

"Got it," he said in obvious satisfaction a minute later. He scanned the article he'd found. After a moment, he raised his head to look at An'gel and Dickce.

"I can tell by your expression that it's bad," An'gel said.

Benjy nodded. "According to the article I found, there were complaints about safety violations on the site where it happened. Some equipment that wasn't up to standard.

Scaffolding, actually. Collapsed with Mr. Jackson, and he fell six stories and died instantly."

"Sounds to me like Nathan Gamble's company could be liable," Dickce said. "There's no excuse for putting workers' lives in danger with shoddy equipment."

"No, there isn't," An'gel said. "I wonder if Mrs. Jackson is planning to sue the company."

"According to the article, the widow is considering a lawsuit," Benjy said. "This is dated about two weeks after the accident. I haven't found a follow-up to it."

"Maybe Alesha Jackson didn't want to wait for the outcome of a lawsuit," Dickce said. "No telling how long it might drag out. Unless the company agreed to settle out of court."

"Based on what we've heard about Nathan Gamble's love of money," An'gel said, "he might not have settled, unless it would be cheaper than going to court. Now that he's out of the way, whoever will be running the company might be more amenable to a hefty settlement. Who knows?"

"There's prime motive for murder," Dickce said. "For someone out for revenge and for a lot of money."

"Alesha Jackson is the most likely suspect

now, isn't she?" Benjy set his laptop aside, and Peanut immediately put his head in the young man's lap. Benjy began to stroke the silky head.

"Probably," An'gel said. "I'm certainly not going to discount Serenity Foster or Truss Wilbanks. Either separately or together, depending on Nathan Gamble's will, they could stand to gain a lot more in terms of money than Alesha Jackson."

"If I had to choose," Benjy said, "I'd rather it was Serenity Foster. She's not nice at all. Alesha Jackson, even though we know she's a fraud, isn't nasty like the other one is."

"I agree with you," Dickce said. "The lawyer, well, I just feel sorry for him. Sounds like he wasn't being treated well by his so-called partner, and having to deal with Serenity . . ." Her voice trailed off.

"True." An'gel grunted in frustration, an unladylike sound to her ears, but it expressed how she felt. "If only we knew how Nathan Gamble died. Plus how the killer got into the room to do it, if the method called for it."

"You're not going to get the information out of Lieutenant Steinberg," Dickce said. "If you think you are, then you ought to give up such a foolish notion."

"I know the man isn't going to tell me, or any of us, anything he doesn't want us to know. Unfortunately that includes how Gamble died." An'gel felt her jaw clench and made herself loosen it. The last thing she needed was damaged teeth, since they were all still her own.

"What about this project you were mentioning earlier, Miss An'gel?" Benjy asked. "You were pretty anxious about it. What is it exactly?"

"I want to find out if there is another way to get into the French room besides the bedroom door and the windows that look onto the second-floor gallery on two sides," An'gel said.

"The problem with that is there isn't space anywhere that I can see for a secret entrance." Dickce frowned. "Other than the wall between the bathroom and the French room."

"Exactly." An'gel thumped the arm of the chair with her right hand. "That bathroom wall. If there's a way through that wall, anyone could slip into the bathroom and get into the French room. As simple as that. Nobody locks the bathroom door unless they're using it at the moment."

Benjy looked puzzled, An'gel noticed. "What is it?" she asked him. "Something wrong?"

He shrugged. "I guess I'm wondering why there has to be a secret door or entrance for the killer to use. Why couldn't the killer simply use the door or one of the windows? I mean, I know they could be, probably were, all locked, but locks can be picked."

"The Nancy Drew effect," Dickce murmured.

An'gel sighed. "Maybe you're right."

"I'm sorry, you lost me," Benjy said. "What's the Nancy Drew effect? Who is she?"

Dickce chuckled. "I'll let Sister explain it to you."

"Nancy Drew is a girl detective," An'gel said. "She's been around since 1930, I think, and still solving mysteries. In books, of course, but there were also movies and a television series."

"Okay," Benjy said. "That Nancy Drew I've heard about. I used to read the Hardy Boys when I was a kid."

"We read Nancy Drew when we were kids," An'gel said. "Many decades ago. At the time there really was no girl like her in the books we read."

"Nancy was fearless. She would go anywhere, do anything, to help people in trouble," Dickce said. "Adults listened to

317

her and respected her, and she solved crimes that the police couldn't crack. She was strong and independent."

"That's why several generations of women admire her and remember the books so fondly," An'gel said. "Especially back in the times when Dickce and I were really young. Girls weren't allowed to behave like that, to do such things on their own."

Benjy nodded. "I get it. She was a great role model is what you're saying."

"Yes," Dickce replied. "Now that you've got that, An'gel can explain about the secret door obsession."

An'gel frowned at her sister. "It's not an obsession, so don't use that word." She turned to look at Benjy. "The second book in the series is called *The Hidden Staircase,* and in it Nancy is helping two sisters who live in an old Civil War–era mansion. Odd things are happening, and they're frightened. It was a particular favorite of both of us."

"And here we are in an old house that might have a hidden staircase," Benjy said. "You want to be like Nancy Drew in your favorite book."

An'gel could tell he was trying hard to suppress a grin. She couldn't blame him because in her heart she knew that he was exactly right. She hadn't allowed herself to realize the truth before, and now that she had, she could see that she had allowed wishful thinking to cloud her judgment.

"That's basically it," An'gel said.

"To be completely fair, though," Dickce said with a quick sideways glance at An'gel, "in the book the villain *was* making use of secret passageways and hiding places to play tricks on the sisters. When Mary Turner asked us for help and told us what was going on, I think we both leapt to the same conclusion."

"That whoever is behind the tricks going on here at Cliffwood is making use of similar passageways and hiding places to *haunt* the house," An'gel said.

"I can see why you might think that," Benjy said. "And it would be so awesome if we did find a hidden staircase."

"My plan was for us to go over the bathroom wall carefully to see if we could find a movable panel or anything that would allow a person to get into the French room. It wouldn't have to be the size of a whole door," An'gel said. "Just big enough for a person to crawl through without getting stuck."

"We can still look for it," Benjy said.

An'gel shook her head. "Now that I've

faced up to reality, I see it isn't likely. You were right when you talked about the killer getting in through either the door or the window. That had to be the way, *if* he or she had to have access to Nathan Gamble in order to kill him."

"We don't know anything about how he spent his evening, do we?" Dickce said. "Whether he went anywhere, ate dinner out, brought food back with him. I don't think Marcelline would have given him dinner, do you?"

"No, I wouldn't think so," An'gel said. "She didn't care for him any more than she cares for Serenity, because he kept pestering Mary Turner about the contents of that room."

"I wonder if anyone saw him last night before he went into that room for the last time," Benjy said.

"Henry Howard wouldn't have," Dickce said. "He left in the afternoon and didn't come back until late. So that leaves everyone else except the three of us."

"I know that Truss Wilbanks saw him, remember?" An'gel said.

"Right, that was embarrassing, wasn't it?" Dickce shook her head.

"Yes, it was." An'gel didn't care to remember the incident in detail. "I'm sure Mary

Turner and Marcelline would be happy to answer questions regarding the period of time we're talking about. Alesha Jackson, maybe. I can't see Serenity Foster being accommodating, though, can you?"

Dickce shook her head. "No, but we could always try."

"And then there's Mr. Wilbanks," Benjy said. "I could try talking to him. I'm a lot less intimidating than you are, Miss An'gel." He gave her a cheeky grin and a wink.

An'gel was too amused to take offense. Also too self-aware. She understood how she came across to many people. She could be intimidating, but mostly when she knew she had to be in order to get a point across or to get a difficult situation resolved.

She looked at Dickce. "What do you think?"

"About you being intimidating?" Dickce laughed. "Of course you are. But you probably meant about Benjy talking to Truss Wilbanks. I think that would be fine."

"Okay, then." Benjy gently moved Peanut's head off his lap and got to his feet. "Might as well look for him now and see if I can get him to talk." He paused a moment. "Do you think I should take Peanut and Endora with me?"

"I think so," An'gel said. "They're usually

better behaved with you. Dickce and I are about to head downstairs again and look for Mary Turner and Marcelline. We have enough time before we're meeting with Alesha Jackson, don't we?" She glanced at her watch. Almost three o'clock now. "Yes, plenty of time."

"I'll check in with you when I have something to report on Mr. Wilbanks." Benjy took hold of Peanut's leash, and Dickce stood with Endora to let the cat climb on Benjy's shoulder. Armed with his laptop and accompanied by the animals, he left the room. An'gel and Dickce followed a couple of minutes later, after Dickce took time to remove some of the cat hair from her dress.

"Marcelline will probably be in the kitchen," An'gel said as they walked down the stairs. "That's where she told me she was headed when she left after we talked."

"Good a place as any to start," Dickce said. "Mary Turner might be there, too, helping with dinner."

An'gel braced herself again for the sudden cold as she moved down the stairs but nothing happened. She glanced at Dickce when she reached the first floor. Dickce shook her head. No cold spot for her either.

They headed down the hall toward the kitchen. When they entered, An'gel saw

Marcelline at the stove, focused on her work. Henry Howard and Mary Turner stood near the back door, obviously engaged in a heated discussion.

An'gel cleared her throat to alert them to her and Dickce's presence. Mary Turner cast a startled glance their way, then with an expression of determination, she marched over to An'gel and Dickce.

Mary Turner pointed back toward her husband, slumped against the wall by the back door, his head down. "Y'all are not going to believe what that idiot of a husband confessed to me." Her eyes blazed with anger, and An'gel felt briefly sorry for Henry Howard. "He told me not two minutes ago that *he* is the ghost that's been moving things around in the French room."

CHAPTER 30

An'gel and Dickce looked at each other. An'gel knew they were thinking the same thing. If Henry Howard had been playing ghost in the French room, was he also responsible for Nathan Gamble's death? The thought made An'gel sick to her stomach. Had they misjudged Henry Howard until now? He had always impressed her as an intelligent, upright young man.

"I'm so furious with him right now," Mary Turner continued, "I can't even look at him. Will you talk to him? I can't any more right now, or I might scratch his eyes out." She didn't wait for an answer and hurried out of the kitchen.

"We certainly will talk to him," An'gel said under her breath. "But not in here." Marcelline didn't need to hear what she had to say to Henry Howard, nor what Henry Howard had to say in his own defense. "Why don't you stay and talk to Marcelline, Sister?"

An'gel said, keeping her voice low.

Dickce nodded and moved toward the housekeeper.

"Henry Howard, why don't you come with me to the library?" An'gel said. "Let's talk about this and give Mary Turner time to cool down a bit."

Henry Howard wouldn't look her in the eye but he nodded and ambled toward her. They walked to the library in silence, but once behind closed doors and seated in chairs near each other, An'gel opened the discussion.

"You were playing ghost in the French room?" An'gel asked.

Henry Howard nodded, still avoiding looking directly at her. "Yes, I did. Stupid idea, I realize that now."

"When did you get this idea?" An'gel said.

"A few months ago," Henry Howard replied.

An'gel waited for him to continue, but when he didn't, she realized she was going to have to keep probing to get the whole story out of him.

"Was it intended simply as a joke, or was there a reason behind it?"

"I had a reason for it," Henry Howard said, then lapsed back into silence. He stared at the floor.

"Would you mind sharing that reason?" An'gel said tartly. She was rapidly losing patience with him. "If you think I'm going to give up and leave you alone, Henry Howard, you ought to know better. You stop acting like an adolescent, and tell me what was behind this silly idea of yours."

Henry Howard didn't respond at first. Then suddenly he straightened in the chair and looked her full in the face. His expression indicated both embarrassment and frustration to An'gel. She had an idea what was bothering him, based on previous conversations, but he needed to unburden himself completely.

"I'm sick and tired of this damn house," he said, almost spitting out the words. "It runs *our* lives, we don't run *it*. Mary Turner is the most wonderful woman in the world, but I married *her*. Not this house." He slumped in the chair again, and his gaze dropped to his hands, clenched in his lap.

"I can understand that," An'gel said. "We talked a little about this already. Have you talked about this with Mary Turner? I mean, sat down and really discussed it with her?"

"I tried once, about six or seven months ago," Henry Howard said. "She got so upset that I told her to forget it. I said I was just tired, and that it was all okay."

"But it wasn't okay, was it?" An'gel asked.

"No, it wasn't," he replied, obviously miserable. "Every day I get more tired of the same old grind, with no end in sight. We make a decent living out of the house, but we don't get much time to enjoy ourselves. We never go anywhere other than out to dinner with friends every once in a while.

"I spent my junior year in college in England. Did you know that?" Henry Howard didn't wait for an answer. "I loved every minute of it. I loved England, and I've wanted to go back ever since. But I've never had the opportunity. Mary Turner has never been, and I'd love to take her there and show her the places I visited." He fell silent.

"But you can't," An'gel said gently.

Henry Howard sighed. "We could, during the time the house is closed to visitors every year. But Mary Turner won't leave the house. She's afraid of anything happening to the house and her not being here to take care of it. I have begged her to take a trip with me, but she won't."

To An'gel, it was beginning to sound like Mary Turner could have a slightly unhealthy attachment to the house, and if that were the case, then she could certainly understand Henry Howard's frustration. That frustration could soon turn into bitterness,

An'gel knew, and that could damage their marriage irreparably.

"Do you think I'm being selfish and unreasonable?" Henry Howard asked. "Mary Turner said I was."

"It's not unreasonable or selfish to want to take a vacation from your responsibilities," An'gel said firmly.

"Thank you," Henry Howard replied.

"What was it you were hoping to accomplish by making Mary Turner think there was a ghost in the French room?" An'gel asked. "Did you think she would be frightened enough that she would want to leave the house?"

Henry Howard shrugged. "Maybe. I think maybe I wanted her to start thinking that the house wasn't as wonderful as she thinks it is. Anything to get her to reevaluate and see that we can't sacrifice the rest of our lives for it."

An'gel thought the whole idea was foolish, but now wasn't the time to tell Henry Howard that. She suspected he already knew it anyway.

"Why the French room?" she asked.

"Because it's like a shrine," Henry Howard said. "Her father was as bad, if not worse, than Mary Turner is about that room. It has to be preserved as it is. You wouldn't believe what we've spent on special dry cleaning and laundering for the linens and the draperies alone. Every year since we've been married."

"Has Mary Turner explained why this room is so important to her?" An'gel asked. She knew it was filled with valuable furniture and objets d'art, but was that the only reason?

"She seems to think that if anything bad happens to the things in that room, she'll lose the house," Henry Howard said. "Like that room is a talisman of some sort against bad fortune."

"So by making her think it was haunted by a ghost, you thought you might change her mind about the importance of the room?" An'gel asked. The idea seemed even more foolish now.

"Yes," Henry Howard said. "I know it's idiotic, but I've been desperate. I feel like I'm going to suffocate if I'm shackled to this place much longer."

An'gel felt bad for him. He was obviously in severe distress, and if Mary Turner persisted in her devotion to the house, An'gel didn't have much hope for the marriage. At some point Henry Howard would have had enough and simply walk away, she feared. Was that what Mary Turner really wanted?

"So it was you who came into the room while I was there and moved my dress and my nightgown?" An'gel asked.

Henry Howard had the grace to look embarrassed now, she noted. "Yes, ma'am," he said. "I'm sorry if I frightened you."

"You didn't really frighten me," An'gel said, "though it was quite disconcerting. I'm not really comfortable with the idea of someone sneaking into my room while I'm sleeping and moving things around. I'm relieved that it wasn't a ghost, however."

"I'm really, really sorry," Henry Howard said. "I guess I thought if I managed to get you spooked enough, you'd talk to Mary Turner. She thinks a lot of you, you know."

"I'm flattered to hear that," An'gel said. "But I have to say, I don't think I would have advised her to sell the house because of your prank."

Henry Howard nodded. "I see that now."

"I'm not angry with you," An'gel said. "I do want to know how you got in and out of the room without anyone seeing or suspecting."

"Through the bathroom next door," Henry Howard said.

An'gel blinked in surprise. She had pretty well given up on the idea of a secret door between the two rooms. "I knew it, I just knew it," she muttered.

Henry Howard frowned. "I'm sorry, what did you say? I couldn't quite catch it."

"Doesn't matter," An'gel said. "Where is this door? I suspected there might be another way into that room."

"I found it by a fluke, I guess you'd call it, about eight months ago when I was repainting the bathroom," Henry Howard said. "You remember where that tall wardrobe is in the French room?" After An'gel nodded, he continued. "Well, that wardrobe is attached to the wall, although you might not realize it. When I was painting the bathroom, I noticed cracks in the paint. The room hadn't been painted in years, you see. I kept thinking the cracks looked like a door, and I was right.

"It isn't a full-sized door." Henry Howard sketched a form in the air with his hands. "Just enough to squeeze through if you stoop a little. Anyway, I got curious and kept poking around it, and I hit something and suddenly the panel swung out. At first I thought it was only some kind of hidden cabinet, but when I got a flashlight, I could see a similar-sized set of cracks in what I thought was part of the wall. Plus there was a small latch. When I slid the panel back, I realized it opened into the wardrobe."

"I'm sure you climbed through it into the French room," An'gel said. She certainly would have.

"I did," Henry Howard said. "I felt like one of the Hardy Boys. I used to read those when I was a kid, and there was even a book in the series called *The Secret Panel.* So there I was, in the French room, and I realized that I could go back and forth between the rooms without anybody knowing about it."

"You didn't tell Mary Turner about your discovery?"

"No, I didn't," Henry Howard said. "I know I should have, but she had never said anything to me about a secret panel. I figured she didn't know about it, and I guess it tickled me that I knew something about the house that she didn't."

"I suppose finding the door gave you the idea to play ghost," An'gel said. She could understand the temptation, though she certainly never would have yielded to it.

"Yes, it did," Henry Howard said a bit sheepishly. "I tried it out a couple of times, going into the room and moving things, and nobody caught on. The maids and Mary Turner all assumed that it was a spirit, because the door and the windows are always kept locked."

"Couldn't you have done the same thing by going through the door or one of the windows?" An'gel asked.

Henry Howard shrugged. "I guess, but it might have been more noticeable. If I went in to use the bathroom, no one would think twice about it if they saw me going in or coming out. I always ran water in the sink and flushed the toilet before I came out of the bathroom."

"Do you think anyone else knows about this secret panel?" An'gel asked.

"I don't think so," Henry Howard said. "I think Mary Turner's father might have known, but if he did, he never told her about it."

"Did you tell her earlier when you confessed to being the ghost?" An'gel asked.

"I didn't get the chance," Henry Howard said. "She blew up at me before I could tell her, and then you and Miss Dickce came into the kitchen."

"I see." An'gel would definitely ask Mary Turner about it. She had one more question for Henry Howard now.

"Did you enter the French room through the secret panel last night in order to murder Nathan Gamble?"

CHAPTER 31

An'gel watched Henry Howard carefully to gauge his reaction to her question.

"No, I most certainly did not kill Nathan Gamble," Henry Howard said, immediately and firmly. He stared An'gel straight in the eye when he said it, and she believed him.

She told him so, and he looked relieved. "But you did sneak into the room through the secret panel last night." She deliberately made it a statement rather than a question.

"How did you know?" Henry Howard said. "Are you sure *you're* not the psychic?" he added in a jocular tone.

"I'm no psychic," An'gel said, "but I do have a good memory. For example, I remember this morning you asked me how I had slept. When I told you that I had slept fine, you seemed a bit taken aback. That seemed an odd reaction, but I didn't think much about it at the time. Once I knew about your ghostly activities, I remembered it and reevaluated it."

"You're right," Henry Howard said. "I did sneak in there last night with the intent to frighten you a little. I had a small flashlight with a weak beam, but I couldn't see well because I had a mask on. I didn't realize it wasn't you in the bed."

"Did you get any kind of reaction from whatever your little performance entailed?" An'gel asked.

Henry Howard frowned. "I'm not really sure. I thought I heard a moan or two, but I'm not even sure that it came from the person on the bed. I didn't get real close to the bed, you see. I stayed close to the wardrobe in case I needed to make a fast exit."

"That's, what, maybe four feet away from the bed?" An'gel asked.

"About that, yes," Henry Howard replied.

"Did you see any movement on the bed?" An'gel wondered whether Nathan Gamble was alive or dead when Henry Howard was in the room.

Henry Howard thought about that for a moment. "No, I don't think so. Does this mean you think he was already dead when I went in?"

"It's entirely possible," An'gel said. "What time was it?"

"A few minutes past midnight," Henry Howard said. "I came home a little before eleven, and Mary Turner was sound asleep in our room. I looked in on her and then went to the library to wait until midnight. I actually read for a while. Then I came back upstairs to do my ghost bit."

"Did you see anybody else when you arrived home last night?" An'gel said. "Notice anyone's lights on, anything that might indicate someone else was up?"

"For an alibi, you mean?" Henry Howard asked.

"Partly," An'gel said.

Henry Howard frowned while he thought about it. "I remember seeing light under a bedroom door when I went up to check on my wife. From Primrose Pace's room, or whatever her real name is."

"Alesha Jackson," An'gel said. "Was the light on both ways? That is, when you went to the room and then when you went downstairs?"

"When I went to the room, I'm sure it was," Henry Howard said. "But I can't remember whether it was on the way back."

"Of course, having a light on in the room doesn't mean she was in there," An'gel said, more to herself than to Henry Howard.

"No, guests go out all the time and leave

lights burning," Henry Howard said.

"While you were in the library, could you hear anyone moving about the house?"

"No," Henry Howard said. "I closed the door to keep the light from shining into the hall, and that cuts off a lot of sound."

"What bedroom is over the library?" An'gel said. "Isn't it the room Alesha Jackson is in?"

"Yes, you're right," Henry Howard said. "So I guess you want to know if I heard anything overhead."

An'gel nodded.

He shook his head. "Not that I recall."

An'gel couldn't think of another question for him. Now came the hard part — persuading him to tell his story to Lieutenant Steinberg.

"Lieutenant Steinberg needs to hear all this," An'gel said. "He doesn't know about the secret panel, and he will want his people to examine it. You say no one else knows about it, but you can't be completely certain. If someone else did use it to get into the French room to murder Nathan Gamble, then there could be evidence, as long as you didn't destroy it when you went through the panel, that is."

Henry Howard appeared dazed by the flood of words. Then his face cleared. "I know you're right, but I don't look forward to telling him. What if he thinks I killed Nathan Gamble?" Now he started to look panicky.

"There's a possibility he could think you're the killer," An'gel said. "But my impression of him is that he's tough and a stickler for doing things right. That includes arresting the right person. Dickce and I will stand behind you, and I'm sure Mary Turner will, too."

"Thank you," Henry Howard said. "I hope you're right about my wife. When she gets as angry as she did when I told her what I'd done, it can take her a long time to cool down, and she's not always reasonable again until she does."

"She'll come around," An'gel said. "Don't you worry." *Because I'll see that she does,* she added silently.

"I guess I'd better get in touch with the lieutenant," Henry Howard said.

"Yes, but before you do, I thought of one more question," An'gel said with a quick smile. "Just to satisfy my curiosity. What kind of mask were you wearing? I want to know what you thought may frighten me."

"It wasn't anything horrible, like a demon or a monster," Henry Howard said. "It's a woman's face that is made up to look like an otherworldly spirit. With a little light shining on it, it's creepy looking, I think."

"That might have spooked me a little," An'gel said. "But it would never have been enough to achieve your purpose."

"I realize that now," Henry Howard said. "I hope you'll forgive me, Miss An'gel."

"I already have," she said. "Now go make that phone call."

Henry Howard rose. "I will, but will you talk to Mary Turner for me?"

"Yes," An'gel said. "I'll go look for her now." She sat for a moment longer, until Henry Howard had left the room. She wasn't sure exactly what she was going to say to Mary Turner in defense of Henry Howard. Perhaps the best strategy was simply to let Mary Turner talk to her, encourage her to let go of everything. She got to her feet. The kitchen was the first place to look, she decided, and she headed there.

Only Marcelline was in the kitchen, An'gel discovered. Upon being questioned about Mary Turner's whereabouts, Marcelline shook her head. "I'm not sure, Miss An'gel. I know she was planning to talk to Serenity, but that was before she found out about Mr. Henry acting like he was a ghost. She was so upset, she might have gone somewhere to cool off."

An'gel said, "Thank you. I might try Mrs. Foster's room, at least to start. Do you know which one she's in?"

"Room four," Marcelline said. "Toward the end away from the house."

"One more question," An'gel said. "Do you know where my sister went?"

"We just finished talking a few minutes ago," Marcelline replied. "I believe she said she was going to look for Benjy."

"All right. Thank you again." An'gel wondered if Dickce had gleaned any useful information from the housekeeper. She checked her watch. She still had about twenty minutes before she was due to meet Alesha Jackson. She might as well see if she could find either Mary Turner or Dickce.

An'gel stepped out the back door into the courtyard. The afternoon was cool, and this side of the house was increasingly in shadow as the sun moved lower in the sky on the other, western-facing side. She walked across the courtyard toward the annex, found Serenity Foster's room, and knocked.

After a moment, Serenity opened the door. An'gel looked past her and saw Mary Turner seated on a chair, her face turned away from the door and her shoulders slumped.

"What do you want?" Serenity asked, her tone verging on hostile.

"I'm looking for Mary Turner," An'gel said. "I need to speak to her about something."

Serenity turned to face Mary Turner. "You might as well leave and go talk to her. I don't have anything more to say to you."

As An'gel watched, Mary Turner rose from the chair. An'gel could see she had been crying.

Mary Turner stumbled toward the door. Serenity moved aside, but as Mary Turner reached the threshold, she paused and stared hard at her cousin.

"This isn't the end of it," Mary Turner said. "I'll find a way to get the money. You're not going to take anything away from me."

Serenity pushed her out and slammed the door. Mary Turner lurched toward An'gel involuntarily but managed to stop herself before knocking into the older woman.

An'gel put out a hand to steady her. "What on earth was going on between you two? You look like you've had terrible news."

Mary Turner nodded. "It is, the worst news possible. I thought she might be easier to deal with than Nathan was, but I was wrong. She's even worse than he ever dared to be." She burst into tears, and An'gel, after a momentary hesitation, drew her away from the door and put her arms around the troubled young woman.

"Whatever it is," An'gel said, "I will help you sort it out. Do you feel like telling me what's happened?"

Mary Turner pulled away after a moment and looked at An'gel, a glimmer of hope in her eyes. "Yes, please. Let's go in the kitchen, though."

"Is it something you can talk about in front of Marcelline?" An'gel asked as they started to walk toward the back door.

"Oh, yes, she already knows about it," Mary Turner said. "She was actually with me when I got the news from Nathan himself last night."

"When was that?" An'gel asked. "I didn't realize you had talked to him last night."

Mary Turner nodded. "He came down to the kitchen about nine thirty last night, I think it was. Marcelline and I were there, talking about things. We often do. Anyway, Nathan asked for a glass of hot milk. Marcelline said she wasn't about to do it. She really loathed him, you know. Well, Nathan got mad, and they started arguing. I tried to stop it, but they wouldn't pay any attention to me. Then finally Nathan said something that stopped Marcelline in her tracks."

They had reached the back door, and Mary Turner stood with her hand on the knob. She had paled suddenly, to An'gel's alarm. Before she could express concern, however, Mary Turner continued in a rush.

"Nathan said she was soon going to be out of a job. He would see to it personally. Marcelline asked him what he meant by that, and he laughed." Mary Turner paused for a moment, and tears began welling in her eyes. "He said he owned the mortgage on the house, and he was going to foreclose on it."

"Mortgage? What mortgage?" An'gel asked.

"I took one out about three years ago when we needed money for some extensive repairs and restoration," Mary Turner said. "I've been struggling a little to pay it back, and I got behind."

"Does Henry Howard know about this?" An'gel asked.

Mary Turner shook her head. "No, I didn't tell him. The house is in my name, so I could do it without his knowledge. I've always handled the finances anyway. He prefers it because he hates dealing with any kind of bookkeeping." She rubbed the tears away with her free hand. The other still clutched the doorknob.

"I went to Serenity just now to beg her to help me, since I figured she probably inherits everything."

"But she said she wouldn't," An'gel said.

"No, she said the moment she owned the house, she was going to sell all the contents and then tear it completely down because that's what Nathan intended to do."

CHAPTER 32

"Did Nathan tell you himself he intended to tear the house down?" An'gel asked.

"No, he didn't," Mary Turner said, her voice catching on a sob. "But it sounds like something he would do."

"I think Serenity is grossly exaggerating the situation, simply because she wants to upset you as much as possible, my dear," An'gel said.

"Exaggerating? How?" Mary Turner asked, a note of hope in her voice.

"Let's go inside, and I'll tell you," An'gel said.

"All right." Mary Turner opened the door, and An'gel followed her into the kitchen. Marcelline was nowhere in sight.

"Now have a seat and let's talk for a minute. I think I can set your fears to rest." An'gel glanced at her watch. Ten minutes until her appointment with Alesha Jackson.

Once they were seated across from each

other at the kitchen table, An'gel explained. "This house is on the National Register of Historic Places, and it's also recognized as a Mississippi landmark. The state historical commission that oversees landmarks would have to meet and agree that the property could be demolished. Frankly, I doubt they would agree to let this house be torn down. Then there's the issue of whether Serenity will inherit the right to control the mortgage. By the time the will gets sorted out, if Nathan left one, you will be able to catch up on your mortgage payments."

Mary Turner's face had brightened the longer An'gel talked, but at An'gel's last sentence, her face fell again.

"I'll never be able to catch up," Mary Turner said. "Business is always pretty slow after the first of the year, until people start reserving rooms for the pilgrimage."

"I imagine I can help you find a way to catch up," An'gel said. She and Dickce would have to see how badly in arrears the mortgage was, of course, before making a final decision, but somehow they would see to it that Mary Turner didn't lose her historic home. An'gel knew she could speak for her sister on this. They couldn't let their old friend's granddaughter down.

Mary Turner smiled through her tears.

"Miss An'gel, you truly are an angel. I don't know how I'd ever repay you, but I'll find a way if you can help me keep my home."

"Stop fretting about it." An'gel checked her watch again. Time to meet Alesha Jackson. "You'll have to excuse me, my dear. I have that appointment to talk to Alesha Jackson. We'll talk more later about your situation."

"Thank you again," Mary Turner said. "I can't wait to tell Marcelline the news. She was as devastated as I was after Nathan dropped his bombshell last night."

An'gel nodded as she rose. "See you later."

During the brief walk to the parlor, An'gel thought about the implications of Nathan Gamble's bombshell and Mary Turner's parting words just now. Marcelline, of course, would have been devastated at the thought of losing her home of the last half century or more. She was a forceful woman in her way. What might she do to protect Mary Turner and Cliffwood? Would she resort to murder?

On that disturbing thought, An'gel walked into the parlor, where she found Alesha Jackson again admiring the mantel. She turned at An'gel's approach and nodded to acknowledge her.

An'gel indicated one of the sofas. "Won't

you have a seat, Ms. Jackson? We might as well be comfortable while we talk."

"All right." The erstwhile medium chose a spot at one end of the sofa and rested her right arm along its arm. She gazed expectantly at An'gel.

Having taken a seat on the sofa opposite Alesha Jackson, An'gel regarded the woman for a moment. She still hadn't figured out exactly what tack would get her the information she wanted. *Might as well start with the business at Riverhill and see how she reacts to that,* she decided.

"My sister and I live in an antebellum house that dates from the 1830s," An'gel said. "Six generations of our family have lived there. Some also have died there over the years."

"Not unusual in a house of that age," Alesha replied.

"Not at all," An'gel said. "Over the years, my sister and I have observed odd things that we could never quite explain. Not things that happen frequently, or if they do happen frequently, we've not noticed. They are more random, I think, but I haven't made a study of them, nor has my sister."

"What kind of odd things?" Alesha asked.

An'gel shrugged. "Mostly an occasional cold spot in a room, sometimes an object is

in a different place or position. A door closing on its own." As she spoke the last words,
she fought the urge to turn and look at the
parlor door at her back.

"Who lives in the house?" Alesha asked.

"Only my sister and I," An'gel said. "We
have a housekeeper who comes daily
through the week, but she has always lived
in her own home, with her family."

"What about the young man — Benjy,
isn't it? — and the two animals?"

"Benjy is a recent addition to the family,"
An'gel said. "As are Peanut and Endora.
Benjy has his own apartment in a remod-
eled outbuilding behind the house, and the
animals generally spend the nights with
him. All three of them are in and out of the
house every day, though."

"How long has your housekeeper been
with you?" Alesha asked.

"Nearly fifty years," An'gel said.

"How long have these odd things been
happening? Or rather, when did you first
start noticing them?"

"As long as I can remember," An'gel said
truthfully. As a child, she hadn't thought
much about things. Neither she nor Dickce
ever talked to their mother about them,
although they did talk to each other. Neither
of them had ever really felt frightened.

"Have these incidents been malicious in any way?" Alesha asked.

"Not that I can recall," An'gel said. "Neither my sister nor I have ever felt threatened or truly frightened."

"It sounds like this activity really doesn't bother you," Alesha said. "What is it you want me to do?"

"You said that you can communicate with spirits," An'gel said. "We're curious to know who this spirit was. Dickce thinks it's our paternal grandmother, but I'm not sure. She was a cranky old lady and not very nice to children."

An'gel hadn't really meant to go into this much detail with the psychic but somehow she found herself telling the woman all these things. Perhaps the spirit's activities had been weighing on her mind more than she realized. This was distracting her from the real purpose of this interview, however, and she needed to redirect the conversation soon.

"I could come and attempt to communicate with this spirit," Alesha Jackson said. "I would have to stay in the house, and I can't say up front how long it might take. So much depends on the willingness of the spirit to communicate."

"I understand," An'gel said, interested

despite her determination to move on to other subjects. "What is your fee?"

"Room and board, and five thousand dollars for up to a week. If it takes longer, then it's twenty-five hundred a week after that."

An'gel was taken aback. Alesha Jackson had quoted Mary Turner a much lower price. For hourly work, however, it was far less than a lawyer's fee, An'gel realized after a little mental arithmetic. Then she had to remind herself that the woman was most likely a con artist. An'gel wasn't about to pay Alesha Jackson a nickel for her services, much less five thousand dollars plus.

"I've been wondering about any references you might have," An'gel said. "Benjy is talented when it comes to finding out things online, and he did a little research on Primrose Pace's activities." She deliberately used the pseudonym rather than the woman's real name.

Alesha Jackson tensed slightly, An'gel noticed. Her gaze, however, remained bland. "I know there are two or three things online that are pretty easy to find. About work I've done in missing persons cases in Louisiana."

"Yes," An'gel said. "I suppose it was through communicating with the spirits of the dead in these cases that led you to the vicinity of where they'd been buried."

"To put it simply, yes, though the situations were all much more complicated than that," Alesha said.

An'gel wondered if Alesha really was Primrose Pace, or had she taken the other woman's identity temporarily for purposes of her own. She realized that Alesha Jackson was intelligent and wouldn't be easily trapped into betraying herself. The police would have to sort out the question of Primrose Pace.

Time to push harder, An'gel thought.

"I found out something else about you, Ms. Jackson," An'gel said. "Marcelline told me that your grandmother once worked here. For Mary Turner's grandmother, to be exact."

"Yes, my grandmother told me about that. It was a long time ago." Alesha's eyes narrowed briefly as she returned An'gel's gaze.

"I wondered if that had anything to do with your coming here," An'gel said. "I'm sure there are other houses with spirits you could communicate with. How did you really happen to choose this one?"

Alesha did not reply right away. Instead she stared at An'gel for a long moment. An'gel figured the woman might get up and walk out, but then Alesha surprised her by speaking.

"Curiosity," Alesha said. "My grandmother didn't work here long, but she encountered the spirit that is in this house while she worked here. I got my abilities from my grandmother, you see. I was at loose ends, and I thought I might come here and see if I could communicate with the spirit. She never would talk to my grandmother."

"Interesting," An'gel said. *If it's all true,* she added to herself. "Is your grandmother still living?"

"Yes," Alesha said. "She's in poor health, but she's still with us, praise His mercy."

"I understand, however, that you recently lost your father," An'gel said. "You have my sympathies on your loss."

"How did . . ." Her voice trailed off. "Online, of course, because there have been articles about the accident." Alesha looked disgusted. "Benjy found all that out for you. What business is it of yours? Why are you so interested in my life and my family's lives?"

"Because a man was murdered in this house," An'gel said simply and waited for a reaction.

"So?" Alesha responded. "It's got nothing to do with me."

"The murdered man owned the company

your father worked for at the time of his death," An'gel said. "The company your mother has been considering bringing a lawsuit against. For wrongful death, I imagine."

"You think I killed him because he was responsible for my father's death?" Alesha asked.

"I think it's possible," An'gel said. "It's a powerful motive, don't you think? Perhaps you thought that, with Nathan out of the way, it would be easier for your family to get his company to make a settlement of some sort. I'm sure that will occur to the police."

Alesha stared at An'gel, her expression now one of hatred. "You have a filthy mind, old woman."

"That may be," An'gel replied, refusing to let the other woman rattle her. "I can't abide murder, you see, and I can't stand the thought of a killer getting away with it."

"So you think you're going to try to pin this on me? You think that arrogant policeman is going to take your word for it?" Alesha laughed.

"He might," An'gel said. "I know he'll be interested when he finds out about your connection to the deceased, if he hasn't already." She paused briefly. "Especially when he finds out it was your own cousin you might have murdered."

CHAPTER 33

An'gel was surprised when Alesha Jackson reacted to her words by laughing. She laughed so hard, in fact, that it took at least a minute for her to stop.

When she did finish, she shook her head at An'gel. "I think you need a serious reality check, lady. Where did you get the idea I'm related to Nathan Gamble? You're out of your mind."

Perhaps her grandmother had never told her father about his true parentage. Or her father never told her, An'gel thought. *Or maybe she's simply bluffing.* Should she tell Alesha Jackson what Marcelline had confided in her?

"I'm serious, lady," Alesha said, her tone becoming heated. "I want to know who's spreading that kind of garbage about me and my family."

An'gel reckoned she had little choice now. She had started this, and now she had to finish it, within limits. "According to my source, when your grandmother worked here, she became pregnant with your father. My source says that Marshall Turner Senior was the father. He's Mary Turner's grandfather and related to the Gamble family."

"Your source is lying," Alesha said. "I don't know why this person made up such a story, but it's absolutely not the truth. My grandparents were married two years before my father was born. That was *after* my grandmother worked here. I've seen their marriage certificate. No way was that old man my grandfather."

An'gel was shaken. If Alesha Jackson was telling the truth — and An'gel was beginning to believe she was — that meant what Marcelline had told her was a lie.

"I apologize, Ms. Jackson," An'gel said after she managed to gather her wits. "It's beginning to sound like I was grossly misinformed."

"It was the housekeeper, wasn't it?" Alesha asked. "She's the only one old enough in this house to have known my grandmother when she worked here. You tell her from me she'd better shut her mouth and stop lying. I'm not going to put up with crap like this about my family."

"I certainly understand that," An'gel said.

"I will speak to her, I can promise you that."

"If it's family you're worried about killing Nathan Gamble," Alesha said, "then maybe you should start with his sister. Ask her what she and her brother were arguing about around eleven thirty last night."

"Where was this?" An'gel asked sharply.

"Upstairs, in his room," Alesha said. "I'll bet she hasn't told the lieutenant about it. Well, I heard them, and I know what time it was. I'm a night owl, and I didn't go to bed until after midnight. I heard people going up and down the hall several times last night."

"Do you remember the times?" An'gel asked.

Alesha thought for a moment. "Once around eleven, I think. Someone came down the hall, and then maybe two minutes later went back toward the stairs. Then maybe twenty minutes later, I heard someone walking down the hall again. I heard this person knocking on a door, and a few minutes after that, the argument. I don't think the door was entirely closed."

"How long did the argument last?" An'gel said.

"Not long," Alesha said. "Maybe five minutes. It stopped, that's all I cared about. I had to go to the bathroom right after that, and that's when I spotted Serenity Foster coming out of her brother's room. I don't think she saw me, though, because I was in the bathroom closing the door when she went by."

"Was that the last time you heard anyone in the hall?" An'gel asked.

"No, I heard someone else coming down the hall around midnight when I was on the verge of sleep. I drifted off and didn't hear anyone go back the other way."

"Did you tell Lieutenant Steinberg any of this?" An'gel asked.

"Yes, I did, all of it," Alesha said. "Now I think we're done with this. You remember what I said about my family." She stood up and walked out of the room, obviously still angry.

An'gel couldn't blame her. She herself felt horribly embarrassed now. The whole situation had woefully backfired, but she had only herself to blame. She should never have questioned Alesha Jackson about the story without having more information to back it up. Marcelline had seemed so sincere, so convincing, and An'gel had taken her at her word because she had known her for many years. But, she realized belatedly, not well enough.

Alesha Jackson could be lying, An'gel

knew. Alesha could still be guilty of murder. Her father's death was due to Nathan Gamble's negligence, allegedly. Whether Alesha Jackson was related to the Gambles through Marshall Turner didn't affect the woman's potential motive. Denying the relationship made no difference in that respect. So why deny it? *Because it wasn't true.* Marcelline had lied.

On the whole, An'gel believed Alesha's denial of the relationship. If Alesha could prove that her grandmother had no contact with Marshall Turner after she left his employment and her son was born after her marriage to another man, that settled it.

Maybe Marcelline had simply confused Alesha Jackson's grandmother with someone else. An'gel found it all so easy to believe that Marshall Turner had impregnated a servant. She wouldn't have put anything past the old goat. At the distance of over fifty years, Marcelline's memory could have failed her and she only thought the woman from the past resembled Alesha.

An'gel thought about it. Marcelline could have read about Alesha's father's death in the paper. She could have seen the obituary, and the name *Arletta Jackson* stuck in her mind, to be confused for that of another woman. That was too convoluted, An'gel decided. The simple answer was that Marcelline had lied.

An'gel was left with the question of why. Had she made up the story out of whole cloth to point suspicion toward Alesha Jackson? Away from herself?

Or away from someone she wanted to protect?

The one person who Marcelline would like to protect was Mary Turner. That thought chilled An'gel. Did Marcelline think Mary Turner murdered her cousin?

An'gel recalled how upset Mary Turner was earlier when she recounted her conversation with Serenity Foster and Serenity's threat. If Mary Turner had really believed that Nathan Gamble meant to destroy her family, her whole birthright really, would she have been angry enough, desperate enough, to kill him?

That didn't jibe with the Mary Turner she thought she knew. She recalled Henry Howard's deep frustration with his wife over her devotion to the house. He obviously felt it was a threat to their marriage. Why else would he have tried such a bizarre scheme to frighten Mary Turner? *And me,* An'gel thought. *He did get under my skin a little, I have to admit that.* But she had never been frightened to the point — and never would have been, she thought — that she would encourage Mary Turner to let go of the house.

Had Henry Howard ever sat down with Mary Turner and shared all his frustration with her? Made her see clearly how it was affecting him, and thus their relationship? Henry Howard had never seemed the type to relish confrontation, in An'gel's opinion, so it wouldn't surprise her if he had been reluctant to force the point with Mary Turner.

Even if he had, An'gel wondered, would Mary Turner have believed him? Or was she so blinded by her obsession with the house that it didn't matter? *Obsession* was a strong word, An'gel knew, and perhaps it was inappropriate and simply wrong in this case, but it was sounding more and more like Mary Turner's sense of proportion was a little out of whack at the very least.

What about Serenity Foster? An'gel thought it was pretty certain what she and her brother had argued about. Money — the money Serenity evidently needed to help her in the custody battle. If Nathan continued to prove obdurate about helping her, Serenity might have decided that the only way to get the money was to get rid of her brother — permanently.

That only worked, however, if Serenity was Nathan Gamble's heir. There was no guarantee that she was. Nathan could have left everything to his partner, Truss Wilbanks. The lawyer was still rather a dark horse in this matter. He might have become so bitter and enraged against his lover for Nathan's treatment of him that he killed him in a moment of anger. Based on what An'gel had seen of the man since yesterday, she somehow doubted the man had it in him to commit a crime of passion.

An'gel ran through the list of suspects in her mind.

Serenity Foster — desperate for money, and her brother refused to help her.

Alesha Jackson — out for revenge for her father's wrongful death, and also money from Nathan's company.

Truss Wilbanks — out of passion from mistreatment by his lover, and perhaps for money as well from the business.

Marcelline Beaupré — in order to protect Mary Turner and her beloved house.

Mary Turner Catlin — out of fear of losing her family home and seeing it razed to the ground.

Henry Howard Catlin — for his wife's sake perhaps, but if he didn't know about

Nathan Gamble's threat, his motive was weak.

One of them did it, An'gel knew, but which one?

If Alesha Jackson were to be believed, Serenity had a loud, potentially violent argument with Nathan Gamble around eleven thirty last night. She could have killed him then. But how? An'gel felt incredibly frustrated by her lack of knowledge about how the man died.

He was either alive or dead when Serenity left him after the argument. Henry Howard was the next person on the scene. He had come upstairs from the library a minute or so past midnight to carry out his performance. He slipped into the room through the secret panel in the wardrobe and attempted to frighten the occupant of the room. He got little reaction, aside from a moan or two that he thought he heard.

Gamble might still have been alive, or he might have been dying. That was a horrible thought, and she hoped it didn't occur to Henry Howard that he might have been able to save the man's life. But Henry Howard, seeing his prank falling flat, had left the room the way he came in. He had gone to bed soon after that.

Had anyone else gone into the French

room after Henry Howard?

An'gel had no way of knowing. She had slept through the comings and goings last night, and she had never heard the argument between the siblings. Neither had Dickce, or she would have mentioned it by now.

Any one of the five could have done it. Mary Turner could have slipped across the hall and killed Nathan, either after his argument with Serenity and before Henry Howard went in to play his prank. Or afterward, when Henry Howard was asleep, and the house was quiet.

Marcelline could have come upstairs at some point. She probably had a passkey, the same one that Henry Howard and Mary Turner had. She had to oversee all the housekeeping, so certainly she had one. An'gel hadn't considered that before.

Last, but to her mind, least, Truss Wilbanks could have gone back to Nathan Gamble's room sometime after midnight, after Henry Howard was in bed.

Any one of them could have done it. An'gel wanted to scream in frustration. If Lieutenant Steinberg had convincing evidence, he would have at least taken one of the five in for questioning at the police station, An'gel felt sure. He hadn't, however, so she figured that meant he had no clear lead to the killer's identity.

She wished she could persuade him to tell her how Nathan Gamble was killed. If he actually knew himself. Perhaps he did know, and had known all along, but was being cagey with all of them when he had originally said the cause of death wasn't immediately apparent. She wouldn't put it past him, nor could she blame him for doing so. It was a good tactic, to keep the murderer in the dark.

An'gel got to her feet. Time to find Dickce and Benjy and share the information from their separate interviews. Maybe Dickce or Benjy had picked up a clue from Marcelline or Truss Wilbanks that could be useful.

She pulled out her cell phone and texted both of them to find out where they were at present. Benjy responded right away to say that he was in his room, and that Dickce was with him. An'gel replied that she was on her way to join them.

As she stepped into the hall, the doorbell rang. An'gel answered it. Lieutenant Steinberg stood on the porch, along with two of his officers.

"I'm glad you're here, Lieutenant," An'gel said. "I have some things to tell you."

"This may surprise you, Miss Ducote,"

the policeman said as he stepped inside, followed by his men, "but I am eager to hear
them."

CHAPTER 34

An'gel was slightly suspicious of Lieutenant Steinberg's change of attitude toward her. What on earth could have brought it about?

"I must say I'm rather surprised, Lieutenant," An'gel said.

Steinberg nodded. "I'll explain everything to you, Miss Ducote, but first I have to speak to Mr. Catlin."

"Here I am, Lieutenant." Henry Howard appeared in the hallway near them, having apparently come from the direction of the kitchen. An'gel had not heard his approach.

"In the library, please," Steinberg said to Henry Howard. To An'gel, he said, "Perhaps you won't mind waiting in the parlor?"

"No, not at all," An'gel said. "I'll be ready when you want to talk." She watched as Steinberg, his men, and Henry Howard moved into the library and closed the door behind them.

She took time to visit the powder room

before she did as the policeman asked and went into the parlor to wait. She texted Dickce and Benjy again, telling them of the lieutenant's arrival and asking them to join her in the parlor. After a moment, she added, When you come through the kitchen, if Marcelline is there, ask her for something to drink.

Dickce acknowledged the texts, and An'gel set aside her phone. While she waited for their arrival, she speculated on what — or who — had changed Steinberg's mind. She was pretty certain that it was Kanesha Berry who had effected the change. Steinberg must have talked further to Kanesha about her, Dickce, and Benjy. She would have to thank Kanesha later for doing so.

Dickce and Benjy arrived in the parlor a few minutes after the text exchange. Peanut and Endora accompanied them. As always, upon sight of An'gel, Peanut got excited and bounded over to her to receive the attention she never failed to provide. Endora, atop Benjy's shoulder, was obviously not in the least interested in An'gel. The moment Dickce took a seat beside An'gel on the sofa, however, the Abyssinian leapt to the floor and then onto Dickce's lap. Benjy chose the nearby armchair. Peanut remained by An'gel's side for the moment.

"Marcelline is going to bring us iced tea and cookies," Dickce said. "She offered to make hot tea, but the iced tea was already made. I said that would be fine."

"Thank you," An'gel said. "I could use a cold glass of tea."

Marcelline brought in a tray with three glasses of iced tea, a plate heaped with both chocolate chip and oatmeal raisin cookies, along with dessert plates and napkins. She set the tray on the coffee table and, without waiting to find out if they wanted anything else, hurried from the room.

After a couple of sips of the sweet tea, chilled to perfection, An'gel said, "I'm not sure how much time we have to talk before the lieutenant finishes with Henry Howard. I told him he had to tell the police about his prank, especially since he was in the French room around midnight last night."

"I suppose he was trying to scare Nathan Gamble," Dickce said.

"No, he was trying to scare me. He didn't know that I'd switched rooms with Gamble, you see. He didn't get a reaction from Gamble, however," An'gel said.

"Do you think Gamble was already dead?" Benjy reached for a cookie and began to munch.

"It's possible," An'gel said. "The interesting thing, however, is how Henry Howard got into the room." She told them about the secret panel in the back of the wardrobe.

Dickce nearly spit out her tea. Once she recovered, she said, "You were right after all, Sister. At some point, after this is all over, I want to see it."

"Me, too," Benjy said.

"That makes three of us," An'gel said.

"Why did he go in that way," Benjy asked, "instead of going through the door? He has a passkey, doesn't he? That seems like the way most people would do it when the person in the room was probably asleep."

"Henry Howard said he wanted to be able to duck back into the wardrobe, rather than have to hurry over to the door, to get out of the room if he needed to," An'gel said. "Or words to that effect." She smiled. "I think he simply liked the drama of it as part of his ghostly behavior."

Next she told Dickce and Benjy about her interviews with Henry Howard and Alesha Jackson. She kept the details to the most pertinent ones, because she wanted to get through it all and still have time to hear the reports of their interviews with Marcelline and Truss Wilbanks before the lieutenant was ready to talk.

"I'll go first," Dickce said. "My talk with

Marcelline didn't last long. According to her, she goes to bed every night around eight thirty. Nine at the latest, because she gets up at five to start preparing breakfast for the guests. Her bedroom is right off the kitchen. She says she sleeps soundly. She takes sleeping pills to make sure she gets enough rest."

"So she didn't hear or see anything unusual last night?" An'gel asked.

"No," Dickce said. "She seemed to be telling the truth, though she was busy rolling out dough while we were talking. I couldn't see her face most of the time, so it was hard to judge."

An'gel turned to Benjy. "Any luck with Mr. Wilbanks?"

"Yes," Benjy said. "You know, I really feel sorry for him. I think basically he's a nice guy, and he's terrified the police are going to try to pin it on him. His words exactly."

"Because of the nature of his relationship with Nathan Gamble?" Dickce asked.

Benjy nodded. "Yes. I didn't try to talk him out of that; there didn't seem to be much use. He's really upset by it, plus I think he's really upset by his partner's death."

"What about his movements last night?" An'gel asked.

"He and Serenity got fast food for dinner last night," Benjy said. "They brought it back to their rooms, or rather Truss brought it back. He went to get it while Serenity stayed in her room. They ate in their own rooms. Truss watched TV for a while, played around on his tablet and his phone, then went to bed around ten." Benjy paused for a sip of tea, then he continued.

"He took something to help him sleep because he was upset and didn't think he could sleep without it. It made him groggy but it didn't really put him out. He says it does him like that sometimes. I asked him whether he heard or saw anything last night, and he said he remembered hearing a door nearby open and close. He thinks it was sometime after eleven. After that he finally passed out and didn't wake up until this morning." Benjy reached for another cookie.

"Did you try to broach the subject of the will?" An'gel asked.

"I did, because he seemed so happy to have someone to talk to," Benjy said. "He may regret it later, but he did talk about his relationship with Nathan. Both the personal and professional side of it. According to Truss, Nathan was really smart at making money, but he wasn't generous with it. Truss earned money as Nathan's lawyer, but not as much as he could have working for some other company. Or so he says."

Benjy finished his cookie and washed it down with more sweet tea before he went on. "I finally came out and asked him what would happen to the business and Nathan's personal money. Truss says another lawyer handled Nathan's will but he's pretty sure everything is divided between him and Serenity."

"So they both have a strong financial motive for killing Nathan," Dickce said.

"Yeah," Benjy replied. "Though I don't think Truss did it. I don't think he'd have to guts to kill anybody, even if he was really angry with them."

"That's my impression of him, too," An'gel said. "Though he can't be counted out simply because we don't think him capable."

"I'd put him in the middle of the list, maybe ahead of Marcelline and Mary Turner, but behind Serenity Foster and Alesha Jackson," Dickce said. "I don't think Henry Howard is in it."

"I haven't told you yet about what I found out from him, and from Mary Turner," An'gel said. "Once you hear it, you might revise your list."

"Good heavens, what did you find out?"

Dickce asked.

An'gel told them about Nathan's gloating over having bought the mortgage to Cliffwood and Serenity's threat earlier that day. "So you see, that moves Mary Turner and Marcelline right up on the list."

"Because Marcelline would do anything to protect Mary Turner," Dickce said.

"Do you really think Mary Turner would kill somebody?" Benjy appeared upset at the idea.

"I hate to think so, Benjy, but based on my talk with her earlier, and on a couple of conversations with Henry Howard, I'm afraid she might be obsessed with this house. Obsessed to the point that she would do something drastic to keep it safe."

"I hope you're wrong about her," Benjy said. "That's all I've got to say."

"I hope I'm wrong, too," An'gel said. "Lieutenant Steinberg isn't going to rule her out, and neither can we."

"This is so upsetting," Dickce said. "To think of that nice young woman, sweet Jessy's granddaughter, as a killer." She shook her head, her expression doleful. "But I have noticed that she is really devoted to the house and its care."

"I have a question for you both," Benjy said. "About this house."

"What is it?" Dickce asked.

"Okay, we know now Henry Howard was playing spook in the French room," Benjy said. "But what about the other things? That shadow you saw, Miss An'gel, and the cold you felt on the stairs, Miss Dickce? And remember the door?" He turned slightly in his chair and pointed toward the parlor entrance. "How do you explain those things?"

"I can't at the moment," An'gel said. "I didn't ask Henry Howard about any of those incidents. I suspect he somehow was responsible for the shadow, though I don't know how he worked it. Maybe this door, too."

"But the cold spot." Dickce shivered. "I don't see how he could do that. It wasn't like cold air blowing on you, from an air conditioner vent or anything like that. It was this sudden feeling of being enveloped in cold."

"Like at Riverhill?" An'gel asked.

Dickce nodded.

"So do you think that cold spot means there really is a spirit in this house?" Benjy asked.

An'gel and Dickce looked at each other. Dickce nodded, then An'gel. "I hate to admit it," An'gel said, "but that's one thing

I can't see any explanation for, especially since we've experienced the same thing at Riverhill."

"I'm not sure I want to feel it," Benjy said, "though it might be interesting. Funny, though, that Peanut and Endora don't react when they go up and down the stairs."

"That may just mean that the spirit isn't there when they do," Dickce said. "It might not care for animals."

Benjy laughed suddenly. "It's too bad we can't get the spirit to tell us who murdered Nathan Gamble. Maybe it was in the French room when the murder happened. Who knows?"

An'gel started to laugh, and then she thought about what Benjy had said about getting the spirit to reveal the killer.

"You know," she said slowly, "that might not be such a bad idea."

CHAPTER 35

An'gel spent at the most twenty minutes sharing what she had learned with Lieutenant Steinberg. She stuck to the main points. She knew he would have to dig into the details anyway and verify everything she told him.

She had been right about the lieutenant talking further with Kanesha Berry. The Athena sheriff's deputy had convinced Steinberg that he would be remiss in his duties should he ignore An'gel and any information she managed to uncover. Steinberg hadn't apologized for his earlier attitude, and An'gel didn't expect him to. The main thing was that he was now listening to her and taking notes.

"That's all," An'gel said when she'd finished.

"That's a lot." Steinberg laid aside his pen. He leaned back in the chair and closed his eyes for a moment. An'gel thought he looked tired.

"Do you have any further questions for me?" An'gel asked. "If not, I'd like to ask you one."

Steinberg's eyes popped open. "No other questions right this minute, Miss Ducote. What is it you want to ask me?"

"Will you tell me how Nathan Gamble died?"

Steinberg looked at her for a long moment. "At this point, I don't see why not. We believe that he was smothered to death. There were signs of asphyxia when the doctor examined him on the scene."

I knew it, he purposely misled us, An'gel thought. *He was playing his cards close to his chest.*

"Further," Steinberg continued, "we think that he may have been drugged into a sound sleep. We will have to wait for the outcome of the toxicological analysis on that to be absolutely sure, but there are indications that he was too out of it to fight back."

"Then that means pretty much anyone could have killed him. They wouldn't have to be particularly strong to do it if he was in no condition to fight them," An'gel said.

"Yes, exactly," Steinberg said. "And there you see my biggest problem. I don't know who did it."

"Do you have any idea where the sleep medication came from?" An'gel asked.

"There was no bottle or container of it in the room," Steinberg said, "so we have to assume it came from someone else. We also don't know whether he took it willingly or if he was unaware. During our search of the house, we discovered that four people had sleeping pills with them."

"Will you tell me who they are?" An'gel asked.

Steinberg hesitated, then said, "The housekeeper, the lawyer, the deceased's sister, and the so-called psychic."

At first An'gel was thankful that he hadn't mentioned Mary Turner, but then she realized that Mary Turner could have easily gotten the pills from Marcelline. How had the killer managed to get Nathan Gamble to take the pills? Or had he taken them himself?

She voiced this question to the policeman. He shrugged. "There was nothing in the room to indicate how, other than a glass and a bottle of water. That bottle hadn't been opened, though, and there was no other bottle or source of water in the room."

"He could have gone to the bathroom to get water from the sink," An'gel said.

"Yes, of course," Steinberg said. "The

autopsy might tell us how the pills were taken but that could be a few weeks."

"You need a break in the case," An'gel said.

"Obviously," Steinberg replied, not bothering to hide the sarcasm.

An'gel ignored the sarcasm. "I have an idea that could yield results, but you might think it too crazy."

"I won't know till I've heard it," Steinberg said. "Shoot."

At first Dickce thought An'gel had gone slightly off her rocker when she first told them her idea for smoking out the killer. A séance? Seriously?

"It's not as crazy as it sounds," An'gel had protested. Benjy seemed enthusiastic about the idea, particularly when An'gel explained what she wanted him to do. His eyes sparkled with mischief. "It will be fun," he said.

Dickce warmed to the idea but she had reservations. "What will you do if something unexpected turns up?"

"Improvise," An'gel said. "You don't seriously think we'll be summoning spirits from beyond the grave, do you? This is more of a psychological exercise than a spiritual one."

"If you say so," Dickce said. As the time neared for the séance to start, however, she grew increasingly curious about exactly what might happen.

Alesha Jackson had agreed to conduct the séance. Dickce knew her sister could be pretty persuasive, but she had to wonder about the psychic's motive in complying with the request. If Alesha Jackson was the killer, Dickce reasoned, she might somehow give herself away during the séance. Though exactly how that might be, Dickce wasn't sure.

They were all at the dinner table that evening when Alesha Jackson startled everyone — except Dickce, An'gel, and Benjy — by announcing that she had received a message from one of her spirit guides that tonight she should hold a séance. The ghost of Cliffwood, they told her, was ready to communicate with her.

"How exciting," An'gel had said immediately, and Dickce joined in. The others looked skeptical at first, but the more they talked about it, the more interested everyone seemed to become.

Alesha Jackson insisted that everyone had to participate in order for the séance to have the desired result. Her spirit guides had been most insistent on that point, she told them. They would convene at ten o'clock in the dining room.

At nine forty-five, Dickce was back in the dining room, along with An'gel and Benjy, waiting for the others to arrive. They began to trickle in shortly before ten, and An'gel directed them to take their seats around the table. Alesha Jackson sat at the head, An'gel at the foot, and Dickce and Benjy at the midpoint on either side.

Henry Howard had added a leaf to the table so that it could accommodate all nine of them. There were two candelabra on the table, each holding three candles. Henry Howard lit them and then turned out the lights.

Dickce glanced around the table. Serenity Foster looked bored. Truss Wilbanks was obviously nervous. Henry Howard appeared to be enjoying himself, while Mary Turner appeared to be a little on edge. Marcelline, however, seemed overwhelmed by the situation. The housekeeper sat between Benjy and Mary Turner, and she shivered a little now and then, Dickce noticed.

"Let us begin." Alesha Jackson's voice interrupted Dickce's perusal of the occupants of the room. "We must now hold hands to form an unbroken connection around the table." She extended her hands to those on either side of her. As soon as she was satisfied that everyone had complied with her instruction, she continued.

Her voice deepened slightly as she talked. "There is a spirit in this house, a restless soul who still wanders this earth. This spirit is a remnant of one who lived in this house long ago, but who lingers. We must focus our thoughts on this spirit and encourage it to reveal itself to us. Please close your eyes and concentrate."

Alesha Jackson began to hum something that sounded like a hymn. Dickce stole a glance at the psychic in the dim light of the candles. Her eyes were closed as she continued to hum. The sound was soothing, almost hypnotic, Dickce thought.

Dickce closed her own eyes and did her best to concentrate her thoughts. She knew that An'gel's plan called for a certain amount of deception, and she hoped she wouldn't give anything away. She tended to giggle sometimes when she was nervous, and An'gel would wring her neck if she giggled tonight and spoiled everything. So she focused as hard as she could on the sound of Alesha Jackson's humming and the idea of the spirit of the house.

The humming continued, the volume increasing and decreasing occasionally. Dickce began to feel relaxed. The sound was soothing. She could feel the hands she clasped. Henry Howard, on her right, seemed calm and focused. Truss Wilbanks on her left, however, trembled now and then. Dickce gave his hand a light squeeze to try to reassure him, and he seemed to be calmer after that.

The humming trailed off, and Alesha Jackson began to speak again.

"Spirit of this house, we are here to help you. To guide you on to the next plane of existence. You no longer have to be confined by the walls of this house. If you will open yourself to us, we can guide you toward the light of eternal peace. Will you allow us to assist you on your way toward the light?"

When the psychic stopped speaking, Dickce could hear only the sounds of breathing. She opened her eyes and glanced quickly around the table. Everyone was still connected, hand to hand, and everyone except An'gel had their eyes closed. An'gel winked at her, then assumed a serious expression.

Alesha Jackson spoke once more. "Spirit of this house, I know you are troubled. Memories of life and of death have bound you to this place, but you can be free of them. Let me guide you on toward the light. Don't be afraid. Nothing more can harm you now."

In the quiet that followed, Dickce heard a soft murmur. Even though she was expecting it, she got goose pimples and had to resist the urge to pull her hands loose to rub her arms. The murmur was only a faint sound at first, but the volume grew slightly, and one word, repeated over and over, became distinct.

"Murder." The syllables were drawn out, the voice a breathy whisper. "Mur-der. Mur-der." The word repeated, over and over, in a near-hypnotic rhythm. Then all at once, the volume rose and rose until it suddenly ended in an unearthly shriek.

Dickce shuddered. She had been present earlier when Benjy recorded the whole thing, but still she felt spooked by it. In the silence she heard ragged breathing all around her.

Then the voice started again, whispered for a moment, then suddenly stopped.

Alesha Jackson spoke, her voice now sounding tense rather than soothing. "What is it you wish to tell us, spirit? Speak to us. Reveal everything to us. We are here to help you."

What happened next came as a complete surprise to Dickce. Her eyes flew open when she felt a rush of air across the table. An'gel hadn't told her about this. All the candles

386

went out, and then a voice began to shriek. "Get it off me. Get it off me. It's trying to kill me."

All at once the room lights came on, and as soon as her eyes could focus, Dickce sought out the source of the screaming.

Serenity Foster, her face distorted by fear, sat shivering in her chair. "Get it off me. Oh dear God, get it off me." Suddenly she pushed her chair back and ran out the door. Straight into the waiting arms of Lieutenant Steinberg.

CHAPTER 36

At breakfast the next morning, An'gel ate with a great deal of satisfaction. Her idea to use a séance to psych out the murderer had worked, even better than she had hoped. Serenity Foster, terrified by the experience, started talking to Lieutenant Steinberg the moment she ran into his arms, and she confessed everything. She kept begging him to *keep it off me,* even as he took her into the library to hear her full confession.

The group had been quiet last night. Everyone went off to bed not long after the séance broke up. Benjy disappeared before An'gel could thank him for his help. He hadn't yet made it to breakfast, although it was nearly eight thirty now. That wasn't like him.

"You were terrific," An'gel told Alesha Jackson for the second time.

The psychic smiled and finally responded to the compliment, her tone tinged with amusement. "I told you I could communicate with the spirit of the house."

An'gel nodded, not really believing her but trying to be polite since the woman had been a great help.

"I was terrified when the candles went out," Mary Turner said. "I thought I was fixing to die I was so scared right that moment."

"That was really spooky, but I figured Miss An'gel had somehow rigged it to happen," Henry Howard said. "How did you manage it?" He looked first at Alesha, then at An'gel. "It was a pretty neat trick."

An'gel frowned. The extinguishing of the candles hadn't been part of her plan. She had no explanation for how it had happened. She said that aloud.

Henry Howard turned back to Alesha. "Did you do it?"

She grinned broadly. "Only in the sense that I convinced the spirit to communicate with us. That was the spirit's doing, not mine."

An'gel wasn't sure she believed the psychic, but she preferred not to dwell on it. The sudden darkness had served her plan beautifully, so she wouldn't question its source. It might even have been what tipped Serenity Foster over the edge.

"Good morning, everyone." Benjy stood at the threshold of the dining room. An'gel was surprised to see that he looked tired, as if he hadn't slept much. He also seemed reluctant to enter the dining room.

Dickce got up and went to him. "Poor boy, you look exhausted. Come have something to eat. You'll feel a lot better." She put an arm around his shoulders.

Benjy nodded and allowed her to lead him to the sideboard. Dickce started heaping a plate with food while he poured himself a cup of coffee. He seated himself at the place where Dickce set his plate, picked up his fork, but then only stared at the food.

"Benjy, what's wrong?" An'gel was concerned. He always had a healthy appetite. "Something is obviously bothering you."

Benjy gazed at her with troubled eyes. "I had trouble sleeping last night after what happened. I was seriously creeped out by it." He turned to look at Alesha Jackson. "Did you feel it, too?"

The psychic nodded. "Yes. You didn't imagine it."

Benjy appeared only slightly relieved by Alesha Jackson's response.

"Feel what?" An'gel asked.

"The cold." Benjy shivered. "I've never felt anything like it, even though it barely touched me."

Dickce said, "I know what you mean. It feels like nothing on earth."

An'gel stared at Benjy. He wasn't putting on an act. He had really felt something last night. She looked at Alesha Jackson. "What exactly happened?"

"We called, and the spirit responded," Alesha said. "The word *murder* evidently had the effect you wanted, but not exactly in the way you expected."

"Are you telling me that the spirit reacted to the word by going after the murderer?" An'gel said, unnerved by the idea. She had believed Serenity Foster cracked under the pressure and the weird nature of the séance last night.

"Yes," Alesha Jackson said. She gazed with sympathy at Benjy. "I felt the spirit the other day on the stairs. That cold aura surrounded me when I wasn't expecting it, and I nearly fell down the stairs." Now she looked at An'gel. "You were there; you saw it when it happened."

An'gel nodded. "I did, but frankly I thought you were putting us on."

"I told you I had felt it there," Dickce said. "I thought you believed me."

"I did," An'gel said. "I know you wouldn't lie to me about it."

"But you thought I was putting on an act," Alesha said. "I'm used to skepticism. I've encountered it every time I have been hired, so you didn't intimidate me. Even when you told me that ridiculous story about my grandmother."

"What are you talking about?" Mary Turner asked. "Do you know Alesha's grandmother, Miss An'gel?"

"No, I don't. I was told something about Alesha's grandmother that turned out not to be true." An'gel stared hard at Marcelline, who had entered the room moments before with another plate of biscuits.

The housekeeper set the plate on the sideboard. She hesitated a moment, then turned to face Mary Turner. "I told a lie, Miss Mary, because I was afraid you had gotten so angry at Nathan that you went and killed him."

"If I hadn't been worried you killed him to protect *me,*" Mary Turner said, "I'd be upset by that, Marcelline."

"I lied, and I'm sorry about that, Ms. Jackson," the housekeeper said. Alesha Jackson stared hard at her for a moment before she nodded to acknowledge the apology. "But I wouldn't ever take a life, Miss Mary, and I should have known you wouldn't either."

"We know that now," An'gel said, "but

both of you were strong suspects, you know, because of what Nathan told you the night he died." She glanced at Henry Howard, then at Mary Turner, an eyebrow raised.

"It's all right, Miss An'gel," Mary Turner said. "I told Henry Howard everything. We stayed up until nearly two a.m. talking things over. I think we understand each other a lot better now."

Henry Howard smiled at her. "We do, and I'm glad." He turned to An'gel. "The only thing now is to figure out how to get out of the financial mess we're in."

"We can talk about that later," An'gel said. "Dickce and I are going to introduce you to a friend of ours who is a banker. I'm sure she will get things sorted out with the mortgage, and you'll do okay. We'll see to it."

"Thank you," Mary Turner said. "I'm not sure we deserve your help, but I'm mighty glad you're on our side."

An'gel smiled but her attention had already shifted elsewhere. They had strayed away from the subject of last night's strange events, and she was concerned about Benjy. He still appeared troubled, though he had finally begun to eat his breakfast. She didn't know what to say or do to reassure him at the moment. She was beginning to come to terms with the idea that what had happened last night had happened, whatever the explanation. She was going to be content with that, and she hoped Benjy could make peace with it.

As if sensing An'gel's thoughts, Alesha Jackson spoke to Benjy. "I know you're troubled by what you saw and felt last night, but that spirit would not have harmed you. I can assure you of that."

Benjy frowned and put down his fork. "I guess I believe you, but I don't understand why it did what it did."

"I think I know," Mary Turner said before the psychic could reply.

"What is your explanation, Mary Turner?" An'gel asked. She saw that everyone was intent on the young woman, awaiting her response.

"You may all think this is silly," Mary Turner said, her tone slightly defensive, "but I think she — and I think it's she, not he — was protecting the house. She knew who killed Nathan, and she wasn't going to let the murderer get away with it. Especially after Serenity threatened to tear the house down."

An'gel wasn't going to argue with Mary Turner. She realized it wouldn't do any good. Whether the spirit had acted to protect the house was not a question she would dwell on for long. The important thing was, Serenity had been so frightened by the experience that she had confessed.

"It was all about the money, wasn't it?" Alesha Jackson asked.

An'gel nodded. "Yes, she killed her brother because he wouldn't give her the money she thought she needed in her battle for joint custody of her children. She thought she could get her hands on it right away, once he was dead. She didn't realize it wasn't so simple."

"How did she do it?" Dickce asked. "No one has told us."

"Lieutenant Steinberg informed me yesterday afternoon that Nathan Gamble was smothered to death and that he was probably drugged with sleeping pills. He was unable to resist when Serenity covered his face and suffocated him with a pillow."

"Was he dead when I went in there?" Henry Howard asked, obviously appalled at the thought. He had paled the moment An'gel explained how Nathan died.

"I don't know," An'gel said. "You told me that you thought you heard a moan or two. He could still have been alive at that point and moaning in his sleep. I believe Serenity somehow got him to take the sleeping pills after they argued, then left him until he went to sleep. Then she came back and killed him when she knew he wouldn't be able to fight back."

"We'll have to wait until the trial to find out, I guess," Mary Turner said. "At this point, though, I'm not sure I even *want* to know any more details about it. I always thought she was hateful and completely self-centered, but I didn't imagine that she could kill her own brother."

"She was more concerned about money than she cared about her brother," Dickce said.

"Speaking of money," Henry Howard said, "what's going to happen to her inheritance? She's not allowed to profit from her crime, is she?"

"No, she isn't," An'gel said. "She forfeited her right to her brother's money when she killed him. That means her heirs can't profit either."

"If Truss hadn't gone home first thing this morning," Mary Turner said, "he could probably tell us what will happen."

Benjy spoke up. "He told me yesterday he thought Nathan had split everything between him and Serenity. I guess maybe he'll get everything now."

"The courts will decide," An'gel said, "but

I believe you're right."

"He's welcome to it," Mary Turner said. "I hope he'll see that Serenity's boys get some of it, though."

"I bet he'll do the right thing," Henry Howard said. "He's an okay guy, I think."

No one spoke after that until Benjy broke the silence with a question directed to Alesha Jackson.

"Is the spirit still here?" He looked uneasily around the room as if he might spot the ghost, An'gel thought.

"I don't believe the spirit is here any longer," Alesha said. "I think we persuaded her that it was okay to move on, especially after what she did."

"I will kind of miss her," Mary Turner said with a faint smile. "The things she did, that is, and not the silly pranks you played." She poked Henry Howard in the side.

"That reminds me," An'gel said. "I won't ask you to explain the cold spot, but what about the shadow I saw?"

"And the parlor door closing by itself?"

Henry Howard laughed. "I can explain the door easily. The shadow I know nothing about."

"What about the door?" Benjy asked.

"If you stand back and look at it long enough, you'll probably see that it's at a very slight angle, just barely noticeable," Henry Howard said. "Part of the front of the house has shifted a tiny bit over the years, and when the door is left open at a certain spot, it will start moving. The weight of it makes it close from that point, or near enough to closing."

"I'm relieved to hear that," An'gel said. "I wish you could explain that shadow, though."

"Sorry." Henry Howard shrugged. "That must have been the spirit's doing."

An'gel glanced at Benjy. He appeared more at ease now, though she could tell he was still bothered by something. After a moment's thought, she decided she knew what might make him feel better.

An'gel didn't wait to consult Dickce. If it made Benjy happier, she knew Dickce would be all for it.

"Alesha," An'gel said. "I'd like to talk to you about coming to Riverhill for a little professional visit."

ABOUT THE AUTHOR

Miranda James is the *New York Times* bestselling author of the Cat in the Stacks Mysteries, including *Twelve Angry Librarians, No Cats Allowed,* and *Arsenic and Old Books,* as well as the Southern Ladies Mysteries, including *Digging up the Dirt* and *Dead with the Wind.* James lives in Mississippi. Visit the author at catinthestacks.com and facebook.com/mirandajamesauthor.